A Thousand Nights

Emily Kate Johnston is a forensic archaeologist. She has lived on four continents, including summers spent in Jordan experiencing the desert first hand. Her inspirations come from her work, travels and her university studies in biblical Hebrew and Arabic. She loves telling stories, and has been doing so across different mediums for over ten years.

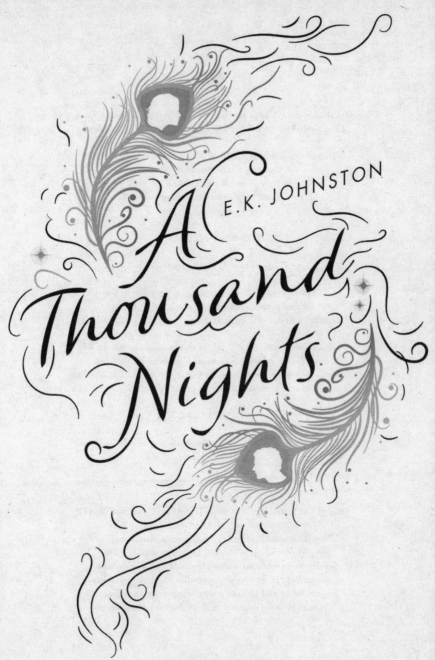

E.K. JOHNSTON

A Thousand Nights

MACMILLAN

First published in the US 2015 by Hyperion, an imprint of Disney Book Group
First published in the UK 2015 by Macmillan Children's Books

This edition published 2016 by Macmillan Children's Books
an imprint of Pan Macmillan
20 New Wharf Road, London N1 9RR
Associated companies throughout the world
www.panmacmillan.com

ISBN 978-1-4472-9037-7

1 3 5 7 9 8 6 4 2

A CIP catalogue record for this book is available from
the British Library.

Designed by Marci Senders

Printed and bound by CPI Group (UK) Ltd, Croydon CR0 4YY

To Dr. Daviau, who took me to the desert, past
and future, and taught me to look for things;
To Jo, Amy, and Melissa, who cheered me on while
I was learning how to write John Druitt;
And to Tessa, who never stops pushing

We do not know why we came from the sea to this hard and dusty earth, but we know that we are better than it.

The creatures that live here crawl beneath a crippling sun, eking what living they can from the sand before they are returned to it, as food for the sand-crows or worse. We are not troubled by the sun, and sand is but a source of momentary discomfort to us. We are stronger, hardier, and better suited to life. Yet we struggled here, when first we came.

The humans were many, and we were few. We did not understand them, nor they us, and they feared us for it. They came at us with crude weapons, heavy stone and bright fire, and we found that our blood could stain the sand as easily as theirs could, until we learned to build bodies that did not bleed. We retreated to the desert, away from the oases, to sun-baked places where they could not follow. From there, we watched. And we bided our time.

They died, and we did not. As our lives measured on, we learned more about them. We watched them tame the auroch and then the horse. We watched them learn to shear the sheep and card the wool. When they spun, we felt the pull of each spindle's twist, and when they wove, we felt a stirring in our bones.

We coveted the things they made, for though we had nothing but time, we had little inclination to master handiwork ourselves. Always, it was easier to take. And so we took. Weavers we kidnapped and brought to our desert homes. We fed them sand and they thought it a feast, and before they died, they made marvels for us. Coppersmiths we pulled from their beds, and set them to fires so hot they blistered their skin. They crafted baubles and blades before they paid with their lives, and we decorated ourselves with their wares.

When they worked, we found ourselves enlivened; and before long, those youngest of us ventured forth to prey upon other artisans. They returned with strength and power, and necklaces made from the finger bones of those whose hands they used to achieve it.

It was never enough for me.

I craved more.

And one day in the desert, I met a hunter who had strayed beyond the reach of his guard.

And I took.

I took.

one

LO-MELKHIIN KILLED three hundred girls before he came to my village looking for a wife.

She that he chose of us would be a hero. She would give the others life. Lo-Melkhiin would not return to the same village until he had married a girl from every camp, from every town, and from each district inside city walls—for that was the law, struck in desperation though it was. She that he chose would give hope of a future, of love, to those of us who stayed behind.

She would be a smallgod for her own people, certainly, in the time after her leaving. She would go out from us, but we would hold on to a piece of her spirit, and nurture it with the power of our memories. Her name would be whispered with reverent hush around new-built shrines to her honor. The other girls would sing hymns of thanksgiving, light voices carried by the desert winds and scattered over the fine-ground sand. Their parents would bring sweet-water flowers, even in the height of the desert wilt, and pickled gage-root to leave as offerings. She that he chose of us would never be forgotten.

She would still be dead.

Every time, the story began the same way: Lo-Melkhiin picked one girl and took her back to his qasr to be his wife. Some in his keeping lasted one night, some as many as thirty, but in the end all were food for the sand-crows. He went to every corner of the land, into every village and city. Each tribe, every family was at risk. He consumed them the way a careful child eats dates: one at a time, ever searching for the sweetest. In turn, he found none of them to suit.

When he came to my village, I was not afraid for myself. I had been long ago resigned to a life in the shadow of my sister, my elder by ten moons and my year-twin. She was the beauty. I was the spare. Before Lo-Melkhiin's law, before the terror of his marriage bed reached across the sand like a parched gage-tree reaches for water, I had known that I would marry after my sister, likely to a brother or cousin of her betrothed. She was a prize, but she was also loath to separate herself from me, and it was well known in our village that we came as a pair. I would not be a lesser wife in her household—our father was too powerful for that—but I would wed a lesser man.

"You are not unlovely," she said to me when we saw the desert burn with the sun of our fourteenth summer, and I knew that it was true.

Our mothers were both beautiful, and our father like- wise handsome. From what I could see of my own self, my sister and I were very much alike. We had skin of burnt bronze, a deeper brown than sand, and duskier where it was exposed to the wind and sky. Our hair was long enough to sit upon, and dark: the color around the stars, when night was at its fullest. I had decided the difference must be in our faces, in the shape of our eyes or the slant of our mouths. I knew my sister's face could take my breath away. I had not ever seen my own. We had little bronze or copper, and the only water was at the bottom of our well.

"I am not you," I said to her. I was not bitter. She had never made me feel the lesser, and she had only scorn for those who did.

"That is true," she said. "And men will lack the imagin- ation to see us as separate beings. For that I am sorry."

"I am not," I told her, and I was not, "for I love you more than I love the rain."

"How remarkable," she said, and laughed, "for you see my face every day and do not tire of it." And we ran together, sure-footed, across the shifting sand.

We were strong together, carrying the water jar between us to share the weight. Its thick ceramic sides made it heavy, even without the weight of the water, but there were four handles, and we had four hands. We learned the trick when we were small, and were rewarded with candied figs for spilling so little water as we walked. Even when we were old enough to carry a jug each, we did the chore together, and more besides. In most things, from weaving to cooking to spearing the poisonous snakes that came to our well, we were equal. My voice was better at the songs and stories our traditions gave us, but my sister could find her own words to say, and did not rely on the deeds of others to make her point. Maybe that fire was what made her beautiful; maybe that was what set my sister's face apart from mine. Maybe that was why I did not tire of it.

I feared that Lo-Melkhiin would think my sister's face was something, something at last, that he too would not tire of. He had married only beautiful girls at first, the daughters of our highest lords and wealthiest merchants. But when his wives began to die, the powerful men of the desert did not like it, and began to look elsewhere for Lo-Melkhiin's brides. They began to scour the villages for women that would suit, and for a time no one paid mind to the host of poorer daughters that went to their deaths. Soon, though, the smaller villages tallied their dead and ceased trade with the cities. From thence, the law was struck: one girl from each village and one from every district inside city walls, and then the cycle would begin again. So many girls had been lost, and I did not wish to lose my sister to him. The stories were very clear about two things: Lo-Melkhiin always took one girl, and she always, always died.

When the dust rose over the desert, we knew that he was coming. He would know our numbers, and he would know who had daughters that must be presented to him. The census was part of the law, the way that men were able to tell themselves that it was fair.

"But it isn't fair," whispered my sister as we lay underneath the sky and watched the stars rise on our seventeenth summer. "They do not marry and die."

"No," I said to her. "They do not."

So we stood in the shadow of our father's tent, and we waited. Around us the air was full of cries and moans; mothers held their daughters; fathers paced, unable to intervene, unwilling to circumvent the law. Our father was not here. He had gone to trade. We had not known that Lo-Melkhiin would come. Our father would return to find his fairest flower gone, and only the weed left for him to use as he saw fit.

My hair was unbound under my veil, and both blew wildly around my face. My sister had tied back her braid and stood with straight shoulders, her veil pulled back and her black hair gleaming in the sun. She was looking out at the coming storm, but there was a storm brewing in her eyes that only made her more beautiful. I could not lose her, and surely once Lo-Melkhiin saw her, she would be lost.

I thought of all the stories I had heard, those whispered at my mother's hearth and those told in the booming voice of our father when the village elders met in his tent for council. I knew them all: where we had come from, who our ancestors had been, what heroes were in my lineage, which smallgods my family had made and loved. I tried to think if there was any one thing in the stories that I could use, but there was not. The world had never seen another like Lo-Melkhiin, and it had no stories to combat him.

Not whole stories, but maybe there was something smaller. A thread in the story of a warrior who laid siege to a walled city. A fragment in the story of a father who had two daughters, and was forced to choose which of them to send into the desert at night. An intrigue in the story of two lovers who wed against the wishes of their fathers. A path in the story of an old woman whose sons were taken, unlawfully, to fight a war they were not part of. There were stories, and then there were stories.

No single tale that I could draw from would save my sister from a short and cruel marriage, but I had pieces aplenty. I held them in my hands like so many grains of sand, and they slipped away from me, running through my fingers, even as I tried to gather more. But I knew sand. I had been born to it and learned to walk on it. It had blown in my face and I had picked it from my food. I knew that I had only to hold it for long enough, to find the right fire, and the sand would harden into glass—into something I could use.

My sister watched the dust cloud for Lo-Melkhiin, but I watched it for the sand. I took strength from her bravery in the face of that storm, and she took my hand and smiled, even though she did not know what I was trying to do. She had accepted that she would be the one to save us, the one to be made a smallgod and sung to after her time of leaving. The one who died. But I would not allow it.

By the time the village elders could see flashes of bronze armor in the dust cloud, and hear the footfalls of horses that rode, too hard, under the sun—by the time the wind pulled at my sister's braid and worked a few strands loose to play with, as though it, too, feared to lose her—by then, I had a plan.

two

WHEN LO-MELKHIIN CAME, some of the girls rent their veils and cut off their hair with sheep-shears. I looked at them and felt their fear. I was the only one with a sister the right age, the only one who was a spare. I could stand beside her and be unseen. The others had no one to shield them this way. They would face Lo-Melkhiin alone, and they disfigured themselves in the hope that this would put them beneath his attention.

Lo-Melkhiin did not always notice, not anymore. Now that he no longer took only the most beautiful, it seemed that he chose at random. It was not as though his bride would last. Our father had heard tales when he was out with the caravan, that Lo-Melkhiin would take his new bride away, to his qasr in the Great Oasis, and she would be given new silks, and perfumed so that she no longer smelled of the desert. It did not matter what she looked like in the dust of her village, for dust could be washed away. But if there was a girl who was like my sister, who drew the eyes of men and smallgods when she walked past with the water jar balanced on her hip, Lo-Melkhiin would be sure to take her.

My sister was dressed in white linen that blistered the eye with the sun's glare. She looked simple and striking, and all the more so because she was surrounded by girls who keened in terror as the horses drew near. I knew that I must work quickly.

I went into her mother's tent, where my sister had been made and born and learned to dance. Her mother sat upon the pillows of her bed, weeping quietly. I went to her and knelt beside her, extending the silk of my veil should she need to wipe her eyes.

"Lady mother," I said to her, for that was how mothers who did not bear you were called. "Lady mother, we must be quick if we are to save your daughter."

My sister's mother looked up and clung to the silk I offered to her.

"How?" she said to me, and I saw a desperate hope burn in her eyes.

11

"Dress me in my sister's clothes," I bade her. "Braid my hair as you would hers, and give me those charms she would not grieve to lose."

"She will grieve to lose her sister," my sister's mother said, but her hands had already begun the work. Like me, she was eager to save her daughter, and was not thinking too much of the cost.

"Someone must be chosen," I said. I was not yet afraid. "My mother has sons."

"Perhaps," my sister's mother said. "But a son is not a daughter."

I did not tell her that a daughter is less than a son. She knew it, for she had brothers of her own. Her daughter, my sister, had no brothers left, and her marriage would be what kept her mother alive should our father die. My mother would survive without me, but without my sister, her mother had no such assurance. I would save more than my sister, though that had not been my intent. I never thought that maybe, maybe, my mother would grieve for me, for no reason other than her heart.

My sister burst into the tent as her mother was fastening the last gilt necklace around my neck. I wore her purple dishdashah, bound at my wrists and waist with braided cord. My sister and I had done the black embroidery on the collar, chest, and arms ourselves, stitching a map of the whispers we spoke to one another as we worked. It had taken us the better part of our fifteenth winter to do it, from raw threads to finished cloth. It was to be her marriage dress, and I had nothing like it. She had told me, as we stitched, that because I had put my hands to making it, it was as much mine as it was hers. There were secrets in this dress—dreams and confessions we had kept even from our mothers—in the weave and weft, and in the decorations and in the dye. It was to be hers, but since she wished us to share it, I looked beautiful, cased in purple and black, and beauty was what I needed.

"No," my sister said to me when her eyes lost their desert-sun haze and she saw me standing clearly before her. She knew, for one time only, the eyes that looked at us would slide past her and fix on me. "No, my sister, you must not."

"It is too late," I said to her. "Lo-Melkhiin's men come for us."

"Thank you, daughter of my heart," my sister's mother breathed. She had always been fair and kind to me when I was a child. She had taught me the ways of mourning alongside my sister, but at that moment I knew that she loved me also. "I will pray to you, when you have gone."

My sister took my hand and pulled me into the sunlight so that Lo-Melkhiin's men would not have cause to drag us from the tent. I would walk to my fate, and she would walk beside me. For the first time, I was the one who drew looks. We rejoined the other girls, all of them staring at me as I

13

walked past them in my finery. I stood at the very front, dark and bright. My sister, who had been so radiant in her simple garb, now looked unfinished at my side. Lovely, but second. I could hear the men whisper.

"Pity," they hissed. "Pity we did not notice she was as beautiful as her sister."

I did not look at them. I held my sister's hand, and we led the way toward the horses that stamped and sweated by the well. We passed the tents of the other families, those with fewer sheep and fewer children. The girls followed us, staying close. They sensed that they could hide in my shadow, my purple oasis, and perhaps be safe. We drew our lives from the well, and now one of us would go to her death by it.

Lo-Melkhiin did not get down from his horse. He sat above us, casting a shadow across the sand where we stood. I could not see his face. When I looked up at him, all I could see was black and sun, and it was too bright to bear. I stared at the horse instead. I would not look at the ground. Behind me stood the other girls, and behind them the village elders held the girls' mothers back. I wondered who held my mother, with my father and brothers gone, but I did not look back to see. I wished to be stone, to be resolute, but fear whispered in my heart. What if my sister was chosen, despite my efforts? What if I was chosen, and died? I pushed those thoughts away, and called on the stories I had woven together to make my plan. Those heroes did not falter. They walked their paths, regardless of what lay before them, and they did not look back.

"Make me a smallgod," I whispered to my sister. "When I have gone."

"I will make you a smallgod now," she said to me, and the tack jingled as Lo-Melkhiin's men dismounted and came near. "What good to be revered when you are dead? We will begin the moment they take you, and you shall be a smallgod before you reach the qasr."

I had prayed to smallgods my whole life. Our father's father's father had been a great herdsman, with more sheep than a man could count in one day. He had traded wool to villages far and near, and it was to him we prayed when our father was away with the caravan. Our father always returned home safely, with gifts for our mothers and work for my brothers and profit for us all, but sometimes I wondered if it was the smallgod's doing. For the first time, I wished that our father was here. I knew he would not have saved me, but I might have asked if he had ever felt the smallgod we prayed to aiding him on the road.

"Thank you, sister," I said. I was unsure if it would help me, but it could not harm me.

Lo-Melkhiin's guard closed his hand on my arm, but I followed him willingly toward the horses. His face was covered by a sand-scarf, but his eyes betrayed him. He wanted to be here no more than I did, yet he did his duty, as did I. When he saw that I would not fight him, he relaxed, and his hand became more a guide than a shackle. I stood straight and did not look back, though I could hear the wails behind me as my mother began to grieve. Perhaps I should have gone to her, instead of my sister's mother. But she would not have helped me. She would have done what my father could not, and she would have tried to keep me safe. She would have cost me my sister.

"I love you," I called out. The words were for everyone, for my mothers, and the words were only for my sister.

My sister was on her knees when they put me on the horse, her white linen browned by the sand and her hair falling forward across her face. She chanted in the family tongue, the one my father's father's father practiced when he tended his sheep, the one we heard at my father's knee as he taught it to my brothers and we sat close by to overhear. My sister's mother knelt beside her and chanted too. I could hear the words, but I could not make them out. I knew they were for me, for I could feel the way the wind pulled at my veil, curious to see the face of the girl who received such fervent prayer.

Lo-Melkhiin sat atop his horse and laughed, for he thought she wept to lose me. But I knew better. I could feel it, in my soul.

three

LO-MELKHIIN'S HORSES WERE SWIFT, like the wind circles that danced on the sand. Our father's tents, and the tents around our well, were swallowed up by the sky before I had time to look back at them. They had been my whole world, before the guard lifted me into the saddle, and now they were lost to me. Never again would I tell my sister stories, using the warm light of the lamp to make shadows with my hands on the canvas. I would be a queen, for however short a time, and I would never live in a tent again.

Lo-Melkhiin rode at the head of the party, and his guards arrayed themselves around me in a loose formation. They need not have bothered. I was new to riding, and spent my concentration staying upright. Even had I been able to get away, I had nowhere to go. If I went home to my village, the guards could simply follow me there, and if I tried to flee into the desert, I would be food for the sand-crows sooner than if I stayed my course. So I watched the guards, how they sat and how they held their legs against their horses' flanks. I did my best to mimic their seat, and after a while my muscles ached. I was glad my veil hid my face. I had no wish for them to see me suffer.

When the sun was high, we halted to water the horses. They were desert-bred, and could ride all day if they had to, but their way would be easier if we let them rest. Lo-Melkhiin wore no spurs. I had always thought that horses must be expensive, because even our father did not have one, and now I knew they must be, because Lo-Melkhiin was kind to his. He held the beast's head himself, and raised the water skin to its lips for it to drink. His hand was light upon the horse's face, and I began to wonder.

What sort of man could have so much blood on his hands that he could choose a wife within moments of seeing her, and know that she would soon be added to the litany of the dead, but would call a halt on the ride home to spare the horses? I had not stopped to think, in my haste to save my sister. I had thought of her life, of her mother's happiness, and I had not thought about what was to be my marriage. One night or thirty, I would know Lo-Melkhiin, who laughed

18

at my sister's tears and watered his horse with his own hands.

We had spoken of marriage, of course, my sister and our mothers and I. We had stitched the purple dishdashah I wore, and filled it with the hopes and dreams of our future. We knew that someday, our father would announce my sister's match, and then mine soon after, and we would move into the tents of our husbands' families. There would be a feast, and songs, and all the old traditions. And there would be the wedding night. I would have none of that, now, except the last.

I looked down from my perch on the horse's back. No one had come to help me dismount, and I was determined not to fall trying. The guard who had pulled me away from my sister was tall, and wore riding leathers much more suited to the desert than my dress. He came toward me, holding out a water skin. I took it from him, drinking only a little before handing it back, and he did not meet my eyes.

"Salt," said Lo-Melkhiin. It was the first word I heard him say.

The guard passed up his salt canister, a small ornate box he carried at his waist. When I held it in my hands, I realized it was wood, and worth more than the cloth I wore. Inside it was the precious mineral that would keep us all alive in the desert sun. I licked my finger and coated it in the coarse white grains. I knew it would taste foul, but I slid my hand under my veil and forced myself to eat it all, and then the guard passed me the water skin again. I took more this time, to cleanse my mouth of the taste, but I was still able to watch him stow the canister away, carefully, securely. Almost lovingly. It was worth more than wood to him.

"Thank you," I said.

Too late, I wondered if that was permitted. Some men did not allow their wives to speak outside the home, and certainly not to other men. I was not a wife yet, but I was as good as wed, and Lo-Melkhiin might be the kind of husband who expected a demure, retiring creature.

"You are welcome," the guard said, and there was no fear in his voice. He still did not look at me, and I knew it was because he pitied me. He pitied my death.

Lo-Melkhiin swung back into his saddle, his heavy robe billowing behind him, and his light boots tucked against the belly of his horse. At that signal the other guards remounted. I shifted, trying to find a place on my seat that did not feel bruised, but could not. I ground my teeth behind my veil, and we rode on.

Time is an odd thing in the desert. They say that in the city, the Skeptics have found a way to measure time with water and glass, but in the desert, the sand goes on forever, and takes time with it. You cannot tell how far you have come, or how far you have to go. The sand is what kills you, if you die in the desert, because the sand is everywhere, and it does not care if you get out. So we rode for hours, but it felt as though we rode for days. We were not on a caravan route, so we passed no travelers or other villages. Had I to guess, I would have said that we were riding in a straight line back to Lo-Melkhiin's qasr, where other travelers would have followed the circuitous route made safe by the oases. But our direction, like our duration, was blown about with the sand.

As the sun drew near the horizon, and the sky turned from blasted blue to a dark and darker red, I saw a distortion in the distance, and knew that we were, finally, close. Lo-Melkhiin's father's father's father had built the qasr of white stone. Our father and brothers had told us of it, for they had seen it when they were out with the caravan, and now that my mother and my sister's mother no longer traveled, they liked to hear tales of the world. In the daytime it gleamed, gathering the sun's rays into itself, heating slowly as the day progressed. As night approached and the desert cooled, the heat came out of the walls and tried to find the sun again, but since the sun was setting, the heat moved in weaving lines, seen from a distance like through a veil of the finest silk, blurred and indistinct. But it was no false vision, seen by one sunstroked and delusional. It was solid, and we were drawing near.

The city was made of three parts. At the heart was the qasr, where Lo-Melkhiin lived, met petitioners, and where

21

the temple stood. Around it were the crooked streets and pale houses, the dust and dirty tents. And around that was the wall, high and strong. There had not been invaders in generations, but the wall was from a less peaceful time. We prospered under Lo-Melkhiin—or, men did, and it was men who kept the accounts of everything, from grain and sheep to life and death.

The city gates stood open, for Lo-Melkhiin was expected. I imagined that at one time the people had come to see Lo-Melkhiin's bride to wish her well. In my village, we sang for prosperity and long life when the bride went past. Those songs were not heard inside the qasr, not for me. There were people in the streets, come to see their momentary queen as I passed under the towers, but they were quiet and did not sing. Most did not look at me for very long. Mothers pulled their children away, hiding them in doorways instead of behind tent flaps, though they looked and dressed the way our mothers did. The guards rode close by me now, but Lo-Melkhiin rode by himself. He had no fear of his own people; most of them he did not rule harshly.

The horses could sense that they were nearing home, and pranced through the streets. The guards sat up straight in their saddles, trying to look the part, though they were covered in dust. I could only cling to the reins and pray that I did not fall. The city had roused me again, lights gleaming warmly. I had the false sense that I was home. The long hours in the desert had numbed me, and I'd forgotten my aching body; now my muscles were screaming. When we came at last to the stables, the guards dismounted and the salt-guard came to take me down. I let myself nearly tumble into his arms, and when he set me on the ground, he waited a moment before releasing me. I straightened my legs and my back, and there was fire along my bones. I bit my tongue against the pain of it, but I would not lean against the guard.

"This one has more than her face to give her spirit," Lo-Melkhiin said. He was not laughing when he said it. I thought it odd, as he had laughed at my sister's discomfort before, but his attention had already turned to a new man in a fine red robe. I took him to be the steward, and his words confirmed my guess.

"Her rooms have been prepared, my lord," he said. "As have yours, if you are ready to go in."

"I shall walk the wall for a time," Lo-Melkhiin said. "I wish to look upon the stars."

"As you say," said the steward with a bow. He gestured to the salt-guard, who still stood next to me. "Come."

The other guards fell away, and the salt-guard took my arm again, gently this time. We followed the steward inside; my hesitation on the steps drew a long gaze from my escort, but no remarks, and we continued down a long corridor and through a garden. There was a sound in the garden I had never heard before, like soft whispering, but it was too dark to see what caused it. It reminded me of something I had heard long ago, but the feel of the city, of the qasr, drove the desert from my memory.

On the other side of the garden, a woman waited. She was old and her cloth was plain, though it was well woven. Her back was unbowed and she smiled at me. It was the first smile I had seen since the morning. She drew me into a well-lit bathing room, waving off the salt-guard and steward, and I followed her toward the smell of heavy perfume and the whispering sound of moving silks. Other women waited for us there, with brushes and oils and cloth so fine it glittered in the light of the lamp.

They would wash and prepare me like a bride, but I knew that I was being dressed for death. Yet there was that sound, pulling at the whirlwind of my thoughts. I decided in that moment that I must live through the night, because I wished to know what made that sound. I walked up the stairs, and into Lo-Melkhiin's harem.

four

WHEN THE SUN BURNED OUT our fifth summer, we had a rainy season like none I have seen since. It began quietly, dark mist on the horizon, and I did not know that it was something to be feared. My sister and I were with the sheep, who did not stray during the hot times because they knew that if they wandered, they would die. The first sign was when the ram took fright, bleating more desperately than if we had been bringing him to the knife for dinner. He butted at us, and at the ewes, and we wept. He had been our pet, and we had made much of him, feeding him the best greens we could find, and leaning up against his flank for sparse shade in the heat of the sun.

He knocked me off my feet and was set to trample me when my brothers arrived. They did not shout at us, nor did they tease, as was their custom. This was the second sign, and when we became truly afraid. They took our staves from us, pushing our small herd back to the village, and when I fell, legs weak from being hit by the ram, the eldest of them—the only full brother my sister had—picked me up in his arms when he might have scorned me. We fled, not to the tents, but to the honeycombed caverns where we enshrined our dead. The sky was much darker now, an odd dark. It was not the black night that I knew; it was grey and boiling, and there was a green around the edges of it that I did not like.

When we reached the caverns, our mothers were waiting for us before the entrance. They were dressed in their priestly-whites, as they were on funerals and feast days, and at their feet lay the scattered remains of a hasty ceremony. We did not come here with the living—or we had not, in my lifetime—and so I knew from my mother's lessons that since we did not bring a body with us today, we must beg for entrance.

Behind us, the rest of my village clambered up the rise, carrying all they could. It was not everything. Below, where the tents were clustered, I could see many beloved objects left behind. Fear took me, though I still did not know why, and I clung to my sister and to my mother's priestly-veil.

"May we go in?" asked our father, his tone the hushed

and reverent one he used when my mother was thus dressed, and not the commanding voice he used in our tent.

Our mothers looked at one another, and something passed between them. They had not yet begun to whisper to us of this office—of the small, terrible power they held with the dead among the village—but I could see it in their eyes, even if I could not decipher it. My mother nodded, and my sister's mother raised her hands.

"We have made the offerings and done the rites," my sister's mother said. "We have not heard the dead speak against us, and so we bid you enter, though there may yet be a price."

"I must risk it," our father said to them, "because the clouds draw nearer, and we have nowhere else to go."

Clouds. The word felt strange against my tongue as I repeated it, and I feared its weight there. They were closer now, dark and heavy, and low in the sky. They waited for us, but they would not wait very much longer.

"Then enter," said my mother. She spoke to our father, but she cast her arms wide to include everyone. "Enter, but be careful where you tread. The dead sleep lightly when there is wind such as this in the air."

We left the sheep outside with my sister's older brother to guard them. We went into the caves, and our mothers spread white cloaks on the ground for us to sit upon. Our father went to each family, advising them where to sit and how best to settle their belongings so they did not disturb the dead. Then he returned to us.

"Come," he said to my sister and to me. "You must see this, so that you will know it."

He had not spoken to us so directly before. Always his orders had come from our mothers, or from my sister's brother. We were the girl-children, born so close together that few men could tell us apart, save that the older of us was already more graceful. We did not know what to do, so my mother pushed us forward and my sister's mother twisted the hem of our father's robes into our hands.

"Do not let go," she said to us. She had spoken before of a price. "No matter what, hold fast and return to us."

We followed our father back to the mouth of the caverns, where my sister's brother waited with the sheep. The clouds were above us now, stretching as far as the eye could see. I did not like the taste of the air, and when I wrinkled my nose, our father smiled.

"Yes, daughter-mine," he said. "Remember this smell. Remember the skies, how they look. Remember how the sheep worried you and tried to knock you down. Remember all of that, and remember what comes next."

He smiled. It was the most he had ever said to me. I was afraid, but I also felt the sand in my heart turn to glass. Whatever was coming, our father wanted my sister and me to see it, to know it, and to be safe from it when it came again. This was how I learned that he loved us.

As we watched, the sky turned to black and finally the clouds could hold no more. They burst with wet, and the sheep reared up and pressed themselves against the hill. It was water, I saw after a moment. And it was deafening. All the water I had ever seen in my life had come from our well. I had bathed with it and drunk it and poured it over melon vines, but I had not ever seen anything like this.

"It is called rain," our father said. "It falls upon green hills far from here, and rushes to us down the dry wadi bed. But when the smallgods will it, the clouds slip free from those green hills and come to us with speed, and with such water as you will see only a few times in your life. We need the water, but it is dangerous, and soon you will see why."

We watched. The rain poured from the sky as from a countless number of jugs. It cut into the rock above us, peeling back the sand and sending it rushing toward the wadi bed. The sheep were soaked through, like how we soaked their wool in dye, and they were giving off a smell I liked even less than the smell before the rain came.

There was a roaring sound behind the tents, where I could not see. Our father looked down at us, at our hands clenched in his hem, and looked to my sister's brother, who stood just beyond the cave wall, as wet as the sheep, but with a burning energy in his eyes that did not speak of fear.

There was another sound, and for a long moment, I did not know what it was. It was my sister screaming. I had

29

never heard her make that sound before, and I stared at her, thinking she must have been injured by the rain. Our father took my face in his hands, and forced me to look back at the tents. Behind them, a great grey wall had risen up where the wadi should have been. It bore down on the circle where we had slept and ate and played, and it crashed down upon it, sweeping through hide and rope like they were nothing.

The wall continued toward us, rushing up the slope toward the caverns. I felt a scream of my own building in my chest. The water had taken the tents and the places where we slept. If it came into the caves, there was no way out. Our father stood in front of us, and we clung to him as the water came. It stretched for us, and for a long moment I thought we would all be taken. But then, as though it had been checked by a smallgod, the surge pulled back, and though it lapped at our father's sandals, it did not take him.

It was then that the ram panicked again. The ewes shifted around him, water swirling around their flanks, and their discomfort heightened his. He charged my sister's brother, who was watching the water surge past us, and butted him hard. With a cry he fell, rolling down the slope, until the water closed over his head and carried him away.

Our father keened, but did not move. Had he tried, he would have pulled my sister and me along behind, and while the water might have spared him, it certainly would have taken us. Instead we watched, helpless, as the dark shape of my brother was pulled farther and farther down the wadi, until he passed beyond our sight.

"Come," our father said then. "There is nothing left for you to see."

The price my mother had warned of was paid, and my sister's mother wailed when our father told her. She held my sister close and wept. The dead had taken their due, and my sister's brother would never lie among them. His bones were lost to the desert, and my sister and I had learned the terrible cost of green and life.

The sound in the garden, I realized as Lo-Melkhiin's women bathed and perfumed me, was the sound we had heard at the beginning of the flood. It was so soft I had not recognized it at first, until the women had put me in the heated tub and pushed me under the surface to wet my hair. Water had rushed into my nose and ears, and I had come up coughing. They pitied that, like they pitied everything else about me. I was a doomed bride, so provincial that I had never even had enough water for a proper bath. But when my eyes cleared, I knew the sound.

It was the sound of death and wet and green. It was the sound of cost and worth. But if I could find something like the hem of our father's robe, if I could find something to hold on to, then it would be the sound of hope.

five

THE BOWER SMELLED OF SAGE and jasmine and fear. There was no hint of sheep or sand, for we were in the center of the qasr, and even the desert struggled to meet me here. I sat on cushions sheathed in the finest silk, and all around me hung draperies and veils of a sheer material I could not name. They must have cleaned it since the last wife died, but something lingered. The air was still and thick, and I could not feel the barest breath of wind. The lamps burned hot and straight, unflickering. And I waited.

They had cut my nails to the quick, finger and toe, and rubbed them with hard grit so that the edges were soft. I could not pluck a thread from my veil, and it would be some days before I could weave again without being as clumsy as a novice. When faced with Lo-Melkhiin's bare skin, I would not be able to mark it. They had checked my teeth, too. The city women cleaned their teeth with mint water, but we scoured ours with fine sand, collected from the wadi bed. The skulls in our catacombs had neat rows of teeth, even those of my kin who had been old when they died. The women who bathed me had gaps in their mouths or crooked smiles. I wondered if they feared that I would bite him, but I suppose there was nothing they could do.

If my sister had been part of my wedding, she would have waited with me, and our mothers as well. They would have whispered secrets, things never said aloud to men, but I was alone. I had not been fed, and I was glad. My nerves thus far were settled, but had I a stomach full of city food, new and unusual to me, I may have been otherwise.

They had not left me a time-candle, and I could not see the sky nor read the water clock that stood in the corner. But I do not think I waited long before he came.

He wore silks, as I did, except his were dark blue against skin paler than mine. Lo-Melkhiin had been a great hunter once, but no longer did he spend very much time beneath the sun. His trousers were caught above his waist in a jeweled belt that wrapped around him three times, and was fastened with a snake's head eating its tail.

The lamplight gleamed on the worked metal of the clasp, finer than any I had seen. His shirt had wide sleeves. My clothing was all simple ties that, once pulled, would reveal my body underneath. I had no idea how I was meant to undress him.

He sat, straight-backed and fine, crossing his ankles and placing his hands upon his knees. He did not look like a predator, except for his eyes, which gleamed as they took me in. I breathed slowly, the way an antelope breathes when it smells a lion in the air.

"My common wife," he said at length. His voice was very soft, as it had been when he spoke to the horse, but I did not expect him to show me the same kindness he had showed it. "You are not afraid of me. Tell me why."

"There is no cause for fear," I told him.

"You do not worry that I will call for your death, right in this room, if you do not please me?" he asked.

"I know you can and might," I said. "The flood will come, fast and without warning, because the ground is not accustomed to it. And therefore it is not worth fearing."

"That much is true," he said, and smiled. His teeth were straight and there were no gaps between them. "But I think you will do better than one night."

"I am yours to command, husband," I said to him, and met his eyes.

When my mother spoke to our father, she often said

that. He liked it, the way she put herself in his hands. Until just now, I had not realized that since my mother was the one who allowed it, she had more power than even he might have realized. Lo-Melkhiin thought I was less than him; but his was not the only tally.

Lo-Melkhiin smiled. "Tell me about your sister," he said to me. "The men whispered that she was fairer, and marveled that I did not choose her. You did that on purpose, and I would know why."

There was something in his smile that lit a flame in my soul. The pieces of the tales I knew came quickly to me, the ones shaped like my sister and the ones to which she could be shaped. They flew about me, and I plucked them from the air.

"There is a fire in my sister," I said to him, "and I did not want you to have it."

"I still might," he said. "You may die quickly, as you have said."

"The law prevents you," I replied. "The men of the city and of the herds will not allow it. If you break it once, and steal a daughter, what is to stop you again?"

"I am patient," Lo-Melkhiin said. "Perhaps I will simply wait."

"She will be too old," I said. "She is my year-twin, and she will be married by the time you return."

"The fiery ones do not marry young," he said. "They

35

wait for fire to match their own. I did not see that in your village."

"My sister finds the fire in others," I said. "Her husband may be the quietest man at the market until he sees her. Then he will burn with a flame to match her own."

"You are so sure of her," he said.

"As sure as my soul," I said.

He laughed, head back and teeth gleaming in the light. I felt something stir again, and my own fire grew hotter. I knew this feeling. I had felt it as I rode away from my village and my sister knelt to pray. Perhaps even now, she wore her mother's priestly-whites and had gathered the other women to her. I leaned toward him.

"In the desert, where the sun burns the hottest, there is a wind that can strip flesh from bones," I said. "When it is in season, we leave old camels out to die. We hide in the safety of our tents, with enough food and water to last until the winds have passed. And we wait.

"The camels moan at first, when the wind starts. They know what is coming. They can smell it. But we tie them hard and they cannot break the bonds that hold them to the earth. They try, though. They try for their lives. They scream when the first blast of hot air strikes them. That is how we know it is no longer safe to go outside, and why we do not kill the camels before the wind comes. They are our last defense against the wind.

"They scream and scream. If the wind is hot enough, it is over quickly, but sometimes it lingers. Once, my sister could bear it no longer. She stole my brother's bow and peeled back the tent flap, holding it outward to protect herself from the wind. The wind was in her favor, and she shot the camel to stop it screaming. Our father was so surprised he could not even scold her."

"So your sister is a fool," Lo-Melkhiin said. "And soft-hearted besides, if she could not bear a camel's suffering."

"No, husband," I said. "My sister is clever. She held the bow against the tent flap so she would not be burned. And she killed the camel before it could panic and try to break free.

"It would have stayed tied, and it would have broken its bones. And we needed the bones to be hard and whole," I said. The fire raged in me with each word I spoke. "We use camel bones as tent poles, to keep the roof above our heads. We use them to prop open the flap that lets the smoke out. The hot wind does not always come. Sometimes an old camel dies, and must be skinned and cleaned in the fashion of antelope, and its bones are useless because they have not been cured by the wind. We cannot use them to build anything. We can hardly even use them for kindling.

"My sister is no fool and she is not tender-hearted," I said. "My sister fights for her home, and takes what risks she must. That is why I put myself before her today—why I would not let you have her. My sister burns, and she does not burn for you."

Lo-Melkhiin was fast, and grabbed my hands before I could even think to move away. It was his right to touch me however he wished, of course, so it was for the best that I did not shift. Where our skin touched, there was fire of a different kind. I thought I could see it, threads of gold and blue, desert sand and desert sky, bleeding from my body into his, but I had been a long time in the sun that day, and did not trust my eyes. He held on for one breath, then five, then ten. A strand of copper fire wound from his fingers to mine, so faint I wondered why I would imagine it at all, and then he released me.

"Well done, wife," he said to me, and stood. "You will do well in my house."

And then he was gone, the heavy air stirring behind him as he went into the night.

I slumped back against the cushions, tired and elated at the same time. I wondered if my sister had felt any of the fire I shared with her tonight. I wonder if she burned, and if she knew why. She must have prayed all day, either to a family smallgod or to the shrine she had promised to make for me. Because I had felt my soul stir, and when Lo-Melkhiin reached for me I had seen the glamor of flames. I did not know what it meant or even what had happened, and I did not care. I could hear the birds in the garden beyond the wall, and though I could not read the water clock, I knew that dawn must be close by. I had spent the night as the wife of Lo-Melkhiin.

And I had survived.

ii.

Lo-Melkhiin rode into the desert as a man, and he was something else when he came out.

He had gone to hunt lions, for his mother was fond of spinning yarn from the hair of their tawny manes, and because they preyed upon the villages around the desert's hem. He rode alone, as befitted a hunter of his class, but Nadarqwi the Farsighted watched his progress from the red stone cliffs, and Sareeyah the Fleetfooted stood beside, ready to dash to Lo-Melkhiin if aid was required.

Some say Lo-Melkhiin met a cruel god in the dunes that day. Others say he bargained with a devil there. The Skeptics looked up from their marble writing slabs and said he had stayed too long in the sun. God, demon, or otherwise, it mattered not. The true difference was me.

When I saw him, I knew he should be mine. He was taller than most, shoulders unstooped; he had never ground his own grain. His cloth was tightly woven, and there was something in his eyes that spoke of power. I wanted it, as I had wanted many things. And so I took.

His mind was harder than I had expected, and it required some effort to slip into the cracks. He loved his people—and he had many of these—well. His sense of duty was strong. He could mend armor and bake bread, though his station rarely required either of him. But at the bottom, underneath the pride he took in his work and home, there was a worry that dragged a chasm through his thoughts.

He was so young. And his father had ruled so poorly. And his mother was so ill.

That is where I set my claws and teeth. I pulled upon his doubts, laying them bare beneath the hot sun. And where he quailed, I set my conquest.

He fought—the best ones fight—but it was too late. I had him and he was mine. I stepped upon his duties and buried his loves. I kept only those pieces of him I wanted. The power. The knowledge. The ability to rule.

When I opened his eyes for the first time, the world was smaller, but it was mine. The air filled his lungs because I let it. I could just as easily have snuffed him out. If I had wanted, I could have made him remove his shoes and let the sand burn his feet.

I kept him in a corner of his mind, which I had not always done before. Usually when I took someone, they burned out fast and left me hungry. But Lo-Melkhiin was different. He was stronger. And it pleased me to hear him scream.

There was a roar, and I stood, leaning on his spear. My spear. I held it in his hands—my hands—as the lion drew near. Lo-Melkhiin knew how to kill them without spoiling the pelt. He could make their deaths swift and painless, and take the mane home to his mother, who loved them even through her illness.

But there were hyenas close by, too, and when I threw his spear—my spear—I pinned down the lion's paw. My prey roared again, this time in pain. The hyenas heard the call and answered, their laughter rolling across the dunes as they spread out to surround the injured beast.

The lion tried to fight them, but the hyenas were too many, their jaws too strong. They tore the golden beast to pieces, hair and blood and bone spread out across the sand, and then they ate him, because they could.

I made Lo-Melkhiin watch.

six

IT WAS A BREEZE THAT WOKE ME, sweet-smelling air untouched by heavy incense. And for a moment, I forgot where it was I slept, but then the serving girl laid the tray beside my pillowed head and I remembered. I breathed the clean air, let in by the open door I had not even seen the night before when the candles had turned my eyes to haze, and sat up.

"Lady-bless," said the serving girl, "you must drink the tea."

I wondered if she had come to bring breakfast to the other girls and found only their corpses in the silk. She showed no surprise at finding me alive, and no relief either.

She held the cup out to me, its ceramic shell so thin I marveled it could hold liquid at all, and I took it from her with both hands. It tasted awful, and I recognized the flavor of the herbs from my mother's description of them. This was the tea that kept a babe from settling. Lo-Melkhiin had only touched my hands, but I drank it down nonetheless.

There had been powers I did not understand in the room with us last night. In the soft sunlight, it was hard to remember, but easier to believe. I still felt the faint stirrings in my chest and knew I could not doubt. The light that had passed between us, first from me to him and then back as different colors, was like nothing of which I had seen or heard. And I did not know who in this place I could ask.

"Lady-bless," said the serving girl, "will you eat?"

I wondered if she expected tears from me, or lamentations. I crossed my ankles, and held out a hand for the bowl instead. She bowed over it, and the bronze was cool in my fingers. The food was simple, as though the cook who prepared it knew that I was desert-born and feared that my new surroundings would make me ill. I folded hummus into bread and ate slowly, and the serving girl watched.

She had my number of summers, I thought, though she was lighter skinned beneath her veils. She had not seen the sun and felt the wind as I had. Her nails were short, like mine, and her hair was bound up neatly in coils around her head. It was a more elaborate style than I had ever attempted, and I wondered how I might duplicate it, since I could not see how it was fastened beneath her silks. Then I remembered the bathhouse the evening before, and remembered that I might never do my own hair again. A queen's hair would be elegant, and put in place by someone else.

When I finished, she set the bowl down on the tray and pulled a cord near the foot of the bed. It rang with a soft chime, calling the other serving girls into the room. They began to open shutters and windows, air and light streaming in, and one took away the dishes. The first girl held her hands out to me, and I let her pull me from the bed. I followed her back along the path, where I could hear the whispering water again. I stopped, to see if she would let me, and when she did not push, I looked at the source of the sound. I had lived the night to see this, and I was not disappointed.

It was a statue of a woman standing tall and proud, with each foot on the back of a lion. In her hands there was a jug, held downwards, and from it poured a thin stream of water, which fell on the multicolored pebbles below. She was beautiful, but there was something in her eyes I did not like, something that did not match her face.

"Lady-bless," said the serving girl. "That is Lo-Melkhiin's mother, as carved by Firh Stonetouched to celebrate her recovery."

Lo-Melkhiin's mother had suffered long and hard; her health leeched from her like bones left out in the sun, white and brittle and bereft of all that gave life. When Lo-Melkhiin had come out of the desert, possessed by whatever demon he found there, he had cured her, but now she went no longer beneath the sun. I wondered if she ever met her son's wives, or if she ignored them.

"Lady-bless," said the serving girl, and I followed her into the bathhouse.

Today they dressed me more simply, and used much less perfume. They combed my hair, and coiled it, and pinned it underneath my veil. I did not know what had become of my sister's purple dishdashah that I had worn here. It had seemed so fine when I put it on, and I did not even really remember when they had taken it off. I wondered if it had simply been discarded, or if it had been passed on to another to wear. I wondered if they had kept it to bury me in.

The dress I wore now was much finer, the silk thinner and the stitching so tiny I had to squint to see it. They painted my face, which they had not done the night before, lining my eyes with black and then blue, to match the color of the dress. With my eyes closed, I saw the people of my village as they woke in the morning and prepared for the day.

Our father, returning, would find his second daughter gone. He might even mourn me, remembering the girl who had held his robe when the floods came, and the woman he might have bartered along with my sister for a marriage match. My brothers would not know what to say. After my

sister and I had reached our tenth summer and came in from
the herds to learn the tent-crafts that would serve us during
marriage, we had seen them infrequently. I looked past them
in my mind's eye, to the tent where my mother and my sister
and my sister's mother now slept together.

I pulled back the tent flap, and leaned in. There was my
sister's shrine, smaller than the one she had made for me in
the caves, but lovingly crafted. It was built of dark stones,
and bound by a circle of purple cloth I knew was from the
dress we had made together, the one I had taken from her
when I saved her life. On it there stood a tallow candle in
place of a lamp. These candles burned more quickly and
were more expensive, but the light was cleaner, and it was
said that smallgods paid more attention to light that more
closely matched the sun.

My sister knelt before the shrine and whispered in the
family tongue. My mother knelt beside her, though she did
not speak. Her face was tear-stained, and I knew that she
would not pray for me until her prayers were made of anger
and hope. Tear-prayers were for the dead, the kind we had
said for my sister's brother when the flood took him, and
for the babies that my mother had lost. My sister's mother
knotted black threads and laid them atop the purple silk, to
finish the binding. I hoped they would remember that my
sister needed a new dress. There was no need for this shrine
to become their lives.

"Lady-bless," said a serving girl, and I opened my eyes.

"I wore a purple dishdashah last night," I said. The words came unbidden, and they were the first I had spoken in hours. The serving girls jumped, but then smoothed their faces.

"Yes, lady-bless," said the girl who had carried my breakfast.

"I would like it back," I said to her. "My sister made it with me, and I do not wish for it to be destroyed."

"Of course, lady-bless," she said to me.

I was not used to idleness, and so the day dragged on. There were no craft tools in my room, and the serving girl who sat with me did not speak. I endured the morning, and a lunch of roasted peppers, and then when evening fell I was taken back to the bathhouse. My face was washed and my hair let down and combed with perfume. Again they wrapped me in fine silks, with ties so fragile that they might leave me bare at any moment, and again they returned me to my room to wait.

Lo-Melkhiin came as he had the night before, and sat down, this time on the bed.

"You still have no fear of me," he said.

"I still have nothing to fear," I told him.

"Tell me more about your sister," he said then. "If you would die for her, she must be worthy of tales."

"She is," I said. "Together, we made a dress that was

beautiful enough to fool a king into picking the magpie instead of the wren."

"That dress is lost to her," Lo-Melkhiin said. "If I wished, I could have it destroyed. I know you have asked for its return."

"My sister will make other dresses," I said to him. "Our father loves her mother well, and brings her the finest silks. Her mother is not so foolish as to waste them on herself, and has taught my sister to make the most delicate skirts and veils, so that when she goes to market, she catches the eyes of everyone who sees her. She will stitch her own secrets now, and they will be all the more powerful, for they will not be shared with anyone, not even with me."

"Maybe I will see her in the market and break the law," Lo-Melkhiin said.

"You will not," I told him. I did not fear him, and thus it was easy to tell him the truth. "You need the merchants. If you break that law in the market, they will wonder what other laws you might bend."

Lo-Melkhiin smiled like a lion, and again he reached for my hands. Again I let him take them without resisting, even though tonight his fingers were clasped more tightly around my wrists. I watched as purple and black fire, silk and secrets, stretched from my hands to his. Blood roared in my ears and the lamps flared more brightly, and then the copper fire came from his fingers to mine. It was no imagined sight, these lights. The cold light was his power, I was sure of it, and somehow the copper fire was mine; tonight it shone even more brightly. My vision and hearing cleared, and I let Lo-Melkhiin see that I would not be cowed. He leaned forward and placed his lips in the center of my forehead. I would not say it was a kiss, but it seemed to be all he required.

"We stitched it together over many desert nights, and wove such secrets with threads as cannot be unbroken." I said the words in my storyteller's voice. His fingers did not lessen their hold. I could sense he wanted to know, that he would compel it from me, yet I felt my own fire and would not be compelled.

The secrets were little things, for the most part. Which of the sheep we would try to ensure were part of her dowry; which of the pots she would take with her when she went wedded from our father's tents; which meals she would never serve, once she had the run of her own household. They were nothing, and they were everything; they were my sister, and I would never tell him what he had missed.

In the morning there was a neatly folded dishdashah, made from purple silk and stitched with black thread, lying at my feet. And I was alive to see it.

seven

IN THE DAYS THAT FOLLOWED, I learned some measure of the qasr's operation. The girls who brought my tea and fresh clothing each morning, and presumably the girls who would shroud my body and sing the last songs when Lo-Melkhiin finally tired of me, were all pretty. They wore simple white gowns with a shift beneath, the color my mother wore when she played priestly roles, but in a much more severe style. Their hair was as dark as my own, but of a shorter length, and braided in a single coil around their heads. I longed for a style of that sort, but each day when I was dressed, the woman who did my hair fell to experimentation. The elabo-rate designs put weight in strange places, and I often had a

51

headache by noon. Also, they itched.

The bathhouse attendants were much the same, though they wore only their shifts when they were at their work. I was given a bath each morning, and I confess I took no small amount of joy in the sheer amount of water that was allotted to me. It was so hot that it steamed, and it seemed that I breathed the water in my lungs as much as I sat in it. If I was to be here, I would enjoy what I could of this place.

I was less enamored of the afternoons. I might walk in the gardens before the sun grew too hot, or again as it began to set and the night flowers bloomed, but I soon tired of the same statues, with their haunted eyes, and the same fountains, though I did love their songs. On the fourth day I caught the hem of a serving girl's dress, when she would have left me.

"Please," I said to her, as I would have spoken to my mother, "is there not some craft that I might do? The hours are long, and I am not accustomed to idleness."

She hesitated, and I knew the reason. As Lo-Melkhiin's wife, I ought to have had the run of the qasr's crafthalls, supervising the embroidery and the weaving. At the same time, they could not give me anything sharp, nor strong weaving cords, lest I turn them upon myself. That left spinning. I supposed I could do some damage with a spindle whorl, but once the distaff was broken, I would have naught but a ceramic disc. I drew myself up, remembering that here,

I was no one's daughter. Here I was a queen, for however long I might last.

"I shall spin," I said, taking the decision from her. "It is my favorite, and I do not wish to interrupt what process your craft-mistresses have established."

"Yes, lady-bless," the girl said, and led me into the corridor.

When we entered the thread room, all heads turned and all conversation ceased. There were some two dozen women sitting grouped at various tasks, and yet if any of them had dropped their needles, the sound would have echoed. The girl looked as though she wished the floor would eat her bones, but I walked proudly. I followed her to the piles of new-carded wool, and she handed me a spindle before moving to take her own seat with the embroiderers.

It took my fingers some time to regain their skill. I had not had much cause to spin at home, being put to embroidery as soon as I was able to understand its worth. Moreover, our wool was a good deal coarser. My mother could have had finer threads, if she wished them, but they were brought to us by our father. We did not make them. My hands were chapped from the desert wind and callused from my earlier years with a shepherd's crook. They snagged my thread and frayed it, and again and again I undid my work.

The others said nothing, but I could feel their eyes on me. Before, I had wanted their attention, had wanted them to remember who, and what, I was. Now they looked upon me still, but they saw a poor desert girl who could not even spin properly, and I wished for it to stop.

"Lady-bless." There was a voice at my elbow. I turned, and there stood an older woman, with gnarled fingers and a kind smile. She held out a pair of soft white gloves, and I took them with a nod of thanks.

"The desert breeds strong," she said. It was an old saying that our father liked to tell my brothers when they complained of the wind and the sand and their herds.

"And we must find ways to live in our father's tent." I finished the words, and her smile grew.

She returned to her seat, and I took up the spindle again. Now the thread grew beneath my fingers, coiling into the basket between my feet in an even strand. I felt the eyes of my companions turn to their own work, and when they no longer looked at me, they forgot that I was there to hear their words.

My mother had told me that when she first married our father, when he had not yet built the fortune to establish a permanent camp in his father's settlement, she and my sister's mother had gone with him in the caravan. It was a harder life for them. In addition to constant travel, they were each night at the mercy of some new trader's wives and mother. The men all respected our father as a merchant who was set to establish himself, but the women were not so sure.

Why had he married, then, if he was not yet wealthy enough to keep his wives at home? And why had he married twice?

Yet every night, my mother and my sister's mother had gone to the women's tents and taken out their thread boxes. There was always mending to do, and sometimes they had finer work, if our father's trades had gone well. The others saw the work they did, saw the work they did together, and they understood that our father was not foolish, and neither were his wives. Then the other women would start to talk to one another. Through them, my mothers learned more of the habits of the men our father traded with than he had ever dreamed of.

"With your eyes on your work," my mother had said to me, thinking to prepare me for a trader's life, "it is easy to forget who is present to hear your mouth. You and your sister must remember that, when you are wed. Do good work, and those you work with will tell you things beyond what you can imagine."

Advice for a trader's wife, perhaps, but it would serve me well in the qasr too. As I spun, the women fell to talking around me. It was quiet at first, like the whispers in water-starved wadi reeds. They did not say anything that day about Lo-Melkhiin, or about the qasr, but they did not hold their tongues when I was present; I knew that, if I lived, I might soon hear something I could put to use.

I focused on the whorl instead. This too was a trick I

had learned from my mother. Spinning does not require a great deal of thought, and when you have become accustomed to the weight of the spindle and the feel of the wool, even your eyes are not necessary. My mother's mother had spun while blind for the last ten years of her life, and yet the threads my mother used to embroider her wedding dishdashah were as fine as any our father might have bought for her later. Spinning is a dreamer's craft, and I wished to dream of my sister, and of a place that was not so closed and full of fear.

My breath slowed to match the rise and fall of the spindle, and my eyes drifted back and forth with the whorl. The thread I spun was raw—they would dye it later—but soon enough I saw the black fire of my sister's dark hair in the dirty-white of the wool.

She was in the caves, the hill where we buried our dead, and where we had first seen the rain. My mother and my sister's mother stood beside her, and all of them were clad in the priestly-whites the women of my family wore in that place. I could see their mouths moving, though I could not hear their words, and I knew that no one had died. My sister was learning the songs, not burying someone, and our mothers were teaching her to follow in their work.

I was puzzled by this. My sister would still marry, surely, and leave our father's tents. If she were to learn the songs to sing to the dead, it would be her husband's songs she sang. If she learned our songs, if she were tied to our family's caves, the dead might not let her leave them. They would always require her to keep them. But I knew the vision before me did not lie. My sister was learning our own death songs, and that meant she would stay in our father's tents forever—and always near my shrine.

I wondered if our father knew what they were doing. I could not imagine that he would give his approval. He respected the dead, of course, not least because his father's father's father was the smallgod to whom he owed his trade. That shrine was the most often visited in our catacombs. Even in the dry season, it had sweet-water flowers on it, and pickled roots. It was not the shrine before which my sister now stood.

This shrine was new, stone still bleached white from the desert sun and not shadowed by time under the earth. On it there was a scattering of purple cloth that I recognized immediately. When we had cut the dishdashah for my sister's wedding, her mother had kept the scraps, to use for luck-pieces in later works. We had not yet begun those, and so the pieces had stayed in her thread box. But now they were on the shrine, laid out for the smallgods to see.

Laid out for *me* to see.

It was my shrine they were teaching her to keep. The shrine that would make me a smallgod when I died, and the same one she had promised to build while I yet lived.

I had seen them praying to another, smaller, shrine in the tent, and thought it the full extent of her vow. She must have told my mother, perhaps to stay her grief, and then they must have decided together to move their worship to our holiest place. She would never leave, not now. She would be mine forever.

"Lady-bless?" said the kind woman from earlier. "Lady-bless, it is time for you to go."

I shook myself from the trance. I was surrounded by dirty-white thread, neatly spun and coiled, and the lamps were lit. It had been hours.

"I thank you," I said to them, all of them. "I will see you tomorrow."

They nodded. It was a pretty wish.

That night, Lo-Melkhiin came to me, and asked me to tell him of my sister,

"My father will be back with the caravan now," I said to him. He had not yet taken my hands, and yet I felt a fire in my skin nonetheless. It spun, burning, like the spindle whorl. "He will have brought with him final news of my sister's marriage."

"Her marriage?" he said to me. "You lie."

"I do not," I said to him, though I did. "These past few seasons my father has sought a husband for my sister, and he has found one to his liking, and to hers."

"He cares so much for her tastes?"

"My sister must love the one she weds," I said, and the heat within me surged. "And in him, she will stir all the fires of creation."

I lied, but I saw the morning all the same.

eight

ON THE SEVENTH MORNING, an old woman brought my tea. She was not old the way the master-weavers were, with their gnarled fingers and stooped shoulders, their white hair braided about their heads in that simple, coiled style of which I was so jealous. She was old like desert rock, bleached and hard, all the impurities worn away. And her hair, which hung loose about her face, was a tawny color the like of which I had never seen.

It was her hair that gave her away. This was Lo-Melkhiin's mother, who had been so ill and then was cured by him in the days after he came back from the desert. Her hair had not recovered as she had, once her sickness was gone, and since no more of it ever grew she had made for herself a wig out of the lion manes she loved so dearly. It could not be braided or oiled, and could no more be tamed than the beasts themselves. It was unearthly to look upon, so early in the morning with the golden sunlight around her, but it was beautiful nonetheless.

I sat up and took the cup from her hand. I wondered if I ought to rise altogether and bow, but before I could move again, she took a seat amongst the cushions at the foot of my bed and tucked her feet beneath her, as though she were a daughter of shepherds herself.

"Seven nights," she said to me. "I suppose I will not be able to avoid you for much longer."

I wondered if she had thought to care at all for her son's wives at the start, and learned to ignore them the way the rest of the qasr seemed to. The women in the thread room still did not speak to me, though they spoke to themselves in louder and less cautious voices. At least they no longer looked so surprised when I appeared each morning, and no longer avoided my gaze when I told them I would see them the next day.

"It is my honor to meet you," I said. I did not know what to do, or even what to call her, so I drank my tea and prayed that I did not give offense.

"My son says that you are not afraid of him," she said to me.

I had not known that they were on speaking terms. I did not know if she approved of his marriages. I did not know if she feared him.

"I do fear him," I said, which was close to the truth. "I fear him as I fear the desert sun and poisonous snakes. They are all part of the life I live. But the sun gives light, and snakes will feed a caravan if they are caught and cooked."

"And under my son's rule, we have peace and prosperity," she said, her voice bitter. Her husband had not ruled well.

"And I have no escape from him," I agreed.

She looked at me for a long time, and I finished my tea.

"I will tell you of my son," she said. "Not the man he is now, for that you know as well as I do. But I will tell you what he was like when he was a boy, and what he was like when he learned to hunt."

I wondered if she meant for me to pity him, but I remembered the others who had lived in this room before me, and my heart was not moved. Still, I had no other business today, and our father had always told my brothers that the best routes are the ones best known.

"I will hear you," I said.

"Come to the gardens when you are dressed, and we will speak," she said to me, and then she left, the wooden screen sliding shut behind her.

The serving girls came in, breathless with excitement, though they did their best to keep their faces blank. Today, at last, my hair was coiled simply about my head, though they twisted it instead of braiding it, which looked better and was more difficult to secure. I thought I might have more pegs in my hair than held our father's tents to the sand by the time they were done. Then they led me to the garden, the one with the fountain I had seen on my first night, and I sat down next to Lo-Melkhiin's mother. There was a basket of figs before us, and a jug of sweet-water.

"I am from the south," she said to me. "Where our desert is blue and looks like water, but will kill you if you drink it."

Our father had told me of this, and my brothers had seen it too. It was their favorite tale to tell to me and to my sister. A great blue and boundless desert, that heaved under the wind and grew or shrank with the size of the moon. Creatures did live in it, underneath the surface, like our burrowing snakes and insects; but if a man drank from it, he went mad and died, the same as if he had tried to drink sand.

"We have different animals there," she continued, and I remembered myself and paid attention. "So when my lord came to marry me, and brought me my first lion skin, I knew that I must follow him back to see the creature that had such glorious fur."

I wondered what it must have been like to be unafraid of lions. When my sister and I first took up the herds, we were told how to kill jackals and hyenas; *but*, my brothers insisted, *should a lioness come, she can take whatever sheep she likes*. The males, I had learned when I was older, were different, but still vicious, particularly when they were alone.

"I loved him, though he was something of a fool," she said. "He was kind and fair-minded. In better times, he would have made a fair ruler. But it was not to be. I grew ill, and whatever makes the water come to us from far away failed. The lords he trusted betrayed him, and lined their own pockets instead of looking after their people in the towns and villages. And then my son was born."

Lo-Melkhiin had, I think, ten summers more than I did. By the time I was born, we were accustomed to the hard times. My father traveled farther and was home less frequently. My mother and my sister's mother had learned to stretch every thread, every loaf, every cut of meat, as far as they could. We did not starve, and neither did any in our father's tents; but in the towns, they did not fare as smoothly.

"My son grew up hard, like the times, but with the kind-ness of his father's smile," she said. "I knew that he would be a better lord than his father, and my husband knew it too. He spent hours ensuring that Lo-Melkhiin had all the best teachers and weapons-masters. If there was a craft my son wished to try his hand at, his father found him a craft-master.

"But what he loved most of all was hunting," she said. "He learned the desert's secrets with the ease a hawk learns to fly. By the time he had twelve summers, he was already bringing home more meat than the qasr's huntsmen, though the pickings were still lean in those times. He traveled far and wide, seeing more of the land and the desert than his father ever did, protected by his loyal guards wherever he went."

I had heard of the guards of which she spoke. Their names were legend now, as was his. Fleetfoot and Farsight had not saved him from whatever-it-was, the day he last went into the desert. His mother spoke fondly of them, though, so I did my best to control the emotions that would otherwise have rioted on my face.

"He took his first lion in his sixteenth summer," she said. "The beast had been stealing sheep from a village close to the city, and there was worry that it would soon develop a taste for children. My husband forbade Lo-Melkhiin to go after it, but he made his guards take him out anyway, and three days later, he returned with a fine pelt.

"After that, it was as though the beasts took to taunting him," she said. "Though I suppose they had no more game than we did, and were forced to find the easy prey of sheep. And every time he rode out, he came home with a pelt. I loved them dearly. They were soft, and they smelled of such wildness. I was fading then, breaking under the sun, and the lion skins my son brought to me were one of the few joys I still had."

She carded her fingers through her wig as she spoke, smiling at the memory.

"And then he went out after one last pelt." The smile disappeared from her face. "And you know what happened after that."

We sat, listening to the fountain, and the sun climbed above us.

"My lady mother," I said at length, not thinking it odd that I should call her the same thing I called my sister's mother. "Why do you tell me this?"

"I would have you know your husband," she said. "It is not fair for you to think him only a monster. The men of the court will tell you that he has done much good for us, and that your death and those of the others are the price we must pay. I wanted to tell you that he was good, before, and that his father and I wished for him to be a better man. He is not that man. But every day you live, I will pray to the smallgods of my house that he will become that man again."

She left me then, and I sat in the garden until the hammer of the sun became so hard that I was forced to seek shade. It still did not matter to me that Lo-Melkhiin had once loved his mother and his people. He shed blood and kept peace, but only the peace was of note. I was not content with that, though I did not wish for some other girl's death to pay the price instead. Seven days in the qasr had made me determined to get seven more, and then more besides. But I had a map of the trade route now, or at least a better one than I did before Lo-Melkhiin's mother told me about her son. Perhaps there was a weakness, a fault, I could exploit in him.

But I thought also of what she had said at the end, of what all the stories said: he is not that man anymore.

nine

I DID NOT GO TO THE thread room that afternoon. Instead, I went through the gardens to see the great statues that Lo-Melkhiin's artists had made. When I saw the statue of his mother again, standing strong and straight on the backs of the lion pair, I stopped. The first day that I saw the statue, I had thought it striking and beautiful. Now, having met the flesh-and-blood woman herself, I was less sure. The statue seemed harder, and not because it was made of stone. The face was more pointed, the mouth drawn down, and the shoulders broader than they were in life.

The worst, though, were the eyes.

I had seen the like on the other statues in the qasr

gardens. It did not seem to matter if they were men, women, or animals. All were carved in an uncomfortable beauty, such that no living creature could duplicate. And all had eyes that were not quite right, staring off into corners as if they expected to find unspoken horrors there. To look too long at any of them was to court madness.

"Do you like this one?" said a voice behind me. I turned, and saw the guardsman who had given me salt in the desert. He was not dressed in his uniform, the leather armor that deflected blades and arrows—and must have been murderous in the sun—but wore linen breeches and a tunic belted at the waist. The carved wooden box hung there, next to his eating knife.

"It is striking," I said to him. "But having met the subject, I do not think I like it."

"I do not like it, either," he confessed, coming to stand beside me. "And I feel I am allowed to say as much, as it was me that carved it."

I choked. I had never met a stone carver before, let alone one as famous as Firh Stonetouched.

"My lord, I am sorry," I said. "I meant no offense."

"I am no lord," he said, "and I spoke true when I told you I do not like it. I do not like many of the statues I have made for Lo-Melkhiin, even though he does me great honor by putting them on display in such fine settings as his own gardens."

"I thought you were a guardsman," I said. I wished, not for the first time in my life, that I had my sister's gift with words. I could tell stories well, if I learned and practiced their telling, but I was not gifted when it came to making them from whole cloth.

"I am," he said. "I came here to serve Lo-Melkhiin's father, right before he died, and then I served Lo-Melkhiin."

"Carving, then, is entertainment to you?" I said. My mother did not approve of idleness, and since my brothers would not lower themselves to sew, many of them whittled bone tools as they sat around the fire at night.

"It was, once," he said. "I could make shafts for arrows, or tent pegs—nothing finer. It kept my hands busy, you see, on long watches when the night was cold."

I looked at the statue. It was a long way from arrows and pegs by the evening's fire to carven rock in the center of Lo-Melkhiin's gardens.

"What turned you to stone?" I asked.

His face darkened.

"I rode with Lo-Melkhiin to fetch a bride," he said. He had forgotten to whom he spoke, and I saw when he remembered, looking at me with a jerk of his head.

"It is all right," I said. "Please continue."

"Very well," he said. "On those rides, we number few, and Lo-Melkhiin takes his turn at keeping watch and saddling the horse, as if he was a common guard. He spoke to us, and we to him, and he watched me carve. He said I had good hands for stone, should I want to; when we returned, I found this great hulk of rock had been quartered to me.

"I ignored it for a good long while. Six wives, I think. Or maybe eight. I apologize, my lady, but sometimes I do not like to keep track."

I could not blame the qasr folk. Lo-Melkhiin's wives numbered in the hundreds, and some had barely survived long enough to make a mark upon the qasr way of life. It was too much to expect them to mourn.

"Each time we rode out, Lo-Melkhiin watched me carve, and told me that I had hands for stone. And each time, I did not listen," he said. "And then one night I dreamed, more vividly than I have ever done, of a statue that was trapped inside a great block—a statue of Lo-Melkhiin's mother, astride a pair of lions.

"When I woke, my tools were already in my hands, and I was halfway to my feet before I thought about it. I had never carved stone before, and the statue I had seen in my dream was beautiful. I knew it was foolish to think that I could make something of that quality on my first attempt. Even arrow shafts take practice.

"I did not stop for food or drink, not even when the sun was high above where I worked. My hands cracked and bled, and my throat screamed for water, and I did not stop. I baked in the sun, and I did not care. I thought only of the statue, the one that I would free from the stone."

If you separate the ram from the ewes when they are in heat, he will go mad trying to get to them. It does not matter how you tie him down. If he can smell them, he will break all his bones, and yours, trying to reach them. It sounded as though the madness that had overtaken the carver was the same.

"At last, it was finished. I came out of my trance and Lo-Melkhiin was there. I think he had watched me for some time, though I had been lost in the work and did not see him arrive," he said. "He looked at it, from top to bottom, and declared it perfect. He thanked me for so wonderful a work in the name of his mother, and named me Firh Stonetouched, because when the stone and I worked together, we wrought beauty. He asked what boon I would have from him, and I told him that I was happy as a guard. I do not love stone, you see, but sand and sky. I did not wish to leave them."

"But the other statues?" I asked. "What about them?"

"Those I carved in fits like madness," he told me. "Sometimes Lo-Melkhiin rides with me, and then gives me stone. And I always carve it, even though I do not like to, and the results haunt me in every garden in this place."

I looked at his hands. They were dark brown from the sun and wind, and callused from his horse's reins and the shaft of the spear he carried when it was his turn to walk the wall. I saw no cuts or damage. It had been seven days since I had come here, and that would not have been enough time for his hands to heal if the carving-madness had overtaken him.

"Did you carve nothing when I came?" I asked him.

He smiled, truly smiled for the first time since he had begun to speak to me.

"I carved arrow shafts, my lady," he said, "in the tradition of my father's father's father. I do not trade them for gold and herds, as he does. Instead I use them to buy my way out of chores in the barracks I would rather not do. Then I have free time to come here, to the garden."

"I am surprised," I said. "I would think, from what you have said, that you would stay as far from your statues as you could."

"You are right, lady-bless," he said. "But the flowers are lovely, despite the stone, and the fountains are still as wondrous to me as they were the day I got here. For those two beauties, I will overlook my dislike of the statues, and of their eyes. I cannot ever seem to fix their eyes."

"The fountains are magnificent," I agreed, but suddenly I was uncomfortable.

Always, it seemed, men would overlook unpleasant things for the sake of those that went well. The statues' eyes for the melodious sounds of the fountain. The deaths of their daughters for the bounty of their trade.

There was great beauty in this qasr, but there was

73

also great ugliness and fear. I would not be like those men who turned their eyes from one to see the other. I would remember what those things cost. Whether he knew it or not, the carver's hands were moving over the lion's bodies, like he was carving them again. Had he his tools, I've no doubt he would have found some new stone to make it into some dreadful semblance of life. Even so, I could not hate him. He had given me salt in the desert, and he had looked at me when the other guards had avoided my gaze. It was possible that he, who had come here to serve a man he loved, was as much a prisoner as I was, though he was held by different promises. I could not be saved from the death that awaited me inside these stone walls, but he might yet find his freedom in sand and sky. I watched as he lost himself to the quiet music and ever-changing patterns of falling water.

"May your hands find what you love," I whispered, too softly for any but my smallgods to hear. "May your work not frighten you, but bring you joy instead, and may it bring joy to others. May you carve for yourself, and not for Lo-Melkhiin."

I left him there, with his hands on the flanks of the lions he disliked and his eyes on the falling water. As I came close to the garden's arch, I heard a rustle in the low shrubs, and knew that one of the serving girls had watched us as we spoke. My marriage might be unconventional, and as yet unconsummated, but it seemed that at least my attendants were certain to mind me. I would not be left unchaperoned with another man, not even one as respected as Firh Stonetouched.

Lo-Melkhiin had given him that name, he said. I wondered what his name had been before, if he had had one—or if the sun had baked it from his mind the day he carved Lo-Melkhiin's mother.

ten

ON THE TENTH MORNING, when I woke alone in my comfortable room and was not dead, I was not surprised. A chill ran through my blood, and the walls closed in around me. I had seen the strange power ebb and flow between Lo-Melkhiin's hands and mine. I suspected that my inevitable death would not be the result of poison, nor a blade, nor his fingers crushing my windpipe. There was something at work here that I did not understand; some wicked smallgod of Lo-Melkhiin's family, or perhaps the demon from the stories, played upon our linked fingers. That would be my end. I could not pray to the smallgod my sister had made of me. The words stuck in my throat. But I could pray as I always had, to the bones of our father's father's father, even though they were very far away.

I breathed deep, as my mother had taught me, and drew the picture of clear blue sky and calm brown sand in my mind. Before, when my sister and I had done this, we had held hands and pinched each other to keep from giggling. We did not lack piety by any means, but we were children, and children will find laughter wherever they can. My mother had frowned, but my sister's mother smiled with us.

"The smallgods hear of so many sad things, so many hopeless wants and desires," she said. "Let them hear laughter for a time."

I did not laugh now, and clouds roiled through the desert in my mind. In vain, I tried to call the blue sky into focus, but it would not come, and the smooth sand was punctured in many places by sharp rock, and by bushes with thorns so long they would pierce a lamb's heart, if the creature stumbled into them. I opened my eyes, and lamented my failure. Perhaps I really was too far away from the places of my dead to pray.

On the top of the wooden chest in the corner of my room, there lay folded the dishdashah that my sister and I had made, the one that someone had brought to me when I wished for it. I rose and crossed the room to get it, bare feet used to rug-covered marble floors at last. Holding it in my hands, I returned to my seat on the bed and closed my eyes once more.

This time, I did not call the desert. Instead I saw my sister's hands as we worked the embroidery into the fine fabric. I heard her voice, whispering in my ear. And there was something more, something else deeper in the vision. I let go of the focus on my breathing, and fell into it.

It was a regular sound, rhythmic and comforting. It was the loom on which the cloth had been made. I did not know who had crafted the cloth—our father had brought it with him when he returned with the caravan—but I could feel her hands on the shuttle, the way her fingers picked apart the strings of the warp to make a pattern for the weft. The cloth of my dishdashah had been of deepest purple, a mark of our father's wealth. The weaving this time was the brightest orange, with fine gold thread added as an accent every half-handspan or so. Though the color was less rich, the pattern and weight of the fabric made it priceless. This would dress a queen.

I felt the strength of the weaving, and called it toward myself. I saw orange fire run from the fabric to my hands, and though the color was not bleached from the cloth, I felt stronger, calmer. I thought I could call the blue sky desert now, but found I no longer needed it.

When I opened my eyes, a serving girl was kneeling at the foot of my bed. I had not seen her before, and wished that there might be some consistency in the women who came into my rooms. She had not interrupted me, and I was glad of it. Her eyes were wide, but I did not know the reason until I looked down at my hands, still holding the dishdashah. It was pale in the sunlight of my room, but undeniable nonetheless: the copper-colored glow that enveloped my hands and the dark purple silk. Alarmed, I opened my fingers and the dishdashah fell, taking that strange light with it.

"Lady-bless," breathed the girl, and I thought she might fully genuflect before me. At least she did not flee in fear.

"Pay no mind to it," I said to her. "The smallgods show favor in ways we cannot always understand."

"Yes, lady-bless," she said, but it was clear that she did not think the light was from a smallgod any more than I did. She took a breath and stood. "My lord will have a grand feast tonight," she said, as though nothing had happened. "There is a star shower, and he has called upon Skeptics and priests to debate the matter. He bids you to come, else he will not see you."

I wondered if that meant I was safe tonight. If I did not go, Lo-Melkhiin would not see me, and could not kill me. If I went, he would surely not kill me in front of the others. I felt that chill again, as when I had awoken, but it was less because of the copper fire I had called to myself. Lo-Melkhiin would not kill me with his hands, I was sure of it. There was some strange power to him, even as there was some strange power to me, and I would not learn of it hiding in my room, or from the women as they crafted.

"I will go," I told her, and she smiled at me.

She helped me to dress then, in a light shift for the morning, as I would soon begin preparing for what was to come. I broke my fast with flatbread and oil, and then was taken away to the baths. The preparations were even more elaborate than they had been for my wedding night, presumably because this occasion called for a more involved hairstyle than had been required on that evening. I sat for hours as I was scrubbed, pumiced, hennaed, plaited, and coiled. It was warm and I could have drifted into the weaving trance, or even called up the blue sky desert, but I was concerned that if I made the attempt, that strange light would reappear. I did not wish to startle my attendants. Instead, I sat and listened to their talk.

"Last year, my lord only called upon the Skeptics," the henna mistress said, dark brown hands working patterns on my skin. "The priests were angry, but of course they could say nothing about it."

"The Skeptics said that the stars are not smallgods, but rock and fire," said the girl whose job it was to pick the bath salts.

"Who lights a fire hot enough to burn rock, then?" said the henna mistress. "And how does it stay aflame in the sky with no one to tend it?"

"I am sure the Skeptics have an answer," the girl said.

"Of course they do." The henna mistress finished with my arms, and began to comb the dye into my hair—for the scent, not the color. "But in hearing their answers and the answers from the priests, we see a clearer picture of the sky."

They continued to argue as they worked on my hair, and I withdrew into my thoughts in spite of my determinations otherwise. We did not have Skeptics in our father's tents. They lived only in the city, and in some of the larger villages. Unlike priests, who can work alone, Skeptics require the company of their fellows so that they can debate the great questions they have set themselves to. Small villages and encampments can spare folk to tend to the bones of the dead and the altars of the smallgods, but they cannot always spare a man to do nothing but think, no matter how great his thoughts. I had never met a Skeptic, and tonight I would.

I was unfamiliar with what, exactly, was accorded to me by my rank. While the servants deferred to me, and Firh Stonetouched had been respectful, I was unsure if I could command. If I spoke to a Skeptic, he would likely disregard me as a simple tent-born girl, come to die at Lo-Melkhiin's hand as all the others before me had done. Perhaps my continued life would be interesting enough to garner me the conversation I required. I wished to ask about the power of smallgods, if any knew how far their power reached. I knew the priest's answer already, because I had had it from my mother, but now I wanted another opinion.

When my hair was done to satisfaction, the women brought me fruit to eat, and took some time to rest before the final steps of my decoration. I learned how to sit with the mass of coiled braids upon my head, and how to handle a cup without ruining the tattoos on my fingers and wrists. The henna mistress watched me closely, and then nodded her approval.

"Do not worry overmuch about courtly manners tonight, lady-bless," she said, her voice low and close to my ear. "It will be torchlight only, and standing to eat. With luck, all eyes will be upon the stars."

"With luck," I said, and smiled. She smiled back, uncertainly at first, but then a true smile when she saw that I was not afraid.

At last it grew dark, and it was time to dress for dinner. The dressing mistress cut me out of the shift I wore, because they could not pull it over my head. A new one was brought, with lacing in the back, and they tied me into it.

"This is a dishdashah for standing," the dressing mistress said to me. "You must not sit unless one of your own attendants is close by to help you stand again. It will not fall apart while you stand, but if you bend, you will loosen the fastenings, and then they will not hold when you move again."

They brought out the garment. I could not keep the

surprise from my face. The light cast by the oil lamps
flickered, but shone brighter than the tallow candles we used
in the tents. It was not murky or dim, because the tiles in
the bathing rooms reflected the light cast by the lamps, and
magnified it so that it was as bright as it had been during the
day. There was no mistaking what I saw, though I blinked
several times to make sure I had not strayed into a vision.

The fabric was as orange as fire, and woven through
with gold so that it, like the tiles, glimmered in the lamplight.
The heavy silk whispered as the dressing mistress wrapped
it around me, stopping now and then to do the fastenings
while her assistants held the cloth in place. Even the pattern
in the warp matched the vision I had seen.

"It was made especially for your coloring, lady-bless,"
the dressing mistress said. She had clearly mistaken the
cause of my awe. "We had not heard about the gold thread,
though. That was a surprise to all."

"Indeed," I said, carefully running one finger across the
fabric. It rippled, variations in color running over the top
of it like wispy clouds through a hot summer sky, but much
more brilliant to look at.

"You will even stand out in the dark," said the henna
mistress. "Perhaps some eyes will stray from the stars after
all."

I stood quietly as they finished, their excitement about
the dishdashah quelling the last of their fears that I would

die tonight. I no longer had that fear either, but a new one was growing in its place. I still wished to speak to a Skeptic, but now I would have to be even more careful about what I said. I had never heard of a person who dreamed the future while they still lived. Sometimes a smallgod gave guidance, but it was always vague. My vision had been strikingly specific. I closed my eyes, and once again reached for that blue sky desert, as I had so many times before I had come to this place. It came as soon as I bade it, but it was different this time than it had been before.

The sky was still a brilliant blue, and the sand a smooth brown, but it was no longer unadorned. I could see, as I had never seen before, how the sky was woven together, how the sand was made a part of the pattern, and how the two pieces were joined at the hem along the far horizon. My heart sped up, and I thought at first that I was afraid; but then I opened my eyes, and I saw how the women looked at me, like I was a queen in truth, and I knew that it was not fear I felt, rushing along with the blood through my veins.

iii.

Lo-Melkhiin knew her well, that first one. He knew what she looked like. Her scent. The shape of her smile. He remembered her for a long time, because he loved her. I remembered her because I stole her.

She was shorter than Lo-Melkhiin was, and her face was lit with joy all throughout the wedding ceremony and the feast that followed. The people did not know what was to come, not yet. They had not even begun to suspect. All they knew was that Lo-Melkhiin was happy to wed, at last, and their lands were slowly recovering from misrule. They did not yet understand that there would be a price. Lo-Melkhiin knew, of course, and he screamed and raged, but he could do nothing to stop me.

When the food was eaten and the songs were sung, they put Lo-Melkhiin and his bride to bed in a silk-hung room with wide windows for the moonlight. Lo-Melkhiin stood in the pale space on the floor, and she came to him, dark hair bleeding color under the silver glow. The night air was desert-cool, but her lips on his were warm. For a moment, Lo-Melkhiin was overcome. He stopped his voiceless screams at her touch, warmed by her kiss. When I tightened his hands on her slim waist, he remembered, and screamed anew.

I was clumsy, that first night. The cold light worked too quickly, and she was too in love with the man she thought she had married. It would take me time, and several more wives, to refine my methods. I think, had I been better able to control myself, she might have lived to see the next day. She might have lived to see the next ten. I would learn in the nights to come that fear burned swiftly, but love burned strong. Both were useful, which was fortunate, because soon enough no one loved Lo-Melkhiin anymore.

None of that mattered that night. I took what I required from her, and made Lo-Melkhiin watch as she shriveled and wilted under his hands. Her dark hair turned grey, then silver, and finally white. Her eyes lost their spirited glow, and became dull things within her skull. Her skin drew tight across her bones, and then sagged as her bones failed within her. My only real complaint was that she never screamed, but Lo-Melkhiin did enough of that for both of them.

In the morning, when the serving girls woke Lo-Melkhiin, it was with cries of fear and distress at the sight of the thing with which I shared his marriage bed. I feigned distress as well, and did so good a

86

job at it that I was believed. She was buried, and I pretended to mourn even while the lands prospered. But a lord cannot be unwed, and before long, the council begged Lo-Melkhiin to set aside his supposed grief and marry again. They did not have to beg very hard.

The second wedding was much the same as were the ones that followed it. If there were rumblings that Lo-Melkhiin should not wed again, they were as quiet as the footfalls of a wild dog hunting in the desert. Time passed and girls died, and eventually there were too many for even the Skeptics to explain away. But the land prospered, and there was peace, and Lo-Melkhiin asked again to be married. The men of the council decided, then, the sort of girls to sacrifice, and the law was handed down.

I cared not for the laws and rules of Lo-Melkhiin's council. I cared only for the strength of the power I took from his wives, as they came to his bed, and for the pain I caused to the body I had taken. In time he twisted; his agony lessened, and became a dull thing that I could barely provoke. My power did not wane, however, and I found I could still taunt him with the fragility of our victims. And so we continued. Together.

eleven

WHEN THE HENNA MISTRESS and the others were done
with me, one of the footmen came and took me to a garden I
had not been into before. It was at the base of the qasr wall,
and its entrance was hidden by a door carved to look as
though it were part of the wall. I had looked at it and never
seen what was hidden there. Lo-Melkhiin's mother waited
for me by a worn statue. It did not have the unsettling eyes
I had become accustomed to seeing in the qasr gardens. For
some reason, it made me feel more at ease, even though I
still had no idea what awaited me this night.

Lo-Melkhiin's mother was even paler in the dark, and
bore no henna on her skin as I did. As always, her head

was crowned with her lion's-mane wig, the sandy-colored hair bleached white under the stars the same way the desert paled under the night sky. Her dishdashah was darker than mine—blue, or maybe purple—I could not tell with such little illumination. It was simply cut and sewed, with no embroidery and no thread like the gold that highlighted mine. I wondered if I was overdressed, but when she saw me she only nodded, and then raised a hand to fix one of the curls that had come loose while I walked.

"Your dresser missed a pin," she said to me. I felt her thin fingers against my scalp as she anchored the curl to the same pin as its neighbor. She pulled my veil forward slightly to cover the mistake. "You must be sure to hold your head still."

"I will, my lady mother," I said to her.

She nodded again and took my arm in hers. We walked away from the comfort of the statue's gaze to the sally port in the qasr wall. This, I realized, was why the garden was hidden. The sally port was likely concealed from the outside as well, to keep enemies unaware of its exact location. I wondered how many within the walls knew of its location. I wondered if Lo-Melkhiin's mother only showed it to me now because she knew that I might die. Even if I lived, there were few whom I could tell.

The qasr walls were wide enough that the sally port was more a tunnel than a door. Lo-Melkhiin's mother did not need a lamp in the darkness under the stones, and I followed her because there was nothing else I could do. We did not go all the way to the exit, which would have taken us outside the qasr walls altogether, but instead turned to the side. There was, to my surprise, a door, and behind that, a narrow stair. This we took to the top of the wall, and I breathed cool night air without palace perfumes for the first time in all the days since I had been taken in my sister's stead.

"Come," said Lo-Melkhiin's mother to me, after I had filled my lungs three times.

We went around the top of the wall. I saw the familiar gardens below me on one side, and the unfamiliar city on the other. The gardens were dark; even the customary lamps were unlit tonight for the star-falling party. The city, stretching out into the desert from the safety of the qasr wall, was lit up with hundreds of little lights. Lo-Melkhiin was no tyrant, it seemed; or at least, not one who would demand a city's darkness for his own sake.

I did my best not to look out at the desert and think about my sister. Did she know that stars would fall this night? Such a thing had not happened before in our lifetimes. If a Skeptic was required to predict the fall, then my sister would know nothing of it. I did not know if the priestly crafts of my mother and of my sister's mother were profound enough to foretell such an event. Would the sheep be unsettled? I did not imagine they would. They would sleep through the entire thing—unless a star landed beside them—and be none the wiser. Would the night watchman see the stars fall and raise the alarm, not knowing what it meant?

In all the preparation, I had not given much thought to the actual event. I did not know if the stars would fall to the sand itself. Lo-Melkhiin's mother was not afraid, which gave me courage, but I did not like the idea that something that was a part of the sky would not remain so. I pushed my fear away. If I was not afraid of the qasr's master, I decided, I would be afraid of nothing else.

At length we came to a wide place atop the wall, where flat stones made a balcony that stretched from an elaborately decorated door to the edge of the wall itself. It was the size of the space between all the tents our father owned, the common area where all the women sat outside to spin and card, and where the night's fire roasted sheep and gave light to the evening tales. There was no fire here, though. And the people who stood about were unfamiliar, and formally attired.

Lo-Melkhiin's mother put a hand on my arm and guided me across the balcony to stand by the door. There we stood and waited as more people arrived. There were priests in white robes and others I took to be Skeptics in robes of varying shades. There was Firh Stonetouched, in breeches and a tunic lined with some decoration I could not see in the dim light. There were others, men of Lo-Melkhiin's court and their wives, all dressed in fine cloth that was wasted without torches and lamps to parade it. Only my dishdashah, with its gold thread, showed its quality. No one looked at me for very long, but they could not help pausing before their eyes slid past me in the dark.

Our father's tents saw no shortage of happy gatherings. We celebrated the Longest Day and the Longest Night, and those two days when the dark and light of the sky were held at balance. We danced for the lambing and again for the shearing. When our father and my brothers returned from the caravan with traded goods instead of carded wool and spun yarn, we welcomed them with fire and song and food. My mother and my sister's mother danced for the dead and for the rain, alone in the sacred caves. Even after my sister's brother died, we sang for the joys of his life, and wished him well wherever his bones had come to their rest.

Lo-Melkhiin's party was not like any of those at all.

It was cold and dark, not just because it was nighttime. In our father's tents, the daytime was for labor and the night-time was for songs and tales, but we had always had the heat from the fire and the light from our poor lamps. As I had seen on our circuitous walk along the wall, all the lights in the qasr had been concealed. The sky was not as bright as it was in the desert, because the city lights still shone, but it was close.

There was a stir, and I looked to the carved door. There

Lo-Melkhiin stood, with an old man beside him. I knew he must be a Skeptic, for his robe was dark, its color stolen by the night. I wondered if it was he who had predicted the star fall, and if that was what accorded him the honor of standing by Lo-Melkhiin's side. Lo-Melkhiin looked at all of us the way a shepherd counts his sheep before moving to another pasture. His eyes were bright, even though there was no light for them to reflect, and few could meet his gaze. His mother held out the longest, and he smiled at her. It was almost kind.

"I am grateful to you all for attending tonight," Lo-Melkhiin said to us. His was the voice of a man who watered his own horse, but I did not trust it. "I know that you weary yourselves during the day to serve me and to serve our kingdom. I thank you for putting off your rest for a time, that you might watch this miracle with me."

They murmured that it was no trouble, of course. There was nothing else they could do.

"Before the sky begins its show," Lo-Melkhiin continued, "we will hear from the Skeptic Sokath, His Eyes Uncovered, as he has won the right to speak before us tonight."

The Skeptic beside Lo-Melkhiin bowed to him, and then to the other Skeptics and priests before walking to the middle of the balcony.

"How does he win the right to speak?" I said to Lo-Melkhiin's mother as softly as I could. It was the voice I used to speak to my sister when we did not wish for any of the other women to hear us. I used it now because I did not wish to show ignorance on this grand a stage.

"They threw dice," she said to me. She used the same voice. I wondered who she might have learned it with. "Thus do they appease both the odds and the gods."

The Skeptic had drawn himself up into a pose I recognized. It was how our father stood when he made a marriage in the village or announced the season's trade route. It was how my brothers stood when they imitated him and gave my sister and me petty orders, which we invariably disobeyed. It was not, I noticed, how Lo-Melkhiin stood. He did not have to draw anyone's eye to earn attention or respect. He could command both, and there was no one who could refuse either.

"Gather, gather," the Skeptic intoned. Instinctively I leaned forward. So did the others. Then Sokath, His Eyes Uncovered looked directly at me. "Listen, and I will tell you the secrets of the skies."

If I had stayed in our father's tents, I would have learned no secrets beyond those of how to run a household with my sister when we were married. The men we wed would have had their own mothers to wear the priestly-whites, and those women their own acolytes to train. I would have learned the secrets of the grain and the sheep, the hearth and the bed, the kitchen and the loom, but nothing else. I had not stayed in our father's tents. My sister learned the songs her mother sang for the dead, and now I might learn the secrets of the sky. If I died, I would not know them for very long, but I would know them. Sokath, His Eyes Uncovered did not seem to mind that the girl he spoke to might not have time to ponder his lesson. I looked back at him, though I wasn't sure if he could tell in the dark, and through my veil, which way my eyes were turned.

"There is a wanderer in the sky," Sokath, His Eyes Uncovered said to us, to me. "It circles us the way we circle the sun, but its journey is far longer than ours. As it travels, it gathers a caravan of stars in its wake, and when it passes above our heads, we see the caravan in the sky."

"How long does it travel, revered Skeptic?" Lo-Melkhiin asked.

"For every night that it is in our sky, it will be gone from us for ten years," the Skeptic said. "And it will light our sky for seven nights, beginning now."

I would not see the caravan of stars return again in my lifetime, I knew then. It did not matter how many nights more I survived Lo-Melkhiin's marriage. Any child I might one day have would never see it at all, unless she lived longer than most born in the desert do. The idea might have frightened me before, but now I understood the dangers of the world with greater clarity than I had when I lived in my father's tents. I might die tonight or tomorrow, but soon, in any case.

"My lords and ladies," said Sokath, His Eyes Uncovered. "I bid you, look up to the sky and see the wonders there."

It began slowly. One moving spark in a sky full of fixed lights, spiraling blue and gold, and then doused by the blackness of the sky. Not all of us saw it, it burned so quickly, but soon there were plenty of lights to marvel at.

I hoped my sister was watching. I hoped she did not fear the sight, but stood in the sand and watched this beauty with her strong heart. Our father and my brothers should be home by now, watching with my mother and my sister's mother as the sky danced above them.

And then I forgot about the stars, because Lo-Melkhiin moved from where he stood and watched. Everyone else, priests and Skeptics, lords and ladies, had their eyes fixed upon the dancing skies, but I saw him. He stalked across the balcony, his hunter's feet stepping lightly as a lion on the sand, and stopped beside where I stood. His mother looked at us, but did not speak. I could not see her expression, nor his, and took some small comfort in the fact that my veil hid my face from him. Then he closed one hand upon my shoulder, crushing the fine weave of my dress, and pulled me into a darkness that was beyond the reach of the stars.

twelve

IT WAS A SMALL ROOM, I could tell that much. The stone against my back was hard. There was a breeze—it had followed us through the door—but no silks or perfumes were stirred by it. This was not a room much used. Lo-Melkhiin loomed above me, his breath heavy with spice from his dinner. One of his hands was at my waist, and the other arm was pressed across my breastbone. If he wished, he had only to shift it upwards and it would crush my throat.

"I am glad you could join us tonight, wife," he said to me. He did not sound threatening, merely careless and unkind. A man who had fine things and did not care for the work it had taken to get them.

97

"I had few alternatives," I said to him. Surely he would not kill me here, not with everyone on the balcony. They might still watch the sky, but they had all seen me. How far, I wondered, did their acceptance of Lo-Melkhiin's murders go? No, we would both go back out onto the balcony, after he had what he wanted. I lamented that the ties on my dress were not likely to hold.

"I suppose your sister watches tonight as well?" he asked, almost conversationally. The arm against my breastbone had not relaxed. Tomorrow, I would have a bruise. I was determined to see it. "Do you think she cowers in fear, thinking the sky will fall down upon her head?"

"My people know the priests' ways, as much as anyone in the city," I told him. Our father walked the desert and my sister was neither foolish nor timid. She was worth ten of Lo-Melkhiin. "My mother and my sister's mother know the songs. They will have known about tonight as much as your priests did, even if they do not have a Skeptic to tell a pretty story about it before it starts."

"I suppose even a common desert girl like you is better than that," he said to me. He pulled back, but I did not relax. If he moved away from me, I was not going to follow him. "Your dress is beautiful. The cloth was only orange when I bought it for you. However did you manage to add the gold?"

I did not answer him. I was not about to tell him that I

had woven it in my dreams, if that is what had happened. I did not like the sudden gleam in his eyes; it flickered, like a lamp left exposed to a breeze. It might flare up and set fire to all surrounding it with no warning.

"It matters not," he went on. "You and I have a ritual to perform, same as every night."

I had not considered it a ritual until he said it. There were no special words or songs. We lit no candles, and I am not sure either of us had any peace from it. Yet every day, every night, we came together. It was not a marriage as I had been taught, but it was something, and he had given me its name.

"My sister does her rituals too; proper ones, far from the city walls," I said to him, though I could not say how I had seen it. "She prepares for her wedding, and leaves offerings for our dead."

I knew that my shrine flourished in the place where our ancestors slept, but I would not tell Lo-Melkhiin that I was held in such regard. The other girls brought offerings there, as did their mothers. In the privacy of their own tents, they had smaller shrines, personal mementos of me that they whispered to without the formality of song. They told me their secrets there, their loves and hopes and dreams, and when I was a smallgod, I would be able to whisper back. Our father would carry my token in his belt pouch, as would my brothers, when they went out to trade again. The scraps from the purple dishdashah would go out into the desert, and the sun would give them strength there.

In the cold of that small stone room, I felt the desert's scouring wind heat my face. I held my hands out to Lo-Melkhiin, and he took them. His face, visible, just barely now that my eyes had adjusted to the darkness, had the look of victory to it. I wondered if mine did too, because I felt like I had won something, but I did not know how both of us could be victorious. I did not know how I could win.

His fingers closed around mine, and the strange light began to move between us. Always before, we had done this in the lamplight of my chamber. Now, in the dark, I could not help but notice that the cold light did not illuminate the room. It was bright enough, but it was of no use to actually see anything by. I had never seen light behave in that way before; like it was only the idea of light and not the real thing. When the copper fire stretched out from him to me as a reply, it was the same; a fire burning without smoke or glow or warmth, but it made me feel like I was growing.

He released me abruptly, and I swayed on my feet. He held out his arm, a mockery of a perfect husband, but I leaned on the wall and did not take it. Instead, I quickly felt each of the knots that held my dress in place. They had, by some luck, not moved. I would be decently covered when we returned. Lo-Melkhiin laughed, and turned toward the door. I followed him out because there was nothing else I could do. I was light-headed, and felt as though my very blood were singing. It did not feel the same as when I was ill. I was rarely sick as a child, but I knew what it felt like. It did not have this draining feeling, as though I were a gage-tree and the wind was pulling the water from my bones. Usually when we did this, I was sitting down, and I did not have to walk anywhere.

"Mother," Lo-Melkhiin said, once we were back on the main balcony. She turned her face from the sky to look at her son, and at me. "I must go and speak with my counselors. Will you see to my wife? I fear the lateness of the hour has stolen some of her vivacity. Perhaps the fruit juice will restore it?"

The light of the stars seemed bright in comparison with the darkness of the stone room. I could see in her face that Lo-Melkhiin's mother did not believe her son entirely, but she waved to a serving girl, and got two cups anyway. Lo-Melkhiin left us without a backward glance, which belied his earlier concern.

I drank the juice. It did not cost me to be obedient, and I was thirsty anyway. Somehow it was cool, beyond the chill offered by the night air, and it did make me feel more grounded. This was fruit I knew, even if it was presented in a different way than when my sister and I shared a pomegranate in our father's tents. There was nothing otherworldly about it. Lo-Melkhiin's mother did not ask me what

I had done with her son only moments before. Perhaps she did not wish to know. I felt her eyes skim over the ties of my dress, though, and when she saw that they were all intact, she frowned. Perhaps she did not like mysteries.

I watched Lo-Melkhiin instead of the sky. He moved from group to group, talking with his advisors and listening to the priests and the Skeptics both, clasping their arms as though they were his comrades and not members of his court. Every time he went from one gathering to another, the knot of men he left would fall to talking in hushed tones, waving their hands at one another as though they were excited by what they spoke of. Before long, it was as though I stood in one of the night gardens, and heard the wind moving through the leaves.

Firh Stonetouched stood apart from the others, his eyes still fixed on the stars. When Lo-Melkhiin came to stand beside him, he flinched, but recovered well enough. They spoke only briefly, and then Lo-Melkhiin put his hand on the carver's shoulder. I saw, as I had not seen when he spoke to the others, the spark of light that was not light as it jumped from my husband's hand to Firh's body. And then Lo-Melkhiin moved on.

I walked to where the carver stood. Lo-Melkhiin's mother did not try to stop me, nor did she follow me. More than anything, I wanted to see the desert, to imagine that if I looked in the right direction, I would see the fires that burned around our father's tents. To imagine that I would see a way back to my sister. Firh Stonetouched stood there instead, and I saw that his hands were shaking before he wrapped his fingers around the crenellations that decorated the top of the wall, and gripped so hard I thought for a moment they might crumble.

"Do you miss the tents of your father, lady-bless?" he asked me.

"I do," I said to him. I had not expected to be gone long enough to miss them. I had thought to die and return to the place where the bones of our father's father's father lay in peace.

"I miss mine as well," he said to me. "I miss them especially on nights like this."

"The Skeptic said that there have been no nights like this while you or I have been living," I reminded him gently.

"No," he said to me. "I meant nights when we come together as a court. When . . ."

His voice trailed away, but I heard the rest of his thought as if he had spoken the words clearly in my ear. He did not like the nights when Lo-Melkhiin came to him and laid his hands upon his shoulder.

"Will you have to carve now?" I asked him.

"I think so," he said to me. "I can't tell what yet, but I know that I will carve something."

I laid my own hands on top of his where they still gripped

the top of the wall. For a heartbeat, they were lit with copper fire, but he did not see it.

"I will tell the serving girls to bring you water," I said to him.

He pulled his hands out from under mine, glancing nervously to see if anyone had seen us, but no one had.

"I will not stop to drink it, lady-bless," he said to me.

"Then I will tell a footman to make you drink," I said to him. "As long as he does not hurt you too much."

Firh Stonetouched laughed. It was not a happy sound. I knew that he would hurt whether he drank or not.

"I am sorry," I said to him. "It is the only way I can think of that I can help."

"I understand, lady-bless," he said to me. He bowed formally, and I returned to stand by Lo-Melkhiin's mother until we were all finally dismissed to find our beds.

In the morning, the carving madness came upon Firh Stonetouched, and he would not be stopped from his work. All day, he stood in the hot sun and set his tools to the stone. Yet whenever a serving girl came into the courtyard with a jug at her waist, he would go to her and drink. Beneath his hands, the statue took shape. The watching guards and footmen were certain that it would be a lion, but the henna mistress said that the shape of the face was wrong. She was correct: by the time the sun had set, a lioness stood proudly in the courtyard.

When Lo-Melkhiin came to me that night, before he went back out to watch the second night of falling stars, he looked at me for a long time before he took my hands. This time, it was not the way a lion stalks a gazelle, but rather the way a ram surveys the ewes.

"I ordered them to move the statue," he said to me, once the fire had faded from our fingers. He did not release my hands. "I will not destroy something that took such work, but it is not like the others."

"Oh?" I said to him. I did not pretend interest; it was genuine.

"Yes," he said to me. "There was something wrong with its eyes."

Then he left me to dream of sand.

thirteen

THE SEVEN NIGHTS OF FALLING STARS had ended, and I was still alive. I had been almost three weeks in Lo-Melkhiin's qasr. There were few now who would not meet my eyes when I called upon them, though they always looked away from my gaze. It befit my status as their queen, so I did not let it trouble me. I missed my sister every day, because she was my sister, and because although I could talk to the women in the spinning room or any of the gardeners, none of them were my friend. I had not seen Firh Stonetouched again since the night of the starfall party. The girl who brought my tea told me that he had been sent out on patrol. I did not find the lioness he had carved, either. Wherever Lo-Melkhiin had hidden it, it was hidden well.

On the morning of the eighteenth day since I was taken from my sister and from our father's tents, I went looking for Sokath, His Eyes Uncovered. I had not sought him out during the starfall. He had been every night upon the walls, watching the skies with the other Skeptics and the priests, and debating with them. Lo-Melkhiin had told me this for no reason that I could determine, but I was never bidden to join them. I liked Lo-Melkhiin little enough in my chamber, with the lamps to show me his face. I did not like him at all in the dark.

Instead, I used the days of the falling stars to find all of the qasr gardens that I could. When I was upon the wall with Lo-Melkhiin's mother, I had seen that the part of the qasr I lived in was in fact very small, and rather isolated from the rest. I was not sure how much longer I would live in this place, but I was determined to learn my way about it. Also, I was very bored.

No one ever tried to halt my wanderings, and so on the morning I went to find Sokath, His Eyes Uncovered, I did not expect to be stopped. I met the same serving girls and footmen as always. They bowed their heads when I passed, and moved to the side of the corridors to let me by if we were in close quarters when we met. I tried to avoid this: it made me uncomfortable to watch them get out of my way, particularly if they labored with some heavy burden, but I knew they would not stop if I asked them to. They looked at me now, because they thought I might just live. And accordingly, they treated me as their queen. If my brief discomfort was the price I paid for living, then I would pay it. The loneliness was less easy to bear, but I was bearing it as best I could.

I walked through the water garden, where the statue of Lo-Melkhiin's mother stood astride the lions. I passed into a little hall, used by the women who brought lamp oil up from the storerooms beneath the qasr. I had learned quite a bit from following them discreetly, and from listening to their talk. They were the ones who went into the most rooms and gardens of the qasr, filling lamps and trimming wicks every day, so that when nighttime came again the lamps would be ready to hold back the darkness. It was not unlike following our goats, when my sister and I had watched them; we could not always tell where the grazing would be, but the goats knew, and would lead us to it—along with the sheep, who were much less wise.

I was content to be a sheep for now, following the lamp-women when they were too busy at their tasks to notice me, and then pretending to be engrossed in some tapestry or vine sculpture if they did. In this way, I learned the rooms closest to mine, and by hearing their talk, I learned what sort of people were likely to be in which

E. K. JOHNSTON

places at certain times every day.

The mornings, so the lamp-women said, were the best time to change the oil in the Skeptics' workrooms. They went out every day to watch the sun rise and break their fasts, and often did not return indoors for several hours, particularly if they were arguing about something that they felt was important. They laughed when they said the last part. Skeptics were useful: they had given us the water clock and the way to make words on paper, but sometimes they wandered into a thicket of their own making, and, like our ram did, tried to push their way out of it instead of just backing up the way they'd come.

I knew the Skeptics would be on the east wall. It was not the highest, but it was high enough to see the sun rise, and there was a small balcony there. It was not half as grand as the one from which we had watched the stars, but it was large enough for them to gather to watch the sun, and there was a cover to keep the sun from baking their thoughts out of their ears before they were finished making them. Sokath, His Eyes Uncovered did not always join them. He tired of their babble, the lamp-women said, and wished to have his own thoughts in peace before the day began. He went by himself to the south wall, where the view was not as grand but the silence was better assured.

I climbed the stairs as quietly as I could, not wishing to disturb his thoughts. It was easy to talk to my mother

109

and to my sister's mother, even when they wore their priestly-whites. I had not ever had occasion to speak to a priest, much less a Skeptic, and it felt a bit like when I spoke to our father. I took a deep breath before I stepped out onto the narrow walkway at the top of the wall, and then stood behind him, breathing as softly as I could while the sun fully cleared the horizon and began its daily trek across the sky.

"Do you know," Sokath, His Eyes Uncovered said to me after a time, "I think the world is round. And I think we are near the side of it, not at the top."

I had never thought what shape the world was. For so long, it had been the shape of our father's tents. The shape of our father's herds. The shape of my sister.

"Why?" I asked of him. I had not meant to pester him with questions, but it seemed that I was invited.

"I have watched the shadows here for many years," he said to me. "You see how tall they are?"

I looked at the flagstones by his feet. The shadows were two full stones out from the high part of the wall, but there were scratches in the stone farther away from there, as well as several that were closer.

"I do," I said to him.

"They do not move very much," he said to me, and pointed. "Here on the Longest Day, here on the Longest Night."

Both marks were placed so that I could have spanned the distance between them with both hands. It did not seem like much distance to travel, especially for something as big as the sun, and I said as much to him.

"If we were closer to the top of the world, the space would be bigger," he said to me. "It is possible that at the very top or very bottom, there might be days with no sun at all."

I looked at the marks on the floor and thought about making shadow animals on the walls of our father's tent.

"Could you not find out?" I asked of him. "I mean, revered Skeptic, if you took a ball and a lamp, could you not tell?"

He laughed then, and winked one eye at me.

"I could," he said to me. "And I have. Never tell the other Skeptics that, for they will think it blasphemous. They would rather argue about it forever."

"But then how will they know?" I asked.

"They do know," he said to me, "more or less. But in arguing, they will ask and answer a dozen other questions."

"I suppose that is worthwhile, then," I said. No wonder he came up here to avoid the babble. I would rather know than talk.

He turned and bowed then, and I bowed back, forgetting who I was to him in this place.

"My queen," he said to me. "Do you seek me out for a reason?"

"Yes," I said to him. "I have questions about the smallgods."

"Those are questions for the priests," he said to me.

"They may be," I said to him. "But I thought to ask a Skeptic first."

"I am intrigued by that, at least," he said to me. "Come, let us get out of the sun."

We went down the stairs and into the garden there. It was a water garden, like the one by my rooms. The fountain sang quietly in one corner, and vines grew up the sides of the walls. There was a canopy and two cushions beneath it, along with a tray of oils and flatbread. Whoever it was that followed me whenever I left my chambers had arranged for enough food for both of us to break our fast, and since my stomach rumbled when I saw the tray, I was grateful.

"I will do my best to answer your questions," said Sokath, His Eyes Uncovered. "In return, I would like a story from your village."

"That is fair," I said to him, and wondered what tale I would tell. "I am not certain we have any great wisdom for you."

"Wisdom is the currency of young men," he said to me. "They seek it, thinking it is something they will find. You are young, and a woman besides, and yet still clever enough to find me here today. That is wisdom few of my own students would have."

He sat, and took an olive from the bowl. He put it in his mouth as I sat down beside him, and then spat the pit across the garden. I could not help myself, and laughed.

"That was no great distance," he said. "When I was a young man, I could have cleared the wall."

I looked up, and knew that he was jesting, but it had been a very long time since anyone had said anything light-hearted to me. I caught myself: it had not been a long time. It had been only the time since I came to the qasr, and that was still short enough that I could number the days.

I took an olive and removed the pit with my thumbnail as I had been taught. Sokath, His Eyes Uncovered looked almost disappointed, so once I had eaten the olive I put the pit in my mouth and spat it out as hard as I could. It barely cleared the cushion, and he laughed again.

"You will learn the trick of it if you practice," he said to me. "Life is too short to pull out olive pits, when spitting them is so much more fun."

He said it in a friendly way, but I looked at his eyes, and they were sad. He had more years than our father, and I would be lucky to live another day. I took another olive, this time wrapped in flatbread. It nearly stuck in my throat, but I forced myself to swallow it, and then spat out the pit.

It went no farther than the first one, but I felt I understood why; it had to do with where I put my tongue.

"Now," said Sokath, His Eyes Uncovered. "Ask me your questions, and we will see if we can find the answers you seek."

fourteen

IN THE FIRE OF OUR TWELFTH SUMMER, before we were proficient enough with our needles to stitch the purple cloth, but after we had come in from the herds, my mother and my sister's mother told us the story of our father's father's father, and how he had become our smallgod. We had heard versions of the tale before, sung around the fire or whispered to his bones when our father was away with the caravan. This time, they promised us, it would be the secret tale. Our father knew it, as was his right, but my brothers did not, which was of course how they bribed us to keep our seats instead of chasing each other off into the desert to play, as we would rather have done.

Our father's father's father had been born on a different wadi, one closer to the city than where we lived now. The wadi's path through the desert was not straight as the sand-crow flies, but it was a safer path. The camels could find water there, and green enough to eat. A good hunter could find prey as come to drink, and when lions came, they came only at night, and roared aplenty to announce themselves. Our father's father's father was not a hunter, save at need, and though he was a good enough shot to keep the hyenas and wild dogs off his herd animals, he was not good enough to get sufficient meat for the whole camp that way. He was content, though, as a herdsman; and by the time he was twenty summers old, he was herd master.

It was the herd master's job to pick which animals were fit to eat and which were fit to mate, and to pick the path the herds would take. A wise man, it was said, followed his goats. A fool was led by his sheep. A master, though, picked his own way, and that is what our father's father's father did. He had no Skeptic to tell him how the water moved in relation to the sun, and no priest to tell him which smallgods to ask for guidance and what offerings to make to catch their attention. He had only himself, and the craft he had learned from his summers under the desert sun.

The wadi was crowded. Many families made their camps along it, and used the water for small fields and for their own use to drink. Our father's father's father's village was small, and their herds suffered because there was not enough space for them at the wells. There were many merchants crammed together as well, and they bought and sold and traded the same goods over and over, until the prices were so high that our father's father's father could not afford them. One of the merchants who had the highest prices also had a camel. It was an older beast, one which knew the desert well. The merchant always left the camel tied to a post in the middle of the market square while he went to talk with the other men. Even when the sun was at its hottest, the camel would stand patiently in the heat and wait for its master.

One day, when the others had taken the sheep and goats, our father's father's father came to the market. He needed to buy a milk goat, because none of his goats were in milk; one of the village women had died in childbirth, and there was no one to feed her baby girl. The only merchant with a milk goat was the man who also owned the camel, and when our father's father's father saw this, he despaired; for surely he could not afford the price, and then he would lose another member of his village, tiny though she was.

Our father's father's father went up to the camel, standing in the hot sun as ever, and stroked its brown nose softly.

"Where is your master?" he said to the camel.

"He has gone to the tents by the wadi, where it is cooler," said the camel.

Now, our father's father's father was surprised. He had

not expected the camel to answer him. But he knew that surprise was no reason to be impolite, so he continued, talking to the camel as he would to the old men who played backgammon in the shade.

"Thank you, revered elder," he said.

"Why do you seek my master?" asked the camel.

"I need a milk goat for a babe in my village," said our father's father's father. "And your master is the only one on the wadi that has one today."

"Buy me instead," said the camel. "I am old, and my master will part with me for less than he will the milk goat."

"But you cannot feed a child," protested our father's father's father.

"Buy me," said the camel again. "Buy me and you will not regret it."

Our father's father's father felt foolish indeed, taking advice from a camel. He did not follow the goats, after all, as lesser herdsmen did. On the other hand, the goats did not actually speak, as the camel had done. So he sighed and went to the tents by the wadi. He haggled with the merchant, who was surprised to be offered anything at all for the camel, and came away with a good price and an old camel.

They walked back along the wadi together. Our father's father's father was sad. The babe had not been fed for almost a day, except on thin porridge, and the women assured him that it would not be enough. And now he had only an old camel to show for his efforts. He was so downhearted that he did not notice when the camel stopped walking until he ran out of rope and was jerked backward.

"Master," said the old camel. "We must go into the desert."

"Camel," said our father's father's father, "if we go into the desert, we will die."

"Master," said the camel again. "We will not."

The camel turned away from the wadi and pulled our father's father's father after him. Though he could have hit the camel and made it turn right, he did not. The camel talked, after all. It must have had a good reason.

They walked into the desert together. Our father's father's father counted his steps as he had been taught, to be sure that he would not walk farther than half his water could sustain. When he reached the number that said he should turn back, he pulled gently on the camel's rope.

"Camel," he said. "I must turn back, or I will run out of water."

"Master," said the camel. "Look ahead."

Our father's father's father looked, and there at the edge of his gaze was a familiar sight. There was a low green line, where oleander bushes grew in clumps. When he got closer, he knew, he would see the pink flowers. Those only grew where there was water. They only grew where there was a wadi.

"Camel!" said our father's father's father. "How did you know that this was here?"

"I am a camel," said the camel. "We can find water."

"Why show it to me?" he asked.

"My old master never listened," said the camel. "You did."

They walked to the wadi together. Our father's father's father's mind teemed with plans. They could move the whole village here. Yes, it was farther from the city walls, but that didn't matter if they had more space, and more water. They could expand the herds and not worry about fighting for their food and drink. All at once, he remembered the baby, and was sore-hearted. He knew that prices must be paid, but this seemed like a very steep one.

"Master," said the camel. "Look again."

Our father's father's father heard it before he saw, and recognized the sound. In the shade of the oleanders there was a goat, laid down to have her kids in the cooler sand on the wadi bank. Our father's father's father knelt beside her, and saw that she was wild and claimed by no one's herd. He helped her birth her kids, and then lifted them up in his arms. The she-goat he placed on the camel's neck, and she lay there as calmly as if she had been born to mind his touch. The kids he bore himself, back across the desert to his tents.

There was great rejoicing that night. Our father's father's

father had gone to market for a milk goat and returned with not only that, but three kids and a camel besides. And even better, he told them of the second wadi. In the morning, they packed up their things and went out from that place. They crossed the burning sand, and found shade under the oleanders where to pitch their tents. Soon enough, they found the cave where to bury their dead.

As our father's father's father had hoped, the herds flourished there. He led the caravans in trade, and oversaw the wealth of the village. When he died, they wrapped him up in fine white cloth and set him in the hillside, next to where he had seen the old camel buried, and then they built the shrine.

"Your father and your brothers," my mother said to us, "pray to your father's father's father because of the way the herds multiplied and the way the trade increased. We pray to him as you do, for those reasons too. But that is not the only reason we pray to him."

"This is the secret," my sister's mother said to us. Her eyes burned the way they did when she wore the priestly-whites and sang with my mother before our father's tents, even though we were only sitting in the shade of the oleanders and spinning thread. "This is the part of the tale that you must keep close to your hearts, all your days."

My sister promised, words spilling from her lips like oil from a jug. I was so in awe of the tale and of the promise of something my brothers could not have, I could only nod.

"The baby that lived because of the milk goat was my mother's mother's mother," my mother said to us. "If she had died, I would not have wed your father, and you, my daughter, would not have been born at all."

"I would not have my dearest friend," my sister's mother said to us. "And you, my daughter, would have no sister."

We clasped hands, my sister and I. We had come so close to never having each other, and we had not known it until that moment. All at once, our bond was even stronger. We had always prayed to our family's smallgod, but now we put our hearts into every word, and our work into every offering we left at the shrine. We gave thanks as much as we asked for blessings, and we made sure to pour out cool water where the bones of the camel were laid. And if we left oil and bread where my mother's mother's mother was buried, we were not the only ones to do so, but that was a secret too.

Until that day in the garden when I sat down with Sokath, His Eyes Uncovered, and learned to spit olive pits through the air, that was all I had known of smallgods.

fifteen

"DO YOU BELIEVE IN SMALLGODS?" I asked of Sokath, His Eyes Uncovered.

"I do not disbelieve them," he said to me. "That is the nature of Skeptics, remember. We would rather debate than know for certain."

"Do you understand how smallgods receive their powers?" I asked then. I had to come at him like the wadi, with its meandering lines. I could not come at him as the sand-crow flew.

"I do," he said to me. "But when Skeptics talk, we often explain things we already know. In the telling, we dredge up the memory of half-forgotten facts or inspire new ones.

So tell me how smallgods are made."

"When a person dies, if he has done something great, his son and his grandsons will build a shrine," I said to him. "They will pray to him and leave offerings of oil and bread. They will carry memories of him with them in the caravan, and he will help them if he can."

Sokath, His Eyes Uncovered was nodding.

"And the more prayers that are said and the more offerings that are laid will increase the smallgod's power," he said. "Until his children's children's children forget him, and he becomes nothing more than a pile of bones in the desert sand."

"That is what the priests say," I said to him.

"What do you say?" he asked of me.

I thought about it, chewing on a piece of bread longer than I needed to before swallowing it down.

"I say that our father and my brothers have always returned to us," I told him. "And that our herds multiply and no one goes hungry in our father's tents, even if there is a season when the wadi does not flood."

"But is that the smallgod?" he asked of me. "Or is it that your father is a good tradesman?"

"Can it not be both?" I asked in return. "Can our father be a pious man and a clever one, who is served by himself and favored by a smallgod?"

"There is no way to test that," he said to me. "And it must be tested to be proven."

I considered his words. I had never thought to prove that a smallgod existed. I had only ever known they had.

"How do you prove that the sun will rise tomorrow?" I asked of him, and he smiled at me like I had won a prize.

"I have observed it many times," he said to me. "But that alone does not guarantee that it will rise again tomorrow."

"The same way that I have observed our father return home with fine silks—it does not mean that the smallgod favors him," I said.

"Yes," he said to me. "However," he continued, "my companion Sokath, His Eyes To The Stars has determined that the world we stand on, in addition to being round as we discussed, also spins like a spindle and whorl, and that is why we have day and night. He has a model that shows that as long as we continue to spin, the sun will continue to come up in the morning."

"I thought you said that Skeptics would rather debate than know," I said to him. I smiled. It was better than talking to our father.

"We all have our own moments of weakness," he said to me. There was a laugh—a real one—in his voice, but then his face darkened. "To be honest, lady-bless, the Skeptics have changed since Lo-Melkhiin took the throne. Debate is no longer enough for the younger ones. They seek only to know, not to think."

"I am not sure why that is so bad," I told him. "I can

think of many things I would like to know."

"Yes, but a knowing mind is a closed one," he said to me. "On that, at least, we Skeptics and priests agree."

"We have the water clock because someone needed to know the time when it was night," I said to him.

"Yes," he said to me, "and because someone needed to know that there would always be water in the qasr cisterns, they built a dam in the wadi which dried up everything downstream of the city. As everything does, knowledge comes with a price."

"The priests agree with you on that too," I said to him, and thought of my sister's brother.

He was quiet for a time, picking olives up one by one, no longer spitting the pits out. He ignored the bread, which was hardening in the heat anyway.

"I think you cannot prove if smallgods have power because they are dead, and you cannot ask them directly," I said to him.

"That is true," he said to me. "The dead cannot speak."

"What would happen if you built a shrine to someone who was alive?" I asked of him. "What would happen if you prayed and left offerings?"

He rolled the olive pit between his fingers.

"I think that person would become lucky," he said. "I do not think it would be enough to notice."

"What if a whole village prayed?" I asked. "What if

traders went out and spoke of this living smallgod to others? What if they sent out a token and built shrines, and more people prayed?"

Now he looked troubled. I wondered if, for all his fine words, he really did believe that smallgods had powers to work on the living.

"That sort of person would be special indeed." He said the words so softly that I barely heard him over the water in the fountain. "That sort of person would have had to do a great deed, and survived it. I do not know what sort of man that would be, or if we would like him very much."

He meant Lo-Melkhiin; I could see it in his face. I had not considered that. It was possible that the men who became richer under Lo-Melkhiin's rule built shrines to him, but I had seen the way his power worked, and it did not look like any smallgod power I had ever seen.

"Men pray in the morning and in the evening," I said to him. "In the heat of the day, they speak to one another. They trade and they talk and they drink cool water."

He looked at me, and for a fraction of a breath, I saw fear in his eyes, but then it was replaced by wonder, and a hope so desperate that it made my heart hurt. Lo-Melkhiin would never have shrines.

"Women pray waking and walking and working," I said to him. "They pray with the spindle's drop and the shuttle's shift. They weave their words into the warp and the weft of the cloth they make, and they send that cloth out into the world where everyone can see it, and remark upon its beauty."

"That would wake the dead," said Sokath, His Eyes Uncovered. His voice was breathless with awe. "I cannot imagine what it would do to the living."

"To a living woman," I said to him.

"To a woman who saved a sister who loved her," he said to me. "And saved all the other girls in her village. And came to the qasr. And did not die in the night."

"Not yet," I said to him.

"When I talk to Lo-Melkhiin, my thoughts run faster than they ever did before," he said to me. "I can see things clearly, and it does not cost me effort. I miss the days when I had to work to see with the same clarity. Other men, though . . . they are glad of the lesser effort."

"Like weaving with wide thread," I said to him. "The cloth is done quickly, but there are gaps where holes can appear, and the decoration is not so fine."

"Yes," he said to me. "It is like that."

"Lo-Melkhiin does not talk to me," I said to him. "Or, rather, he does, but he mocks my home even as he asks for stories of it."

"He does not understand what he has got, this time," he said to me.

"I think he might," I said to him. I thought of the ram's

look in my husband's eyes. "Every night, he takes my hands, and a cold-fire light runs from my skin to his. I saw the same sparks the night of the starfall party when he moved amongst the men there, only the sparks jumped from him to them."

"Did that happen to Firh Stonetouched?" For the first time, there was urgency in his voice, and he leaned toward me.

"Yes," I said to him. "It happened to everyone. It happened to you."

I knew, then, that this was a debate he had labored over for months, but never shared. It had gone on only in his head, round and round in circles, like sheep when the dogs bring them in, until he had caught a piece of proof from me, a direction that made sense, and followed it.

"Does anything else happen when Lo-Melkhiin comes to you?" he asked of me.

It was an impertinent question, if I chose to misinterpret it, but I did not. I knew exactly what he meant in the asking, and decided to tell him the truth.

"Yes," I said to him. "Always Lo-Melkhiin takes my hands, and the cold-fire blooms from me to him. Sometimes there are pictures in it: my village, my sister, things he would like to take and burn away. And then, when it is done, thin copper lines stretch from his fingertips to mine, and I feel like my heart grows in my chest. I do not know if he sees the cold-fire as I do, but I know he does not see the copper at all—it is as though we trade, though he does not mean to."

Again, there was silence from Sokath, His Eyes Uncovered. The olives were gone, and the bread was too hard for even me, with my desert-scoured teeth, to chew. I sat and waited, though suddenly it galled me. It was still morning, yes, but the day would wear on and then I might die, and here I sat while an old man who did not even believe in smallgods wasted thoughts with no action.

"My queen," he said to me at last. His tone was quite formal, and I lamented that the easiness of our conversation was gone. He no longer spoke to me as though I were one of his students. "I am sorry that I do not have better answers for you, or better answers to guide your thoughts. I know that you do not know how much time you have left, but I need just that to consider."

"Revered Skeptic," I said to him, returning his formality, though I did not much like it. I stood, preparing to leave the garden. "I hear your words. Should you have more later, I will hear them too."

"Lady-bless." He was just an old man spitting olive pits again, and despite the title he gave me, he might have been talking with a girl instead of a queen. "I do not have answers or questions for you, but I do have some advice."

"I will take it gladly," I said to him, and let the warmth back into my tone. At the same time, I was done with talking.

Unaccountably, I chafed at my inaction. I knew it was futile. I was a prisoner of the walls, and though the spinning room was open to me, I was not content to spend my days making thread. I missed stitching and weaving. I missed grinding grain and kneading dough. I missed being useful and part of a family. I missed my sister, her eyes and her spirit and our fingers meeting as we worked. I felt anger burn hotly in my chest, though I fought to master it and gave no outward sign. Sokath, His Eyes Uncovered had been nothing but polite and considerate to me. It was not his fault that I was trapped in this nightmare of Lo-Melkhiin's making.

"I think," he said to me, "that you are going to need a ball. And a lamp."

iv.

When men give you their fear, it is easy to steer them on the path you wish them to travel. When men show you their worth, it is easy to determine what you will freely take. When men do both, it is easy to play upon their hearts as deftly as a musician might play upon his pipes.

One dead girl was nothing. Two, only a little more. Ten was something to consider, at the very least, but it was not until I had used Lo-Melkhiin's hands to kill fifteen of them that their fathers and brothers began to take notice. They enacted their puny law: one girl from every village and from every district within the city walls. It took them a full waning of the moon to do it, and by then my count numbered twenty-five.

They were second and third daughters, or servants within the house passed off as kin by then. No one could turn Lo-Melkhiin down, of course, not even when he sought his bride before the family had finished the rites for her sister. Men clung to the chance of it, the idea that their houses would be linked with their lord's. The women knew better.

Their fear was a delicious thing, so raw and powerful that I could not steer it. It could only be consumed. Their terror gave me power before I was strong enough to bend the men of the court to my will. By the time the law was brought to bear, I did not need the girls so much anymore: I had stores of power to last. I did not stop, though. There was no reason to, not so long as they served their daughters up to me for the asking.

Lo-Melkhiin hated it, of course. Hated that I used his hands for murder, and frivolous murder at that. Hated that I used his voice to give commands. Hated that I used his body to sit on his throne and issue edicts of my own. He did not care that I was a wise ruler, and kept well those of his people that I did not kill. He screamed and screamed inside his own head, and at times I was tempted to burn him out completely, as had been the custom of my people, but I enjoyed his suffering, and so I did not.

We rebuilt from the follies of his father's reign, and that is why the men of the court let us do it, no matter the cost. Our Skeptics saw answers where before they had been content with questions, and built devices as wondrous as they were beautiful. Our priests had money for their temples and shrines, and the best bread and oil to leave as

133

offerings for the dead they called smallgods. Our people did not go hungry. Our army and our walls were strong.

That was what men needed. I required something else.

I found a carver who might have spent his days fletching arrows, and raised him up to be one of the greatest artisans of the age. I found a Skeptic who had labored with sand and glass as a way to tell the time, and gave him water and small wheels so that he, and any who looked at his clock, would always know the hour. My cook had once been a simple miller, his hands used to grind grain for others. When I brought him to my kitchens, he learned the craft, and before long his experiments had given us a flatbread that stayed fresh for days longer.

A smith, a mathematician, an architect, a breaker-of-horses. The list went on.

They were burning up, and they didn't even know they were afire.

I had chosen my kingdom well, when I took Lo-Melkhin for my own in the desert. There were other kings and other lands in the world, but his had been a people on the edge of greatness. Two generations, perhaps three, had stood between them and the master craft, science and mathematics. I had given it to them now, cutting the corners and speeding them along wherever I could. Had I wanted to conquer, I could have done so, but I was content with what I had.

None of them wondered why it happened so quickly. They were too pleased with the results, and raced ahead of me with all the enthusiasm of frisking colts. They made and wrought and calculated as though there were nothing that could stop them. If there was weakness *left in a bridge too quickly made, or if a well was drained forever, I did not care. When I had power enough to last me, I would leave them. I did not care if they burned.*

None of them wondered how my wives died, save in their darkest dreams and most secret thoughts. As they did with their crafting, they simply accepted the deaths. The men stopped counting, as did I. No one paid any mind to the line of dark-haired, dark-skinned girls who came to the qasr, and met their end there. They were nameless and faceless under their veils. Sometimes I looked at them; sometimes I touched them. Sometimes I simply burned them, and then rode out for another.

Until I got one that did not die. The first night she was mine, I did not bring the full force of my power to bear upon her. I was curious. This one had spirit. She had drawn my attention deliberately, and I did not know why until she was ahorse and we rode away. She had put herself before me to spare her sister, and that was something that had not happened before.

The second night she did not die, I mocked her and made her speak to me. The third night, I gave her all of the fire I had, and still she lived.

She was not of my kind, yet there was some power to her that was not human, not quite. She did not die, and I wondered if I might at last have found a queen for whom I could set the desert on fire.

sixteen

ON THE THIRTIETH NIGHT after I wed Lo-Melkhiin, he came to my rooms and did not leave them after he released my hands.

Instead, he settled back on the soft silk pillows at the head of my bed. I still sat at the foot, dressed for sleep. The serving girls had extinguished all the lamps but the one that burned next to us, and the hour-candle that stood in the corner. The air was heavy with perfume, a scent I did not care for, and I did not like the weight of it in my lungs. I was not wearing my veil, could not hide my face from him, so I thought of a stone that did not move and held myself still. He smiled his hunter-smile at me.

"You have lived with me longer now than any have, my wife," he said to me. "Why do you think that is?"

I could not tell if he knew the reason, or if he expected me to know. He did not mock me anymore when he spoke to me. Rather, he was hard and cruel, like a desert storm: visible for hours before it struck, but only to be endured, not evaded. I had preferred the mocking. At least then, he had not paid me much heed.

"I do not know, my lord," I said to him. "Perhaps my smallgod smiles on me, and his power is greater than yours."

Now he smiled like a viper, like I had poked him with a stick.

"The others had smallgods," he said to me. "That did not save them."

He said words like Sokath, His Eyes Uncovered might have done, but in his mouth, they were harsh. When the Skeptic spoke, it was to encourage new thought. When Lo-Melkhiin spoke, it was to obliterate through fear.

"Our father's father's father was a good man when he lived," I said to him. "We have prayed to him for many years, and left him great offerings."

"I wonder, what do you think would happen to your smallgod if I ordered your burying hill burned?" He said blasphemy like it was nothing. To him, it was. "Have you seen burning bone, my wife? It starts like a roasted goat, but then the meat strips away to feed the fire until the bone is left naked and alone. It twists and shatters, marrow leaking onto the flames, until only dust is left."

"That is what happens to everything, my lord," I said to him. "If only the fire can be made hot enough."

"Would you like to see it?" he asked.

"No," I said to him. "I have seen it before, when we have collected marrow for our use. I do not need to see waste."

"You are not curious?" he asked. "You do not wish to know how the world works?"

"I am, and I do," I said to him. "But I would rather be patient and learn things in their own time, than force knowledge where it causes destruction."

"Did the sheep teach you such common sense?" he asked.

"No, my lord." For the first time since he had dropped my hands, I looked into his face. "I learned that from the goats."

He laughed, a true laugh with his head thrown back and his mouth wide, and I could not hide my surprise. The cruelty was gone—no monster could have made that noise—and I thought about what Lo-Melkhiin's mother had said to me the night of the starfall watching. If there was a good man in Lo-Melkhiin somewhere, I had just seen my first real glimpse of him.

No, my second. He had watered his horse with his own hands when we crossed the desert, and had not pushed the animals beyond their endurance.

"Why did you heal your mother?" I asked him then.

He sat up, surprised at my question, all trace of laughter gone from his eyes.

"It is what any good son would do," he said to me. "Is it not?"

"It is," I said to him. "But you are not her good son."

He looked at me sharply. He had tested me before, as goats test a new minder, and now I was testing him. I was not even sure what my question had meant, only that the words had come to me when I needed them—threads from Sokath, His Eyes Uncovered and from Lo-Melkhiin's mother both. It was clear to me that the words had meant a great deal to *him*, though, and now I had another puzzle, regardless of his answer.

"I cured my mother because I had the power to do it, and because she was ill, and because it suited me," he said to me. "Does that answer suit you?"

"Yes, my lord," I said to him, the picture of meekness. It was the way my mother spoke to our father when she had won, but wanted to let him preserve his dignity.

Lo-Melkhiin smiled at me, not a hunter or a viper this time, but not quite a man either—or at least, not the kind of man I wanted in my bed.

"I think we will do very well together, my wife," he said to me.

"If I do not die," I said to him.

"If you do not die," he said to me. He reached out and wound one hand into the fabric of my sleeping gown, pulling it toward him. "Now, come up here and go to sleep on your pillows. If the serving girls find you down there in the morning, they will think you have angered me. Rather, I find you a delight."

There was no way to do it without crawling, which irked me. If he had let me go, I might have stood and walked, but he didn't, so I was forced on my hands and knees like a babe. I put my head on the pillow, as far from his as I could, and he smoothed the gown back over my knees before lying down beside me. Though he was within arm's reach, he did not touch me. Instead, he leaned over to put out the lamp. Just before the darkness swallowed us both, I saw that copper fire leap from him to me, though we did not make contact.

Was this the last night, then, I could not help but wonder. There were so many ways to kill a person while they slept. He did not have a knife on his person, I was certain, but his robe was in reach of the bed, and if there was a knife there, he might stab me while I slumbered. He could wrap his long fingers around my neck, or use the ties from the bed hangings to cut off the air to my lungs. He could place one of the pillows over my nose and mouth.

He did none of those things. He turned on his side, facing away from me, and I counted his breaths until they were even. As determined as I was to stay awake, the softness of his breathing lulled me, and I drifted between one blink and the next. I saw the line of his shoulders faintly silhouetted by the hour-candle when my eyes were open, and my sister's strong hands with a grinding stone when they were shut. I wanted my sister, wanted her spirit and her sharp tongue, and the comfort her presence gave me. My blinks became longer, until I saw Lo-Melkhiin no longer.

I knew it for a dream, because my sister was there, and I was with her and not with her at the same time. She was grinding shells to fine white powder, the basalt stone heavy in her hands as she crushed her work into the stone trough. Her mouth was moving, though I could not hear her. She was singing, I guessed. Or praying. I had never done this sort of work, but I saw how she did it. It was the same as grinding grain, except the grinding stone was long, flat on the bottom, and arched under her hands; the pestle was too heavy to balance on her knees, like the one we used for spices. This was priestly work.

Our mothers sat close by her, weaving broadcloth by passing the shuttle back and forth between them. It was not fine work, but it was good work, the sort I had hoped to emulate when I was a child. While I watched, my sister's mother looked at the shells and shook her head. They were not fine enough, I knew, though I had not heard her say it. They must be ground so hard that they forgot the animals they used to house, the place where they used to live. There must be nothing of their old power left. Only then could they be put to priestly use.

My sister ground the shells again. I put my ghostly hands on her shoulders, and felt the tired ache there. Grinding was rough work, even a small amount. My mother and my sister's mother were always careful to make sure that the grinding of grain was a job shared by many, because if one person did it too often, it would twist their whole body. We were lucky to be healthy and to have enough men and women to do the job. My brothers had told us that others, not so well-off as us, were forced to spend so much time grinding that they could not lie flat on their backs, nor spread their fingers out, nor even walk properly any longer.

I did not know who did that job in the qasr. I had not yet ventured into the kitchens. I did not know if Lo-Melkhiin bought flour. He could afford it, surely. I had not set hand to a grinding-stone, nor to any work harder than spinning, since I had left our father's tents. I had grown city-soft. Perhaps the desert sun would break me, if I ever went outside the walls again. The dream began to fade, my eyes clouding over, as I doubted myself. I did not want to lose this vision of my sister, but I did not know how to hold on to it.

Sokath, His Eyes Uncovered had called me strong,

and I had not died, so maybe he was right. I tightened my fingers on my sister's shoulders, the way I had touched Firh Stonetouched the night of the starfall party, and the dream became clear to me again. I could feel her muscles now, and the heat of her skin under her shirt. In the tent with just our mothers, they had taken off their veils and tunics. It was cooler that way, and easier to work in the desert heat.

I kneaded my sister's shoulders the way my mother kneaded bread dough, and felt the ache lessen. Her breath came to her lungs, and she pushed the stones together harder than she had before. We did the work together, like we had when we stitched the dishdashah, only this time we whispered no secrets to one another. I did not think she would hear me, even if I tried, and by the time I thought to, my sister's mother had taken the stone from her hands, nodding and smiling at a job well done. I would have to remember, when next I dreamed, to see if I could talk as well as touch.

My sister raised one hand to her shoulder, as though to massage her aches herself. Her fingers passed right through mine, but I felt them do it. For just a breath, I thought she might feel them too, but she shook herself, and that shook me back into my bed in Lo-Melkhiin's qasr, far away.

It was daylight when I woke, still reaching for my

sister's touch. Lo-Melkhiin was gone. A new hour-candle burned on the table, and there was my tea, steaming beside it. The lamp was unlit—there was no need for it when the sun was up—but it was polished brightly. Beside it, painted gold, was a wooden ball.

seventeen

I RETURNED TO THE SPINNING ROOM, and found I was made welcome there. Grief and resilience are odd emotions, I was coming to understand. Before, the women had not wanted to become attached to me, as they assumed I would not survive. Now that I did not die, they were letting their guard down. I wondered what would happen when I did die, and how long it would take their hearts to soften again afterward. If I had been a nobler sort, I might have scorned their friendship to spare them future pain, but I was lonely, and as common as our father's goats.

Before, they had talked around me, and I had learned from them. Now, they tried to include me in their conversation as much as they could, though there were, of course, some things we did not discuss. They were all city born, though, and hungered to hear my stories about growing up in the desert.

"Will it make you homesick to tell?" one of the weavers asked.

"No, I do not think so," I said to her. "It makes me happy to remember."

I did not tell them any of our special stories, the ones that my mother and my sister's mother whispered to my sister and me over the fire when our father and brothers were away on caravan. Nor did I tell them the stories I spun for Lo-Melkhiin. Instead, I told them of the great silver-colored birds that tried to take goats and even sheep from the herds my sister and I had watched when we were children.

"My sister had better aim than I did," I said to them. "But I could throw a rock farther. When the great birds came, we shouted and waved our arms, and threw stones. Even if we hit them, the birds were so big that we could not injure them too badly. They would fly away and leave our flocks in peace."

"Lady-bless, that sounds terrifying!" a spinner said. "Big enough to carry you off, and you only armed with stones!"

"They do not have a taste for children," I told her. "In the desert, the only things that do are lions and snakes, and both of those creatures will hunt anything. The birds only came for the flocks, and we drove them off."

"Where do they live?" This from the embroiderer who specialized in stitching desert flowers into the hems of dresses for city women. I had no notion of where the birds lived, but I was in the rhythm of a story now, and could feel the word-threads coming together for an answer.

"Far away to the north of us, beyond the sand desert and the scrub desert, there is a range of mountains, higher than anything you can imagine." A Skeptic had lectured about mountains at dinner a few nights ago, and shown pictures of them, incised on baked clay tablets. His mountains were by the blue desert, though, where Lo-Melkhiin's mother had come from.

"And they come all this way for food?" the embroiderer asked.

"Sometimes there are too many of them in the mountains," I said to her. "So they pick the youngest and strongest birds, and send them out across the desert to look for food."

"Poor things, to come so far for nothing," said the spinner.

I smiled at her. "Our father gives them the oldest sheep, who would be too tough for us to eat, and whose wool has failed," I said. "He knows what it is like to go out with the caravan and provide for a family at home."

"What makes them so big?" a weaver asked. "We've large sand-crows here, but nothing so big as that."

Again, I did not know, and again, I felt the story-threads

come to me when I wished for them.

"There is a metal in those mountains that we do not have in the desert," I said to them. "It is in the rocks there, and when the water in the mountain wadis rushes over them, part of the metal goes into the water. The birds drink of it, and grow strong."

"That sounds like Skeptic talk," said one of the oldest weavers. "Lady-bless, you are no Skeptic."

"I am not," I said to her. "But I have the stories of my village, and our father has traveled widely to bring us even more tales. It may not be the truth, but it is what I know."

"You are wise, lady-bless," the old weaver said. "And you are desert-strong."

"Perhaps that is why she—" The spinner who had started to speak cut off abruptly. Her spindle thudded to the ground, as though someone had kicked her and she'd dropped it in her surprise. All her thread was unwound. She would have to start again.

I had been embroidering; my hands were finally soft enough to use the silk thread without snagging it at every turn. When I started talking I had stopped paying attention to what I worked, but the work had not stopped.

Needlecraft, whether carding, spinning, weaving, or embroidering, is a craft of the eyes. Talk is easy when you work, because you can talk without taking your eyes from your task. Until the clatter of the dropped spindle, we had all been looking at our laps or hands, where we held hoops, raw yarn, or small looms. Even the women who worked the bigger floor looms in the corner could talk with us without looking away from what they were doing. Now, they all stared at me, and there was fear in their eyes. Surely they did not think I would be so cruel as to punish a girl for speaking what everyone already knew.

Then I saw that they weren't looking at my face. They were looking at my hands.

I looked down at my hoop. I had meant to make a caravan: camels and men, all brightly colored on the desert sand, beneath an endless blue sky. I had done the sky right enough, and the sand, because I had done them before I started to tell my story. But where I had meant to do camels, I had instead done sheep. They were scattered on the ground, running away. The shepherd—no, the hunter with them—had his bow trained on the sky, but I knew he would not be able to fire his arrow in time.

Plummeting out of the blue was an enormous bird, wings extended longer than the man was tall, and terrible talons stretching for its prey. There was no way to be sure— embroidery does not let you make pictures of people's faces in great detail—but I knew in my heart that the hunter was Lo-Melkhiin.

"Lady-bless," began the spinner.

"Will you hush, woman?" said the old weaver. She looked at me with an awed expression on her face. "Lady-bless, your work is very good, but perhaps that is all you should do today?"

She was terrified. I could hear it in the polite way she spoke, and the others in the room fairly quivered with it. They were like the sheep before the rainstorm that had flooded the wadi and taken my sister's brother. This was strange to them, and they knew, somehow, that a storm was coming.

"Perhaps you are right," I said to her. "I am unused to such a long time at one craft. In our father's tents, we had too many tasks to spend so long at only one."

It was not a very good excuse, but it was good enough to get me from the room. I held the hoop and the embroidered cloth tightly against my chest, blocking it from the view of any that I passed. When I got outside and reached the large vats where the dyers boiled the colorant we used to dye yarn and cloth, I threw the work, hoop and all, into the fire, and it burned just the same as any cloth would do.

I returned to my room, anxious to not meet anyone in the gardens in case they had heard about what I had done. In our father's tents, gossip spread quicker than fire, and I

E. K. JOHNSTON

knew that here would be no different. The women, at least, would all know by the time the sun set; and if the men did not, it would be because they did not care to, or because they did not believe what the women said. Whether Lo-Melkhiin would hear, or believe, I did not know. And I did not know what his reaction would be.

I stared at the hour-candle in my room and prayed to the smallgods. I asked our father's father's father for his strength and luck. To my mother's mother's mother, I prayed for survival. She had survived when she should not have, thanks to a talking camel. I did not think I was worthy of such a miracle, but I prayed for one all the same. Neither of the smallgods had saved themselves, in the end. Both had been saved by other forces. Perhaps it was enough to do your best, and know when to ask for aid.

There was a clamor in the garden outside my rooms. On the other side of the garden was the bathhouse I used. It was not the only one in the qasr, but it was the most private. I had never seen anyone else use it, and I knew only one person could be using it now.

I pulled on my darkest veil. They would see me, undoubtedly, standing in the sun, but I did not want them to see my face. I stood in my door and watched four guards, Firh Stonetouched among them, carry a litter into the bathhouse. On the litter, his dark skin pale and his fine clothes dark with blood, was Lo-Melkhiin. I fled as they disappeared into the bath, and did not see another soul until the serving girl brought me my dinner.

"What is happening?" I asked her. "What is going on?"

She was pale too, though her dark hair was still neatly bound up and her dress hung perfectly about her body. The cup on my dinner tray had clattered against the finger bowl when she set it down, and I knew that her hands shook, though now she had them balled up inside the pleats in the front of her shift.

"Lady-bless," she said. "They say a monster attacked Lo-Melkhiin while he was hunting in the desert."

"How is this possible?" I demanded, though I thought I might know. If she had heard the story of my embroidery, she gave no sign of it.

"A giant demon in the form of a bird," she said. "Lady-bless, they say it came out of the sky so quickly that not even Fleetfoot could have matched it for speed. Lo-Melkhiin had a bow, but he could not fire fast enough, and the monster gored him in the side."

"Surely he has been wounded hunting before," I said to her.

"No, lady-bless," she said to me. "Sometimes a graze, maybe, but there have been hunts where the lions took four guards, and Lo-Melkhiin came back without a scratch."

"You may go," I said to her, straightening myself where I sat. "Should my husband send for me, I will of course go, but leaving that aside, I do not wish to be disturbed again tonight—understood?"

She murmured her acquiescence and fled back to the comfortable safety of the kitchen.

I ate my dinner slowly, rolling the pieces of spiced goat in bread and dipping them in oil before taking a bite, and then chewing with more care than I might have needed.

This was like the gown, I realized; only, I had woven men and birds, not gold thread. I had not just seen it, I had caused it. I looked at the golden ball that had awaited me when I woke up that morning. I had made that, too. I held my breath.

It was not enough to wander, to set my power loose like the goats and hope that it found good grazing, and heeded my call when I bid it to return. I needed it to be like that storm. Something I could see coming, something I could prepare for. I would have to try again, and see if I could do this work on purpose.

Lo-Melkhiin did not rise from his sickbed that night, and so I slept alone. When I woke in the morning, there was a new-made lamp next to the golden ball.

eighteen

I HAD NOT TOLD THE WOMEN in the spinning room the truth about the great birds from the mountains. When my sister and I were six years old and the fire of summer had burned down to embers, we saw the birds for the first time. They came in a great flock, not in ones and twos, and they flew above us when we took the sheep and goats out to graze. They reminded me of our father's caravan—a long line of men with purpose, but who tired and sometimes grew sad when they were away from home.

My sister had her sling and a rock in her hands, at the ready in case one of them dropped down for a sheep. I had nothing.

"Sister," she said to me, "where is your sling? You must help me if the birds are hungry."

"I will not," I said to her. "They are on a caravan, can you not see? If we turn them away, we have broken the laws of hospitality."

My sister looked at me as if I had spent too long in the sun and suggested that we might eat sand for sweetmeats. Then the birds started to call, a hard and lonely sound, and one of them dropped like a stone from the sky.

"Sister!" my sister shouted, but she did not raise her sling.

The sheep panicked and tried to run, but the bird was faster. I thought it would snag its talons in the wool and fly away, but instead it landed on a sheep's back and slit its throat with a great claw. The beast slumped to the side as the bird began to eat.

We looked aloft. If a sand-crow finds prey in the desert sand, more will join it and fight over the meal. If these birds were the same, my sister and I and the sheep would be in trouble. The dogs barked and barked, bringing the sheep under control again even as the great bird feasted, but the goats were gone. We could only hope they would come back. We had some small luck; none of the other birds came down from the sky. They circled and watched, as though they were waiting for something.

At last, the grounded bird gave another terrible cry and

took to wing, dragging the carcass of the sheep into the air, trailing blood. On the ground where it had sat was an egg. It was bigger than my sister's head, and we stared at it in awe.

"Sister," she said to me, "you were wise. It was hospitality."

"Come," I said to her. "Let us take the egg to our mothers. The goats will find their own ways home, and the sheep will graze no more today."

It took the pair of us trading off to carry it. We could not share the weight, as we did with the water jars, because of the odd shape. One of us had to wrap her arms around the egg, not too firmly lest we crush it, while the other minded the dogs and the flock. We switched when the egg bearer's arms grew too tired to keep a steady grip.

"Daughters, are you ill?" called my sister's mother when we came in sight of the tents. "Why have you come back while the sun is still so high?"

We were too worn out to speak at first, and set the egg down at my sister's mother's feet. She called for my mother, and for cool water, and by the time both had arrived, we were able to tell the story of what had happened.

"We saw the birds," my mother said. "We hoped they would leave the flock alone. They flew so high we wondered if they would even see it."

"Were we right, mother of my heart?" I asked her. "Was it the same as hospitality?"

"I think you were right," she said to me. "And look what they have given in thanks!"

The egg was too large for our biggest jars and cooking pots, even the dormouse pot that our father had brought back in the caravan from far away, that we only used for special meals. In the end, our mothers settled for pushing the egg into the fire, right atop the coals, and then rolling it out with a long bronze dagger when they decided it was done.

By then our father and my brothers had returned, and were told the tale. Our father thanked us for being so wise, with a bright light in his eyes. We knew then that he thought it was funny, that we had thought the birds deserved hospitality, but also that he was proud of us.

"Look at what your sisters hunted!" he told my brothers as he turned away from us. "And they did not hunt with spears or arrows, but with their own minds."

My mother cut the egg in half the long way, and scooped out the white and yellow insides. There was enough that everyone in the village could have some, and there was still some left over to offer the dead. When the shell was empty, she faced the two halves back to the fire to dry them out. In the morning, my mother and my sister's mother went to the caves to offer the cooked egg to the dead. They took the shell with them, and afterward, told us that they had used them to hold the lamps that burned over the shrine of our father's father's father.

The dead share with one another, and do not mind as long as proper respect is paid. When my mother told us about my mother's mother's mother, my sister and I moved one of the eggshell lamps to her small shrine. I had seen my sister building a shrine for me, but I had not been able to see what she had used to make it. I knew that the older objects would have the most power, but since I was not yet dead, I did not know if she would be able to use them.

There was a cord in my room that would bring a serving girl to me. I had never used it, because I had never needed anything I did not have. I used it now, and if the girl was startled she gave no sign. Perhaps she was fearful of me now, and called stone into her face to hide it, as I did when I faced Lo-Melkhiin. In any case, when I asked for a spindle and something to spin into yarn, she said nothing, only nodded and fled to do as I had asked.

When she was gone I lit the other lamps, including the new one I had found that morning. It was decorated with goats, with round circles I took to be balls, and with images of the sun. It was very finely made, and would have taken hours to cast and fire, had it been made in the usual way. It was not as expensive as the ball—wood was hard to come by in the desert, and a piece that could be carved into a ball even more so—but it was a good piece, nonetheless.

I dressed myself quickly in a light gown, twisting my hair around my head as the spinners did to keep their

E. K. JOHNSTON

long braids from mucking up their work. The serving girl
returned with my spindle and a basket of undyed wool, and
I dismissed her with as much kindness as I could muster.
I did not wish for people to fear me. There was a cushion
next to my low table, and I sat on it with the basket beside
me, my dress pulled out of the way of the spindle. The lamp
burned strongly, giving out clear light even though the room
was already lit by the sun. The ball did not roll, but rather
sat next to the lamp and cast shadows on the table top.

I attached raw wool to the leading thread and spun a
handspan or so, to be sure I had enough of it to start. Holding the whorl to keep the work from unraveling, I took a
deep breath, and then another, and began to spin.

At first, nothing happened except that the yarn grew
under my fingers. Without thinking, I began to match my
breath to the rise and fall of the spindle, and my heartbeat
followed suit. Between one blink of the eye and the next,
I was flying over the desert sand, faster than any horse or
sand-crow, toward our father's tents. Toward my sister.

Our father's camels were gone, and I knew that I was
seeing the days that had gone before, as I had wished to.
These were the days after I had left with Lo-Melkhiin,
yet before our father had returned with the caravan. My
mother's tent flew a purple flag, which was not the color of
mourning. There were no piles of pickled gage-root or desert
flowers on either side of the tent flap, to remind her that the

dead wanted for nothing. They were not mourning me as one who had died, though they were grieving my absence from them. My sister knew I yet lived, and she was spreading the word of my survival down the wadi like a flood.

I found my sister in our tent, the one we had shared and the one where she now slept alone. Her bedroll and rugs were all pushed to the side, exposing hard-packed desert sand beneath. She walked in a long circle, trailing the shell-powder behind her as she went, until she closed the loop. Then she turned and knelt in front of the objects she had put in the center of her circle. There was my first spindle whorl, my favorite of my mother's colored bowls, my shepherd's staff, and the bronze knife I had used to cut my meat. My sister unwrapped a small bundle I knew held my stitching kit, and added it to the collection. Then she began to chant.

I could not hear her words, but I could see the power come into her circle. Before, it had been dirt on dirt, colors mixing as they shifted on the ground. Now, the white of the powder was heightened until it blazed against the sand. It sent tendrils out toward each of the items, and to my sister, wrapping them and sealing them to her use.

Just before the circle was too bright for me to look at, my sister reached into the bag beside her and pulled forth one of the two half-shell lamps, adding it to the rest. It already blazed with the prayers that had been said to it. Now it seared my eyes, and I rocked back from its harsh glare.

As soon as I moved, I was flying again, across the desert to Lo-Melkhiin's qasr and the room where I was spinning yarn. I blinked, my eyes still glamored by the brightness of my sister's work. My lamp burned with a white light, and my ball glowed with it. My lap was full of yarn. Though I had started with raw wool, I had spun it as white as it if had been bleached for days. I hurried to finish the end, so that my work would not undo itself, and then wound it tightly around a skein that I found at the bottom of the basket.

I had asked for a vision, and done the work for one, and I had received it. The sun had moved to a different window, and the hour-candle had burned down to midday, yet I had none of the stiffness I would have expected from spinning for so long without moving. I was exhausted, though, and stumbled when I stood. I went back to my bed and lay down upon it, and if Lo-Melkhiin himself had summoned me, I could not have risen again.

The darkness claimed me, but it was a soft and friendly one, edged in that familiar white light.

nineteen

I SLEPT THROUGH THE hottest part of the day, and when I woke and missed the desert, I went to the water garden. The sound of the fountain was like nothing I might find at home, and yet it soothed me. It had a rhythm, one I could feel in my fingers, the same way I had felt the spindle and the thread. The evening flowers were just beginning to blossom, and their light scent wakened me from the last of my exhaustion.

I was not alone. Lo-Melkhiin's mother sat under one of the date palms on a broad cushion, a pitcher of watered wine at her elbow. When I met her gaze, she gestured to the space at her side, and I crossed the walkway to sit. My place was not quite shaded, but the sun no longer hammered down, and it did not seem so bright after what I had seen in my vision.

"When my son began to hunt, I feared for his safety," she said to me when I had settled. She did not offer me a cup.

"The desert is a hard place," I said to her. "It is full of many dangers."

"Your words are true," she said to me. "Yet my son did not fall prey to any of them. Even when he first went into the desert, it loved him and did not harm him."

"He must be wise to its ways," I told her. "Our father is like that. He goes out with the caravan and comes back, and is only marked by the dust of the road."

"My son studied the desert well," she agreed. "But when his spirit was changed, he began to flaunt his desert wisdom."

I thought about what the women in the spinning room had said. Lo-Melkhiin might go into the desert and return unscathed, but his men did not. Our father's pride was not only in his own resilience, but in the strength of the whole caravan, down to the sheep they took with them to trade.

"The desert does not like to be mocked," I said to her. "It will always take a price in the end."

"And now at last my son has paid," she said to me. "A great bird attacked him, sliced him with silver-colored talons so bright the other huntsmen could not look at them, and now he lies abed as he has not done in months and months, and does not know the sky from the sand."

I remembered the ease with which I had seen the great bird slit the throat of the sheep my sister and I had watched over, and did not doubt her.

"Are the wounds so deep as to be fevered already?" I asked.

"He has no fever," she said to me. "There is no infection that our healers can see. The cuts are more like scratches, barely bleeding now that the compresses have been laid, and yet he does not wake."

At last, she poured a cup of wine and passed it to me. I took it with thanks and drank it slowly. It tasted bitter on my tongue, and as I drank, I felt the world sharpen around me. The white light of my vision faded and the rhythm with it, though I could still hear the echo in the fountain's song.

"The women say you stitched it in thread, before you could have known," Lo-Melkhiin's mother said to me.

I did not answer. Before, the story-threads had come to me easily, but now that I was not focused on a task, I had nothing.

"When a king dies, there is always a scramble, even when there is an heir," she said to me. "When there is no heir, it is madness, and can ruin a city and a realm."

Our boss-ram had died in the dark of my eighth winter. The ewes would not leave him, and the other rams had fought for days until one of them, the youngest of them, had died too—his horns were not yet strong enough to protect his skull, and still he would not stay out of the fighting. I imagined that with men it was worse.

"My son is no longer a good man," she said to me, "but he is a good king. If your desert power has caused this, I beg you to fix it. Fix him, if you can."

"If he dies, I can return to our father's tents," I said to her. I did not mean the words to be cruel, but she flinched at them anyway. "I would be a widow, and the laws of men say I must be allowed to go. I would no longer fear death at Lo-Melkhiin's hands. I would go home, and take the priestly role from my sister, that she might wed."

"You could do that," she said to me. Her words were slow, like it pained her to speak them. "But the city would be in chaos, and chaos crosses sand like the sand-crows do. Your family would not escape it, however well your father trades."

When Lo-Melkhiin's father died, our father had not gone trading for a full year. The roads were not safe, he had said to my mother and my sister's mother, when he thought we could not hear him. He would not risk the caravan, and we had enough to get by, if we were careful. Three of the lambs died, and one camel, but we survived. If there were no new king, no one would hold the roads and enforce the trading laws. Our father would stay at home until he was forced out, and then he might pay too high a price for trading.

"What could I do?" I asked of her.

"You stitched this and knew it as it was happening," Lo-Melkhiin's mother said to me. "I do not know if you saw it or if you caused it, but come and look at my son, and perhaps you will know how to wake him from his illness."

I wanted to refuse her. I could see my home with such clarity that I could smell the sheep and taste the roasting meat on the fire. I could hear my brothers wrestling with each other to see who would have the unwanted chores. I could feel my sister's hand in mine as we watched them, giggling at their antics. I would not heal Lo-Melkhiin for his own sake.

"I will come," I said to her.

She stood, her lion's-mane wig a tawny contrast to her dark skin, and pulled me to my feet. I went to my room for a veil and over-robe, and pinned up the locks of hair that had come loose while I slept. Then she led me into the bathhouse, past the steaming pools and the dressing room I used, and into the room where Lo-Melkhiin was kept.

He tossed fitfully on a high table, rather than on pillows on the floor. The table was covered with white linen, and it looked like his skin had borrowed some of that color. His pallor extended from the crown of his head to his fingers and toes. His face showed pain, though his eyes were closed. I thought that if he were awake, he would be screaming with it. I was almost sad that he slept.

"Lady-bless," said the healer who stood at the head of the table. He bowed to me, but I thought it was to Lo-Melkhiin's mother that he spoke.

"May I take some of your time for questions?" I asked. "I do not wish to distract you."

"Lady-bless, I have done all that I can," he said to me. "When he was awake, even though he was thrashing, it seemed like I had ideas how to make him better, but now that he is asleep, I can think of nothing but to wait."

I went and stood beside Lo-Melkhiin, and took Lo-Melkhiin's hand in mine. For the first time, I saw the cold light without his prompting, and felt something settle in my skin. The copper fire was there, and wound itself around his fingers.

"I know you have tried," I said to to the healer. "Can you tell me what you did?"

"I have cleaned the wounds with water and bound them up to stop the bleeding," he said to me. "The herbs in the bindings are to help the skin regrow, though he may scar."

"My son is a hunter," said Lo-Melkhiin's mother. "He will not mind the scars."

The healer bowed to her.

"Will it damage the wound for me to see it unbound?" I asked. The healer hesitated, and I laid my other hand on his. The copper fire shone. "Only in the desert have I seen such wounds before."

167

I did not lie, exactly. I had seen the wounds, but the sheep was already dead. In any case, the healer was so desperate he agreed, and carefully pulled back the bindings. Unbound, they were gruesome-looking.

"Have they always been this vibrant?" I asked.

"No, lady-bless." The healer pointed to a charcoal mark on Lo-Melkhiin's arm. "Here is the extent of the coloring two hours ago. It has spread a handspan since then."

He offered me clean oil, that I might touch the wounds without causing infection. When I touched Lo-Melkhiin, no fire passed between us, but I could feel the rhythm of his blood. It was like the fountain, like the spindle, and like my own heart. I closed my eyes, and tried to match my breathing to his, but it was too shallow. Instead, for every three of his breaths, I took one, and that helped me sink into his blood.

It was not like spinning. That was orderly and productive. This was a mess of blood and marrow and bone, and a spark that linked them all together that I did not want to touch. The blood was heavy, too heavy for the body to carry. It moved through his veins sluggishly, carrying the weight toward his heart. I did not like to think what would happen when the weight reached its destination. Shifting, I found myself in an artery, rushing fast now, through his body and to his brain. It was like a lightning storm there, except for one corner that was friendly and dark. I tried to look at my own brain, and saw no dark spots like his, but the movement pulled me out of the trance, back to Lo-Melkhiin's side.

I could say nothing, and he would die. I could return to our father's tents, and we would endure while the men of the city fought over the throne. I could say nothing, but others would suffer: other traders, the women and children in other tents, the villages that were closer to the border than they were to the qasr. I could say nothing, or I could make sure that when Lo-Melkhiin woke up, he would owe his life to me.

"His blood is poisoned," I said to the healer. "The bird must have had something on its talons."

"But the horse isn't ill," said the healer. "And neither is the guard, who was also scratched."

"Perhaps it only affects Lo-Melkhiin, but I tell you, his blood is poisoned," I said to him. And that would be a good poison to know.

"Cut the wounds," Lo-Melkhiin's mother said. "I know it is dangerous, but it may be the only way."

The healer looked at both of us helplessly, and then began to roll up his sleeves. I saw the copper fire run up his arms, toward his heart and his mind. He would do it.

"I beg you both, leave us," he said. "This will not be pleasant to see."

I pulled Lo-Melkhiin's mother from the room as the

healer summoned his aide and they began to heat their blades in the fire. I knew when they began to cut, though, without seeing them, because that is when Lo-Melkhiin woke up, and at last began to scream.

twenty

LO-MELKHIIN DID NOT DIE that night, nor the next. It took three full nights of bleeding before the poison was leeched from him and he woke, and knew the sky from the sand. I found a pot of desert flowers in my rooms that day, and knew they were a sign of gratitude from Lo-Melkhiin's mother. I put them in the sun so that they wilted and died, rootless as they were. I wanted no memory of what I had done.

The girls who came to do my hair and bathe me bowed low, and would not meet my eyes. They did not make idle chatter as they had before, and they did not speak directly to me either, save to ask if a pin vexed me or if the design was good. They were afraid, or perhaps they thought I was a fool. I had saved Lo-Melkhiin, after all, for reasons of men, and the women who lived in the qasr would suffer for it. I would pay with my life, as like as anything. I was short-tempered, and did not hold that back from my answers to them. By the time I was dressed, we were all upset. At least they could flee.

I went into the water garden, thinking that the fountain would soothe me as it had the day before, and found once again that I was not alone there. This time, it was Sokath, His Eyes Uncovered who waited for me, and he had break-fast for two spread on the blanket where he sat in the shade. I sat across from him, and did not speak.

"In times gone past," said Sokath, His Eyes Uncovered, "a person who saved a king or a queen would be richly rewarded. Nothing their heart desired would be too large. Yet here you sit, lady-bless, with a hard heart in your chest."

"Should I rejoice?" I asked him. "Am I not a silly sheep who cannot think for herself, and goes willingly to the pen rather than face the possibility of jackals in the night?

"I think rather that you are a goat," said Sokath, His Eyes Uncovered. "You go to the pen because it is your home, but you could think your way out of it, should you need to."

I made an impolite sound that would have galled my sister's mother to hear.

"Tell me what you saw when you healed him," said Sokath, His Eyes Uncovered. "I shall be the sun, and you the ball, and together we will judge the shadows."

I told him about the heaviness in Lo-Melkhiin's blood and the dark spot in his brain that had seemed so unlike the rest of it.

"Unlike in what manner?" he asked.

I considered the words I might use to describe it to him. The threads were there, I found, in the rhythm of the fountain's falling water.

"When we slaughter animals for our feast days, we set aside the head for our offerings," I said to him. "My mother and my sister's mother wait until the skulls have dried, and then they crack them open. That is how I know what the brain looks like. I have seen sheep and goat, and once a camel. In Lo-Melkhiin's brain, it is like there is a viper, but the corner is that of a camel."

Sokath, His Eyes Uncovered rolled an olive between his fingers.

"And the camel-section was dark, like it was asleep," I continued. "The viper section was full of lightning."

"That lightning is what the priests might call your soul," he said. "The Skeptics think it is like the sun on green plants, making them grow tall and strong."

"Does that mean the dark part does not have a soul?" I asked.

"Or that it is being held back," said Sokath, His Eyes

Uncovered. "Do you know the story of how Lo-Melkhiin became like he is?"

"I do," I said to him. "He went into the desert and came back changed."

"You must never tell my colleagues," he said to me, "but I think they are wrong. The sun can bake a man's thoughts for a time, but if it does not kill him, he becomes cool-headed again. I think the priests are right. There was a demon in the dunes that day, and it came back instead of Lo-Melkhiin."

"Not instead of," I said to him. "As well as. If it was instead of, the whole brain would be the same."

"That is true, I suppose," he said to me. "It does not matter, in the end. The demon is too strong."

"Not so strong that I am dead," I reminded him.

"That is what gives me hope," he said. "We must have Lo-Melkhiin until there is an heir. An heir can have a regent, and a regent can step aside. An heir can be taught, molded. Without an heir, the powerful men of the court will step in, and we will be generations without peace as they squabble."

I knew the laws of men. A regent must be a priest or a Skeptic. Often, it was one of each. They were always old, so that they would not hold on to their lives for too much longer after the heir came of age and took his place. An heir would bring peace, but there was only one way to get one, and the idea made my blood cold. I felt nauseated even thinking of it.

"I know it is not fair to ask," said Sokath, His Eyes Uncovered. "It is not fair to ask a price I cannot pay. But it is the only solution that I can see."

He rose, knees creaking, and bowed, then turned to leave me in the water garden. If he expected an answer, he gave no sign of it, and I gave him none. I thought of the tea I had drunk this morning. It tasted so foul, and now I craved it more than anything I had ever had before. I must find my way into the tea stores and take some, I thought, in case someone orders the women to stop bringing it to me in the morning. So far, Lo-Melkhiin had touched little besides my hands, but I would take no chances.

My stomach heaved, and I vomited my breakfast into the bowl it had been served in. The serving girl heard me, and came at a run. It took some time to assure her that I was well enough, that I just required plain bread and water to settle my stomach. I had ruined the breakfast tray, so I helped her wrap it in the blanket before she took it away.

There will be no heir. I will not pay that price for them. I am finished with the laws of men. I will find another way.

I followed at a distance, hoping she would lead me to the kitchens, and she did. The cook took one look at the bundle she carried and ordered it consigned to the fire. When he saw me, he would have made a fuss, but I raised a hand to forestall him.

"Revered bread-minder," I said to him. "I know that you

are busy with the day's meals. Plain bread and a quiet corner are all I ask."

"Of course, lady-bless," he said to me, and guided me to a stool by the window, far enough from the hearth fires that it would be out of the path of the blasts of heat, and near enough a window to catch the breeze.

There I sat, chewing the bread and drinking the cool fruit juice he set on a low table next to me. I watched him and his helpers as they worked. At first, it looked like an unordered melee, but as I sat, I saw the patterns emerge as surely as they did in weaving or in spinning.

Lo-Melkhiin's mother had begged me to fix him, and I had. Sokath, His Eyes Uncovered wished for an heir, but he would get none from me. Lo-Melkhiin ruled because men let him, regardless of the price. I had lived in his qasr nearly two moons' wanings now, and I did not die. I had called the bird. But now I did not know what to do, so I sat in the kitchen, and watched the boy whose job it was to turn the goats upon their spits so they cooked evenly.

As I watched, the chief cook came to the boy and looked at the meat. He nodded, telling the lad that his job was well done, and then took his knife and pointed to a part of the roast that was a different color than the rest.

"You see, it was bad when we put it on, and we knew it, but sometimes cooking can save it," he said to the boy. "But this cannot be saved. If a man ate this, he would be sick.

Remember this color, boy, in case you see it when I am not here, or in your own kitchen someday. This color goes to the dogs."

With quick and practiced strokes he cut the spoiled meat free, and whistled. The hounds who turned the largest roasts—cattle, I assumed—perked up their ears and sat down, paws folded before them as neatly as though they sat at the king's high table. The cook threw the scraps he'd cut in front of them, and then whistled again. At the second signal, the dogs began to eat, licking their teeth to get every morsel until they were done, and then returning to their work before the side of beef began to burn.

"Even the spoiled bits have their uses, lady-bless," the cook said to me, smiling. "And the lads appreciate the treat whether they've two legs or four, eh?"

I watched as he passed a sweet-roll to the boy who turned the goat spit, and then went back to his work at the kneading tables.

Sokath, His Eyes Uncovered thought that the demon was too strong, but perhaps I had found a weakness when I saw the dark spot in the first place. Lo-Melkhiin's mother was certain that her son, her good son, still lived. The dark spot had felt kindly when I saw it. Perhaps it was the lightning that gave the demon control.

"Fix him," Lo-Melkhiin's mother had said to me, and fix him I had. But I had only fixed his body. The dark spot in his brain was still there. If it were bigger, perhaps Lo-Melkhiin would return to the way he had been before he met the demon in the sand dunes. I could not cut with a knife, the way the head cook had, to separate the two pieces from one another, but I did not need to. I had reached my sister across the desert, and I had called a great bird from the sky. The lightning inside Lo-Melkhiin had scared me before I knew what it was, but I knew my soul was strong and could grapple with his if need be.

The men needed a king. Most were content with the one they had. The Skeptics wished for another to put in his place—treason, should anyone hear of it. I would not settle for the king we had, but neither would I give them an heir. Sokath, His Eyes Uncovered had bid me to be the ball, and he the sun, but I would do that no longer. I would be the sun, now, and I would test the limits of what this strange power could do. I would call upon the prayers my sister offered at my shrine, and I would change what I saw fit to change.

v.

I had kept Lo-Melkhiin in a corner of his own mind, for my own amusement at first. I grew accustomed to his screaming and pleading, and then his sullen silence when he became inured to each horror in its turn. When the bird attacked us, I found a new use for that corner.

I had felt pain before—not as myself, but only once I had entered Lo-Melkhiin's body. He might have stiff legs from a day's ride, or cut himself with his eating knife. It was interesting, this pain. It made me feel alive inside his body, and I rather liked it. The day the great bird took us, though, I felt something entirely new. It seared me, inside and out, as though I were cooking and could not find the fire to put it out before it engulfed me. I had thought we might die.

179

I pulled myself out of his hands and his feet and his chest. His own awareness, so long caged, rushed in to take my place, and only found too late the trap I had set. Now the pain was his alone, save for the small amount that boiled in his head, and I had to bear very little of it.

I did not think I would ever tire of his screaming, but he screamed so much that day that I made him go to sleep. I expected that we would heal, and then I would wake him again, but though I had poured as much of my power into the healer as I dared, the healing did not come. There was something in the blood, something put there by the foul carrion—carried from the mountains in its wretched claws— that would not be healed. I was loath to leave Lo-Melkhiin if he could be saved, but he was no good to me dead, so I prepared myself for the long trip back to the hottest part of the desert. I would have power enough for a while there at least, though of course I craved more.

Then there was the lightest of touches on Lo-Melkhiin's skin. A cool compress, where the healer's craft had only sealed the burning in. I waited, and did not leave Lo-Melkhiin yet, as that coolness spread through the blood and the brain, and then retreated as it had come.

It was her.

When she left us, the compresses were removed, and then came a new pain, sharp and sure. We bled, but I felt the poison leaving us, and decided that I could endure a little longer if it meant not leaving Lo-Melkhiin's body on the table where it lay. I let him have that pain, too. I had had enough to suit me forever more.

I woke three days later, weak but whole. The healers filled me with soups and fruit juice until I thought I would burst, but each swallow restored me. On the fourth day, I could walk again. On the fifth, I overheard two of the serving girls whispering as they cleaned the room where they thought I slept.

"She stitched it, before she could have known," one said to the other.

"She couldn't have," said the second.

"She burned it, so no one would see," said the first. "Only, the spinners all saw, and weavers too."

"Did she see it, then?" said the second. "Or did she cause it?"

They hushed each other as I shifted, hardly able to keep still, and then fled. I was sure the creature I had married was human, common and sun-hammered like the rest of them, but if the girls were right, then she did have some power to her use, whether she knew it or not.

I thought of the cool touch that had come before the knives. That had been her hand. She had come into my blood and seen the damage there, and then told the healers how to fix it. She had let me live. I would not have done the same for her.

Power twists men's minds so easily. They bend toward it like a tree reaches for light and water. That was why I had chosen Lo-Melkhiin's body and Lo-Melkhiin's hands; his were the most powerful. The merchant-lords of his court, the Skeptics and the priests, the artisans and laborers and their sons, had all turned to him—to us—the way sand follows the direction of the wind.

I had spent all the years I had been in Lo-Melkhiin's body giving power to men who I thought would use it in ways that might serve me. I had given them great art and great thoughts, and they never guessed that they fed a terrible hunger in me that would require feeding until they died trying to sate it. They had done great things and made great tales, but I had been blind.

All of this time, I had had access to more power than I had imagined, and I had missed it because I saw with men's eyes. I had forgotten the girls who scrubbed the floors and spun the yarn. I had forgotten the women who dyed the cloth and worked with henna. I had married three hundred girls, and as much as eaten them all before they were done cooking.

She knew. She knew, and yet she saved me anyway, when I lay weak and dying in front of her. She had not struck me as malleable, but she must have been. Only a fool or a puppet would save a man who might kill him, and I knew she was no fool.

Better, she had had a taste of it. Whether she had seen that bird or called it down on me, she would have felt the power of it, and power was something I could spin as easily as she spun thread. I had taken the hearts of so many men in my time in Lo-Melkhiin's body that it had become easy, too easy. Now I had a challenge ready-made. I did not know how to bend the heart of a woman, but Lo-Melkhiin did.

twenty-one

WHEN HE RECOVERED, LO-MELKHIIN dined with me in my room. The serving girls brought in a second table—larger than the one where I ate, and where I kept my lamp and ball—and covered it with a soft blue cloth edged in gold. One girl trimmed all the wicks, and brought in more lamps so that we could see each other clearly as we ate. I watched their preparations with a sick heart. Even if we did not eat for an hour while they prepared, we would still have two hours between dinner and the time I went to sleep. I doubted he would leave me, particularly not if his mother had told him I had woven the attack as it happened, but I had no desire to learn what Lo-Melkhiin did to pass his evenings.

The henna mistress came and took my hands in hers. She drew me out of the room and across the garden, to the bath. She did not have time, she said, for a full wash, but she could do my hands and my hair.

I sat patiently while she worked henna into my hair, reddening it. Where her fingers brushed my neck, ears, and forehead, I knew she would leave henna prints on my skin. This she did on purpose, so that smallgods who were not in my family would know I had put the color in my hair. If it were done too neatly, they might think I had been born an oddity, and mark me for their purpose. I did not tell her that her efforts were in vain. I was purpose-marked already.

She left my hair, and took up her stylus to draw the symbols on my hands. I could only watch in silence for a few moments before my curiosity overwhelmed me.

"Henna mistress," I said to her. "What are these symbols that you draw?"

"Some I will tell you," she said to me. "But, lady-bless, some are my family's own secrets. Blessings of our smallgods that we are permitted to draw on others as gifts. Those, I will not give up."

"I understand," I said to her.

I had wondered what set a good henna artist apart from a lesser one. The mistress always worked on me, though I knew she had several apprentices and at least one daughter—a child of herding-age, had she lived in our

184

father's tents. Those girls might draw upon one another, or upon the spinners, but they did not touch me, even for practice. Now I knew why. If the henna mistress drew signs of power on my skin, she would want no others to interfere.

"This one is for luck," she said to me, and pointed at a wide circle with wings on it. There were several of them on my forearms, hidden in the pattern. "And these are for strength."

A tree started at the base of each of my palms, growing leafy branches into each of my fingers. She traced a line I knew to be the desert, and our father's tents: my history. Then she turned my hands palm up, brought them together, and pulled them toward her own body. I looked down at the pale side of my forearms, pressed together by the way she held me. They were birds, half on each arm, and recognizable only when my hands were held as she had them now.

"Lady-bless," she said, and released me.

"Thank you," I said to her.

If I dined with my husband, I would take all the aid I might receive.

She did not explain any other symbols to me, but I could feel each one as she drew it on. They burned, like skin put too near a candle, when she started them. When she finished each one, the ache sank into my skin and ceased. Every one of them made me stronger, even if I did not know their meaning.

At last she finished, and clapped her hands sharply. The other girls appeared as she folded away her kit, and began to coil my hair in the elaborate styles I had, at last, become accustomed to. Here again, there were patterns in plaits and pins, and I felt each bit woven and then sealed against me as the girls braided, looped, and secured.

They brought out my dress, a blue that was several shades darker than the cloth that covered the table, but not yet so dark as the starless sky, and wrapped it around me. It covered the henna mistress's birds, but I could feel them on my skin as though they flapped their wings against it. The dress was embroidered in dark purple thread as well, making the patterns difficult to see. Again, I needed no eyes and no touch to tell their path. I could not tell if any besides the henna mistress had done this on purpose, but I was as armored as I could be to face dinner and whatever followed with Lo-Melkhiin.

The girls left me when their tasks were done. They were still afraid of me—though perhaps they were more afraid of the henna mistress, who supervised their work with eagle's eyes—but they did not shirk. The last girl, who pinned my hem above my slippers after she put them on my feet, hesitated before she left. This was the girl who had brought me my tea on the very first day; though I had seen her several times since, we had not spoken since that time. She passed me a package, wrapped in silk scraps she must have begged from the weavers. Its smell betrayed it to me, and I bowed my head to her. I had not been able to find the tea myself, despite repeated trips to the kitchen and several conversations with the cook and the boys who ran his errands. She had brought it to me.

"Thank you," I said to her.

"You are welcome, lady-bless," she said to me.

"Shoo, now, little bird," said the henna mistress. I was not exactly sure to whom she spoke, and she sounded so like my sister's mother that I moved before I thought. That made her laugh, to command her lady thus, and the serving girl was smiling as she took her leave. The henna mistress held out a hand. "I will take the tea, lady-bless," she said to me. "They may search your rooms, but they do not search mine. If you need it, send for me. You always have an excuse to, because you can say you want the henna."

I passed the package to her, and she tucked it into her dress. There was too much of my own self that I could not control, but I had these women, and I would have this.

"Now you must go," she said to me. "Sit straight on your cushion. Speak only if he addresses you. Take small bites and chew them overlong before you swallow. Do not drink the tea until it has cooled, and if your hands shake, sit on them."

She did not lecture me for manners' sake, but for fear's. I nodded, mouth dry in the heavy warmth of the bath, and she embraced me as she would her own daughter.

"Thank you," I said to her.

"May your smallgods find you, lady-bless," she said to me. I had longed for conversation since coming to Lo-Melkhiin's qasr, and it seemed that at last, some of the women were willing to risk attachment to me. I smiled at the henna mistress, and then she turned me around by my shoulders and pushed me out the door.

The air in the corridor of the bathhouse was still full of that heavy heat, but the air in the water garden was cool. The sun was over the qasr walls, and all was shaded. A light breeze blew the scent of the evening-blossom flowers toward my rooms, which had all their doors and windows open to catch the wind. I could not linger, though, for Lo-Melkhiin waited for me at the entrance. When he saw me, he extended a hand, the perfect picture of courtliness, and I crossed the garden to meet him.

"My wife," he said to me, his warm fingers closing around mine. He did not pinch, and there was no fire. He merely took my hand. "Thank you for dining with me this night."

He said it as though he had invited me and I had agreed to it, rather than the invasion that had taken place.

"I apologize that we have not dined together yet, save for the night of the starfall," he continued. "I confess, the realm takes up so much of my time, and you were so patient with me that I was inattentive. I beg your forgiveness."

I did my best not to look at him. I wondered if he had spent too long in the sun, or if I had. If he thought to charm me, he would have an uphill path to walk.

"Come," he said to me when it became apparent that I would not play with him. "The meal is laid."

In our father's tents, we eat well. There is meat every evening, and lentils and chickpeas to fill the bowls. We have bread and oil, and our father brings back spices when he travels, because my mother loves to experiment. We eat everything together, sharing and knocking fingers in the serving trays, and there is laughter and family at every meal.

This was nothing like that. There was bread and oil, but they were set in dishes so fine, I thought if I held the ceramic up to the sun I might see through it. There was a decanter made of glass—more than I had seen in one place in my whole life—filled with wine, and a jug of water next to it for mixing. The meat was cut into small pieces, and arranged to look like the body of one of the mean-spirited long-feathered birds I sometimes found in the garden. The bird's real neck and head completed the display at the front, while behind, its plumage matched the blue of the table cloth. I did not recognize the smell of the spices, and there were other dishes I could not recognize.

"I must remember to speak with the cook tomorrow," Lo-Melkhiin said, still as conversationally as he had in the garden. "Usually he presents each course, so that we might appreciate its artistry, but tonight I do not wish to be disturbed. Please, my wife, take your seat."

I sank onto one of the cushions, my spine as straight as I could manage, thanks to the henna mistress's instructions, and tucked my feet neatly into my dress. When I put my ankles together, I felt the matching signs the henna mistress had drawn on my heels recognize each other, and they warmed my cold blood.

Lo-Melkhiin sat beside me. If we had sat across from one another, we would not have been able to see each other because of the bird. I could see the raised platform where my bed was, but I did my best not to think about it.

I sat still as Lo-Melkhiin poured and mixed the wine, and set each kind of food on a plate. There was one cup and one bowl. We would share. If he tried to feed me with his own hands, I would bite off his fingers. He took a long drink of the wine, and passed it to me. My drink was much shorter, barely wetting my mouth. It was stronger than I liked, in any case.

He began to eat, making no move toward me, and so I ate too. I took pieces of bread and wrapped them around each morsel I ate, chewing for as long as I could.

"I cannot make you afraid of me," he said. I was glad I had taken a small bite; otherwise I might have choked. Instead, I swallowed neatly, and took a sip of the too-strong wine before I looked at him.

"I do not waste my fear," I said to him. "I have told you that."

"I know," he said to me. "You fear nothing because the desert will get you in the end, regardless. It is predictable, like the water clock. I had thought to be unpredictable, and see if that would set you off."

"I have herded goats, my lord," I said to him. "They have taught me what it means to be unpredictable."

"You have studied birds, too," he said to me. His eyes were like the far horizon when a sand storm lurks beyond it.

"I have studied nothing," I said to him. "I am no Skeptic. If the desert has taught me and I lived, then it is because I learned."

"Yes," he said to me. His hand closed around an eating knife he did not need. "Somehow, you live."

twenty-two

MY OWN EATING KNIFE WAS too far away for me to reach without being obvious that it was my intent to seize it. Since the food was already cut, I had seen no reason to keep it close. If I lived, I promised that I would never be so thoughtless as to let Lo-Melkhiin get his knife while I didn't have mine again. I did not think I could defeat him, but I could slash his face and give him a memory of what my death cost him.

Lo-Melkhiin twisted the handle, and then balanced the blade upon one of his fingers. It did not cut his skin. The lamplight gleamed on the bright bronze as he spun it, throwing spots of light on the walls of my room and then twirling them into a spiral. It might have been pretty, had I not imagined spots of blood following in their wake.

The only thing I had within easy reach was the salt cellar. It was still full, and the grains were coarse. It would be as though I threw sand in his face, if I hurled it at him. It might buy me time to get the knife.

Lo-Melkhiin threw the knife up in the air, and it spun in a whirl of light. I leaned toward the salt, ready, but when he grabbed the hilt again, it was only to twist it down and stick the point into the table. I hovered, unsure of what he might do next, and then he bent toward me.

"It won't be a knife, my love," he said to me. His voice was low. "I can promise you that."

He sat up and clapped his hands. The serving girls came back and cleared the table, except for the wine, and then a man came with a packet. Lo-Melkhiin took it and waved him away. He opened it, and I saw maps of the desert. Where the qasr was, and where all the villages were marked. Many of the places had a red mark through them, and I felt what little supper I had managed roil in my stomach. Those were the places that had given him a wife.

"Would you like to see how I plan a hunt, my wife?" he said to me.

"No, my lord," I said to him. "I have my own tasks."

It was not precisely true, but I did have the spindle and the white thread I had spun when I had gone into the vision to see my sister. I could weave it, I supposed, though I did not have a lap loom, so I was not sure what I would use. The serving girl who carried away the ruined table cloth saw me with the thread in my hands and nodded. She returned with a loom shortly, and I sat down to weave while Lo-Melkhiin plotted his desert horrors.

There are two ways to sit while you are weaving. My mother and my sister's mother had made sure that my sister and I learned both. The first way I much preferred, as I was meant to, because it was more comfortable. I could sit that way for hours, at need, but if I did that tonight, there was the possibility that I might slip into the weaving trance, and I did not wish to do that while Lo-Melkhiin could watch. The second way, I sat on my own foot, and if I did not shift sides every now and then, breaking my concentration, the foot would fall asleep and I would get a cramp. The first way was how my mother and my sister's mother wove when they were together. The second way was how they wove when they sat in the tents of our father's caravan, weaving with the women while he traded with the men.

"Your cloth will be the same quality," my sister's mother said to us, "but your ears will hear better."

I tucked one foot beneath me. Since it was concealed by my dress, it was impossible for any but a weaver to tell how I sat. My shoulders and the slant of my hips might betray me, but I doubted Lo-Melkhiin knew to look for that. I would merely have to ensure he was not watching me when I shifted.

I began to set the warp. Since I was making nothing in particular, I put the threads as close together as I could, leaving just enough slack in them that I might pass my fingers through, leading the thread. This would be finely woven cloth when I was done. Perhaps they would shroud me in it, if I finished enough to cover my face before Lo-Melkhiin strangled me.

He labored over his maps, to what end I did not care to guess, and drank freely from the decanter without mixing. I hoped that meant he would fall asleep at the table and not make it to the bed, but in my heart I knew better. He would no more take risks with me than I did with him. At least the knives were gone. Despite what he said, I knew that it was much easier to slit something's throat than it was to smother it.

Once the warp was set to my liking, I took a long loop of thread off of the skein and coiled it around my fingers. My mother told me that her mother had had to use a needle to pull a fine warp apart, because her fingers were so gnarled with age, but mine were still fine and thin. I could pass the thread through the warp using my fingers to pull up the threads I wanted, and push back those I didn't. I simply had to be careful not to stretch it too far.

I switched feet, and began to weave.

When my sister and I had seen ten winters each, she became ill with a fever, and I did not share it. This was not our way. We had always done everything together, and though I was hale while she burned and wept for her mother, I longed to join her on the pallet. My brothers told me I was foolish, and in my heart I knew it, but she was my sister, and I missed her when I walked to the well on my own.

On the third day after she fell into a fever, my mother sent me for water again. I went willingly enough, as I was glad to do my part to heal her, but I knew I could not carry as much water by myself, and wished she would send one of my brothers instead. Our father insisted that they be out with the cattle, as they were calving. So to the well I went, with a smaller jar and a heavy heart.

I drew water as easily as I could have done alone, and had just got the pail to the crest of the well when a sound in the bushes on the far side made me look up. My heavy heart stopped beating altogether. There was a sand viper, and I knew that if there was one, there had to be another somewhere close by; they do not hunt alone.

We stared at one another for a long moment, the snake and I, and no second one revealed itself. I had no stones with me, as I could not carry them and the water jar at the same time. The snake did not move again, and after a long, hot moment in the desert sun, I dared to move. I poured the water into my jar, and released the pail back into the well. Then I bent and picked up the jar, and walked backward, keeping my eye on the viper as I went. It watched me go, motionless as ever, and finally disappeared back into the bushes when it realized I had gone outside its striking distance.

I told my sister when she was well again, after our father had cut away all the bushes around the well so that no snakes might hide in them.

"Perhaps it saw that you were alone and did not strike," she said to me. "Perhaps it was alone too, and knew you shared a spirit at that moment."

"Perhaps I am very lucky," I said to her. "Or perhaps I do not look like I would taste very good."

She laughed.

The weft snaked through the warp as I bid it, and I felt the viper again. I looked up in Lo-Melkhiin's eyes, though he still sat at his table and his maps. I switched feet, not caring if he saw me do it, and bent back to my work. I had no stones, and I could not stop a viper, but I could be patient.

He watched me for a time, and then went back to his work. When I felt his eyes were no longer on me, I breathed in a long breath. The snake did not always strike. Sometimes it waited. Maybe I did not taste very good. The thought made me smile, in spite of the danger, and I let myself sink a little bit deeper into the weaving, though I still sat upon my foot to make sure I worked nothing strange. My fingers found the rhythm and my threads followed it.

We had many working songs and prayer chants. Some were meant only for the ears of my sister and my mother and my sister's mother, but some I might sing for my brothers or any of the relatives who lived in our father's tents. There were other songs for when a caravan came to visit us, though that did not happen very often, and there were songs that we girls made up to suit ourselves as we worked when our mothers were not with us.

I picked one of my favorites now. It had a soft melody that belied its natural rhythm. A man might think it a lullaby, fit only to soothe a child to sleep, but when its steady beat was put to thread, it helped to guide, to lead even the newest of weavers through the steps to a finished cloth. We had sung it together, my sister and me, and all the girls with fair voices who sometimes wove with us. It was not meant to be sung alone, and was missing parts, but I liked it enough that I could put in the pieces that were not there, even if Lo-Melkhiin could not.

I was halfway through the third verse when I felt a shadow, and knew he stood beside me. I forced myself to finish the line I wove, hands as steady as I could manage, though the viper hovered even closer. When I was done, I set the loom aside, and looked up at him.

"My love, you sing a man to sleep," he said to me. He

had not seen the real purpose of the song, and that made me glad. "Come to bed, then."

He did not touch me. I took the pins from my hair, and shed the dress so that I stood before him in henna and shift alone. If he knew what the symbols meant, he gave no sign. I did not think he did. Men did not, usually. It was only women's art, after all.

"Come to bed," he said to me again.

I turned my heart to stone, and climbed into bed with the viper.

twenty-three

FOR FOUR MORE NIGHTS, Lo-Melkhiin came to me for supper, then the evening's work, and then to bed. The henna mistress drew her signs on me each time, and the girls coiled my hair and pinned it, and put me in a dress of fine make. Each night, the henna burned a little stronger, the pins stuck fast to my hair, and each dress had the embroidery of the most delicate touch.

Lo-Melkhiin's maps were marked, and the cloth grew under my hands. I kept the eating knife close to me when I could, and sang the songs from our father's tent when I could not. If he noticed, he did not care. Each time he invited me to bed, it was the last thing he said to me, and never once

E. K. JOHNSTON

did he touch me. There was none of his cold light, nor any of my copper fire, yet I did not feel at all weakened. The henna kept my copper fire strong. Each morning, he was gone before I woke to a steaming cup of tea on the table beside my bed.

When I woke, I went to the bathhouse. It was empty when I arrived, but before I could take off my shift one of the attendants appeared as always, like I had rung a bell for them. They took the shift away and brought me a new one while I soaked the night's henna away. It did not disappear entirely. Often the henna mistress merely traced over lines, renewing them and their power in my skin. Perhaps that is why they burned with greater intensity when she put them on my body. It was the same for my hair. While I sat in the bath, they brought a trough of heated water to the ledge behind my head. If I put my head back, they combed my hair in the water. It leeched some of the color, but not all of it.

When I was dried and dressed, I went to the weaving room. I opened the door without knocking, as was my custom, and was surprised to find that all the women looked up at me, rather than keeping their eyes on their work.

"Oh, lady-bless," said the oldest weaver, "it is only you."

"Only me?" I said to her, taking an empty seat amongst the spinners. They passed me a basket, whorl, and leader thread, and I began my work.

"Lady-bless, Lo-Melkhiin has come here every day since

201

he woke up from his illness." This from the spinner who often spoke before she thought. "He watches us, and sometimes lays a hand upon us, and tells us our work is good."

The old weaver made an impolite sound. My hands were busy, so I couldn't use them to cover my mouth. Instead, I stopped my smile before it showed. The old weaver did not think that Lo-Melkhiin would know good thread if it tripped him.

"I swear, lady-bless, we did not tempt him here," said the spinner. "He just appears."

"The lady does not care if he finds one of you pretty," the old weaver said.

Again, I had to hide my smile. Jealousy was the last emotion I would feel if Lo-Melkhiin took to pursuing the spinner-girls. I was more concerned with what they had made after he touched them.

"Tell me," I said to the spinner. "Where is the thread you spun after he came and saw you?"

"I burned it, lady-bless," she said, looking down at her spindle at last, though it did not spin. "It was not fit for use."

"And her three years in this room," said the old weaver. "She has not muddled her thread since she first came to me. He scared her that much."

They showed me the other pieces then. An embroidery full of snarls, more lumpy thread, wool carded so badly it might not have been carded at all, and a loom that they had been forced to cut the warp from so that they could start afresh.

I watched the spinner. Her thread was clean now, and even as ever, though her hands shook slightly as she fed wool into her work as the spindle dropped. She had seen the viper in him, I knew, and she worked still, because she did not know what else to do. I caught her whorl so it would not undo, and put my hands on hers. Copper fire spread between us, more than when I had touched the healer, and she stopped shaking.

"There," I said to her. "Everything will be all right now. When Lo-Melkhiin comes, send a girl for me, and I will come after, and help you clean up the mess."

The weaver made another impolite noise, and this time I did smile. I raised my hand to touch her, but before I could, the copper fire leapt from me to her, lighting her eyes and straightening her spine. She coughed once, and I started in surprise, and then bent back to rethreading the loom as though nothing had happened. She worked much faster now.

I took my seat with the spinners again, and thought about how I might help them. I had spun for a vision, once. Perhaps now I could spin the copper fire into the thread. My mother and my sister's mother had laid down lines of strange-smelling salts that our father brought from far away in circles around each of our father's tents. They did not stop ants and bees from coming in, but they did stop scorpions.

And vipers. Lo-Melkhiin would come in—I could not keep him out—but I wondered if I could spin copper fire to keep his cold light from frightening the work again.

I took up my basket of wool again, and reached for the whorl. I began to spin, and let myself fall into the trance without fighting between one blink and the next.

This time, instead of flying across the desert, I hovered in the ceiling of the room, where hot, scented air rose and idled before it found its way out the screened windows. I looked down and saw all the looms at work, all the whorls spinning, and all the needles as they flashed in and out, pulling the silk threads behind.

I could see traces of Lo-Melkhiin's cold light. Unsurprisingly, they collected near the prettiest of the spinners, the quickest of the stitchers, and the most talented of the weavers. At least he had some measure of craft-knowledge. I dropped the thread I spun on each light, smothering it in fire, and then moved my whorl onto the next one. When I had cleaned up the leavings, I turned my thoughts to how I might protect the room.

My mother had left a circle of salts, and that was enough, but scorpions were much shorter than Lo-Melkhiin. Still, that was the best place to begin. Perched on the air near the ceiling, I trailed the new copper-spun thread behind the whorl as I moved it slowly around the room. Then, because I could not think of another way, I repeated the process near the ceiling, level with where I floated. The two lines of copper fire reached for one another, but stayed in place where I left them. As I relaxed my hold, the lines blurred. I tightened my grip again, like I would hold a goat's legs to keep it from straying, but they fought me harder than any goat I had ever restrained.

I could not stay in the ceiling of the spinning room forever. If my first idea had failed, I would have to let it go, and then try to come up with another. I released the copper fires. To my surprise and relief, the lines stayed where I had set them. Threads of fire broke loose, reaching up from the floor and down from the ceiling, the way a gage-tree's roots stretched for water. They intertwined with one another and flared strong in my vision. I recoiled from the brightness, and dropped the whorl. I fell as it did, and woke up in my seat, the old weaver shaking me by the shoulders.

"Lady-bless!" she hissed. She did not wish to shout and cause alarm. I knew if I did not wake, she would pinch me, or worse.

"I am here," I said to her. "It is done."

"It certainly is," she said to me, and I looked down at my hands.

I had been spinning undyed thread, as we all were, but that was not the color I had spun and wrapped about the skein at the bottom of my basket. As I had spun white thread when I sought my sister, I had spun copper thread now, so bright even inside the room that it seemed to have its own fire.

"Lady-bless!" said the spinner.

"You will still your tongue," said the old weaver. She looked around the room. "You will all still your tongues. This stays between you and your smallgods."

They murmured their agreement, and I felt a stirring in my blood. The old weaver said *their* smallgods, but I knew at least some of them sent their whispers out to *me*, though I could not say how I knew it. I nodded to the old weaver, and left them to their work and their prayers. My blood hummed as I went out from them.

In the cooler air of the garden, I paused. Before, Lo-Melkhiin had been content to take his power from men, and inspire their creations. Now, it seemed, he had turned his efforts to the women who lived in the qasr as well. He was not desperate for power; I could tell by the strength of the cold light in the spinning room. More likely, he had forgotten that women do work, too—useful work. He thought he could hasten them along as he had the men, and he had, but at too steep a cost. I hoped he stayed away from the kitchens. The head cook did well under Lo-Melkhiin's influence, but many of his assistants were women or boys, and I had no desire to eat burned or raw bread.

He had not touched me in five days. Had he learned that my power was made stronger by his? Had he tried to find another source, in hope of weakening me? If he had, it had been a failure. The henna mistress and the women who dressed my hair had more than enough power in their work to keep me strong. I did not like that in order for my strength to increase, his must too. I did not like that I relied on him for anything, least of all this. Perhaps it was time to visit my sister in the present, not seek out visions of her past, and see if the cult of my smallgod had done what she hoped it might.

I was halfway back to my room and the weaving there when it occurred to me that Lo-Melkhiin would have visited more rooms than the spinning room. I had warded that place, but I knew that he must have left his mark on others, and that the work done there would be just as muddled. A qasr needs a king; so went the saying. That was what men thought. A king needed a qasr just as much, and the qasr had to operate smoothly, sheep to the wadi, or the flock would disintegrate.

I needed more wool, I thought, and if I could find a way to spin it without turning it impossible colors, so much the better. I resolved to send for a basket, or more, when I had the time and the privacy to lose myself in a spinning trance. It could not be today. The sun was well past its highest point, which meant I must dress for supper; and then the uncomfortable weaving, with the viper watching me whenever I moved; and then another still night in bed with Lo-Melkhiin.

twenty-four

I WAS NOT DEAD IN THE MORNING, but when I woke, I thought I might be the next thing to it. I could barely sit up to drink my tea; I was weak as a newborn lamb. When my breakfast was brought, the smell of it made me heave up all I had drunk.

"It's all right, lady-bless," cooed the serving girl, as she helped me back to my bed. "If you miss one day, it will still work."

"I do not feel all right," I told her. The world spun around me, and I could not make it stop.

"You look very pale," she said to me. "I will fetch a cold cloth and the healer, and tell the cook. He does not like it when we vomit. He says that is the first sign that the sun has been too much."

When she said it, it sounded straightforward. I had seen men felled by the sun if they worked through the heat of the day or if they did not drink enough. Yet I knew that could not be the cause of my illness. I had not spent enough time in the sun. The girl was gone before I could say any of that to her, though, so I waited in my bed, and hoped my head would not split in half before she returned.

I dozed, and when I dreamt, I saw a lion. It drank at an oasis in the cool of the morning. I knew that it was the oasis from Lo-Melkhiin's map. He had pored over it, planning every angle of this hunt. I had thought he might be plotting where to find his next bride, but I ought to have known better: he did not care from whence we came.

There were no tents in this oasis, and it was far from a path of trade. Only a madman or a man with very good horses would ride so far, to an oasis on the way to nowhere. Lo-Melkhiin was not mad, easy as it might have been to accept him if he were, but he did have good mounts.

The lion was old, its mane tawny and bright in the sun. Its back and face were scarred with long claw marks. It had fought to keep this oasis, and driven off or killed younger lions to do it. He kept no pride in his old age, but he kept his home in the desert.

Lo-Melkhiin hunted him for no reason other than to kill him, and he had nowhere to go.

I saw the other guardsmen draw back, an empty saddle where Lo-Melkhiin had left them behind to do the hunt alone. Before the demon, Lo-Melkhiin had hunted lions that were a threat. This old creature was too smart to harry the villages and oases of men. And now he would grow no older.

As I watched, Lo-Melkhiin came down to the water of the oasis, across from where the lion stood. The old beast stared at him, wise enough to know that fleeing would get him nothing. For a moment I thought Lo-Melkhiin might spare the beast, but then he hefted his spear in one hand, and between one breath and the next, landed it between the old lion's eyes.

It fell face-first in the water, fouling it with its blood. Lo-Melkhiin drew a knife and whistled for the men to come, and I knew he meant to skin it. That I would not watch. I felt the vomit rise in my stomach again, though I did not think I had anything left; and then I was in my bed, and the serving girl held my hair as I emptied my stomach again. This time, only white water came out. The cook watched me, shaking his head.

"Juice, lady-bless," he said to me. "As much as you can."

"I wish you would mind your own craft," snapped the healer.

"I'll fetch it," said the girl, but the cook shook his head.

She had to stay as long as one of the men was with me.

The healer examined me quickly, a soft hand on my forehead and a light touch at my wrist.

"Lady-bless, did you have wine?" he asked me.

"No," I said to him. My voice was hoarse. "I drank water, and ate what was brought."

"Did you sit in the sun?" he asked.

"No," I said.

"Perhaps she is only tired?" the serving girl suggested. "She spent the whole afternoon in the spinning room yesterday, and the girls there said she spun without stopping for hours."

As soon as she said the word "spinning", my stomach heaved again. She was so fast, turning me and holding my hair back from the bowl. I had nothing to bring up, but I appreciated her efforts in any case.

"Perhaps that is what has taken the water from your body," the healer said. He was not entirely incorrect, but it was not for the right reason. "Today you must stay abed, drink everything that busybody from the kitchen brings you, and touch no craft."

I nodded, miserable, and the serving girl put another cool cloth to my head.

It was the copper fire that had done this—or rather, the fact that I had done so much spinning with it. It had been too much. Once the healer left and the serving girl went to fetch a comb, I could not stop myself from crying. I had only been able to protect one room. I could not shield the other work rooms if this was the result.

Soft hands undid my braids, and began to work through my hair with the comb. I forced myself to breathe softly, hoping that I would fall asleep and rest without dreaming. I had no wish to see more lions meet their end. Not even the thought that I might see my sister tempted me to seek a dream. I wanted only blackness and oblivion.

A finger brushed my skull. It was much too big to be the serving girl's. I tried to move before I remembered the consequences, and then struggled weakly while Lo-Melkhiin wound his fingers tightly into my hair.

"I went out for a lion this morning, my wife," he said to me. It was the over-friendly tone I hated. My head already ached, and his grip on my hair exacerbated it. "But you know this. I would tell you that the beast ravaged poor men's sheep and stole poor women's children, but you know better."

I said nothing, and his hands tightened. "Tell me!" he commanded.

"I saw," I said to him, spitting the words the way a viper spits poison. "I saw you kill the old lion, far away from where he might have done harm."

"Good," he said to me. "I do not like to kill without an audience."

He released my hair, but I was too weak to get away from him. I would be easy to smother now, if he wanted. He could display my hair next to his new lion mane. Instead, he spread my hair back out on the pillow and began to comb it.

"Your sister did this," he said to me. "When you were small."

"Yes," I said to him. I hated to tell him any truths, but hating gave me strength now. "She would do it still, if I still lived in our father's tents, and I would comb her hair as well."

"We have not spoken of her in some time," he said to me. "Did you see the maps I had? They show where all of my wives have come from."

"I saw," I said to him. "There have been very many of us."

"There have," he agreed. "So many that soon I may start again. I do not have to go in order, you know. I might return to any village I like. I might return for your sister."

"She will be married by then," I told him. I would make it true if it killed me to do it. "Our father brings a man back with him in the caravan, and she will love him."

"Then who will keep your dead?" he asked me.

I barely heard him. As soon as I spoke my tale to him, my head raged again. It was like the copper fire, only worse. If I were a well in the desert, then I had been in use for generations, and I had nothing but a scraped bottom to offer any who came to fill their water jars.

The viper struck.

He left the comb and my hair, and held my hands beside my face. He used his own weight to hold me down, even though I could no more get away from him than I could fly. I felt every hard muscle of his body pressing against mine. He was, I thought in the part of my mind that did not scream, very lucky I had already vomited up everything I had in my stomach, or he would have worn it on his face as he hovered mere inches from me.

"Have you not learned, star of my skies?" he said to me. His voice hissed in my ears. I did not see a man's face, but a viper's hood. "We are the same, you and I. That is why I cannot kill you, and why you do not die."

I would not believe him. He was no smallgod and I was no demon. We were not the same. We were the opposite. He must know that.

"You think it is not true?" he said to me. "You think I do not speak words to men and have them come true the way you speak words to women? You think I could not reach into your soul and take it, as easily as you reach into the soul of your sister, and bend her to your will?"

No! That was not how I did my work at all. I spun and made things new. He forced out craft where there was no want of it, and sped it up so fast that its makers could not control it. I might have changed the path of my sister's life, but I took no one's soul.

"You doubt me, but I will prove it to you," he said to me.

He rolled off of me, the absence of his weight a welcome relief, but he did not let go of my hands, and so the relief was short-lived as he pulled me to sit in front of him. My head screamed and my stomach heaved, but he did not stop. He called the cold light, and I recoiled, thinking it would burn me worse than I already was.

Instead, the light flared and my head cleared. It was as though a cool drink had been poured down my throat and cool water put all over my body. My stomach settled and the pain stopped. I watched, horror-struck, as the cold light licked my arms like fire consuming dry wood in a camp hearth, reaching as high up as my elbows before returning back to Lo-Melkhiin's hands.

Then the copper fire coiled between us, and my breathing stilled. I was a gage-tree, roots scrambling for water, and the wadi was at its highest flood. I traced the water's source, expecting to find my way back to my sister. Instead, it was as though every wadi in the desert was feeding me. I wanted more and more, and Lo-Melkhiin was making me strong enough to get it. This was more fire than I had used to ward the spinning room. This was enough fire to shield the whole qasr, with enough left over besides. I thought of my sister and the husband I had conjured for her. Now he would come, as surely as the sun would rise tomorrow.

Lo-Melkhiin sank his fingernails deep into my skin,

bringing small crescents of blood welling up around them. This new pain brought me back to him, and away from foolish desert dreams. His viper's smile was uncontrollable now, and he leered at me like I was his perfect thing, to do with as he liked.

I would not, I swore. I would never.

"Well, my love," he said to me, passing me a cup of juice, "it seems we will need each other for a little bit longer after all."

twenty-five

AFTER LO-MELKHIIN HAD cleared my head with his cold
fire, he left me, and I finally ventured out into the day. It
was after noon, and I was terrified to meet anyone who
might guess what I had done, so I did not venture past
the water garden. The fountain's song did not soothe me
today. Instead, it reminded me that I was not in the desert;
that such a thing could only exist near Lo-Melkhiin, thanks
to his power. It sang and played when no one watched it,
surely, but it was his. And so was I.

I went into the baths. At this time of day, there was but
one attendant, and she dozed in the heat by the coal basket,
ready to stoke the fires that heated the water if need be,

but otherwise resting. I did not wake her. I passed into the room with the hot steam, leaving my shift on the floor as I climbed the steps to reach the bench. It was not hot like the air of the desert, which dried as it blew past one, but hot like soup—like blood—and as I breathed it in, I wilted.

I slid off the bench, trying to get to the cooler air at the door. My skin was slick with sweat and it took me a moment to find my feet, but I stumbled back down the steps, gasping as the air cooled. The attendant was there, woken by my clumsy flailing. She helped me into the hot pool, and brought me a cup of cool hibiscus tea.

"Lady-bless, you must be careful in the steam room," she said to me. "Stand closer to the door next time."

I nodded. I wasn't sure if I ever wanted to go back in the room again. The pool I sat in might have been a cooking pot, the water was so hot, and that was enough for me. When she thought I had borne enough, the attendant took me to a cooler pool, and laid down soap and a soft brush by the side of it.

"I wish for a harder brush," I said to her.

She looked at me as a spinner eyes wool, or like a cook weighs flour.

"Lady-bless, you do not need it," she said to me. "Your skin—"

I held up a hand and she stopped. "I know," I said to her. "You and the others who labor here have done well

218

turning my desert hide into a city skin." She blushed, and I continued to speak. "But I wish for a harder brush."

She nodded, and left to fetch it. She was right. I did not need it. My skin had lost its desert roughness, even my hands, which had been worked the hardest. But I could feel Lo-Melkhiin's touch, the cold fire up to my elbows, and worse, the press of him against me as he held me down, and I wanted to be rid of that.

The attendant returned with the brush, and I lathered it with soap. I began to scrub, a sandstorm on my bare skin— no, the storm that hardened the camel bones—pressing down as hard as I could and dragging mercilessly across the surface. I was not content to wash away Lo-Melkhiin. I wanted the whole qasr, the whole *city* gone from my memory.

"Lady-bless!" cried the attendant, returning with a fresh shift. Heedless of her own clothing, she plunged into the pool beside me, and wrestled the brush away. I fought her. The girl who had herded sheep and who had raced across the desert sands with my sister, our dark hair flying in the wind, might have won, but I was in the city now, soft and kept and wrapped in silk, and no match for a girl who carried coal.

She threw the brush clear of the pool so I could not reach it, and examined my arms and back and belly. There were scratches there, but nothing bled. I had not had time to start my legs.

"No more of this today," she said to me, and pulled me from the tub. I did not resist her.

She took me to a stone platform and made me lie down on it. I thought it would be cold against my skin, but the fire that heated the water must have heated it too. This was the constant warmth of stone, radiating out to soothe me where the steam and water had failed. The attendant got out a soft brush, and soap scented with lavender, and washed me like I was a child. She poured water out of a bowl to rinse me, rather than send me back to the pool, and washed my front when she finished my back. Only when she had touched nearly every part of me, from my forehead to my toes, did she send me back to the pool. I did not like to admit it, but I felt better.

"Is that how you wash the sick and the old, when they come here?" I asked her. I pulled my hands lazily through the water, and laid my head back on the side where the stone was wet.

"No, lady-bless," she said to me. She had taken a comb and was sitting behind me to brush out my hair. "That is how we would wash the queen, if she would let us."

They had only ever put me in the pool before, but I knew if they had tried this when I was in a mood to fight them, I would not have let them. I raised my chin so that I could see her as she sat behind me, combing my hair. She was smiling.

"It was well done," I said to her. "Thank you."

"Only, be sure you eat," she said to me. "Or you will feel ill again."

She coiled my braid in a simple loop, apologizing as she pinned it that she had no skill with hair, and helped me dry and dress. I went back to the water garden and sat in the shade until the sun went behind the walls. Then the henna mistress found me and bustled me inside.

"Lady-bless, we must hurry," she said to me. "It is well you bathed already today, for now we have no time."

"What has happened?" I asked her. I let her steer me to a seat and watched her light the lamps and lay out her pots and stylus on a cloth.

"A caravan has come, and asked for an audience with Lo-Melkhiin," she said to me. "He has granted it to them, and said that you must join him too."

I must play queen, is what he meant. I had spent enough time upset with Lo-Melkhiin today. I would not spend any more, unless he gave me good reason.

The henna mistress drew her designs quickly. She only marked my skin where it would be seen, instead of putting on the secret symbols to wear under my dress as she had done before. Though she was swift, her work was not sloppy. She made not a single brushstroke out of place. The instant she was done, I was swarmed by the women who did my hair and dress, as if I stood at the center of the flock with a salt-lick in my hands and the goats had finally noticed it.

They did not chatter as they worked, and there was none of the soft comfort in their hands that I had come to look forward to, but they were efficient and neat; before long, I was inked and dressed and veiled, and ready to go out to whatever awaited me.

I stepped into slippers so fine they might have been spun by silk-spiders. The henna mistress kissed me between my eyes, the only place my veil did not cover my face.

"You are ready," she said to me. "Sit straight. They will look at you and see only a veil, even the king. Hear everything, and remember that if you smile or grimace, they will not see you. Only stay silent, and they will never know your heart."

She was correct, of course, and I made myself relax. The veil I wore now was heavier than the one I usually had on when Lo-Melkhiin came to my rooms. That was gauze and whispers, meant to hide nothing. Dressed as I was now, I was hidden from everyone. They might stare at me for an hour, admire the fine red fabric of my dishdashah, and the bright gold embroidery that lined the hems and collar, but they would never know my thoughts.

A serving girl took me to the hall where Lo-Melkhiin gave audience. He did not do it often, preferring to meet his supplicants informally. I knew the truth of that, though. He did not need to awe any of his own subjects: they were already afraid of him. He did have to touch them to influence them, however, and that was difficult in the audience hall. Whoever it was that came tonight, they must not be from the city.

Lo-Melkhiin stood at a doorway, waiting for me. His tunic was gold, embroidered in red, and his breeches were red as well. We would look a matched set, and remind all who gazed upon us that gold and blood were two things Lo-Melkhiin had aplenty.

"Star of my skies, you take my breath from my body," he said to me, and held out his arm. I took it. "Come, see how it is to be a queen."

He led me through the door and into a broad, bright room I had not seen during my explorations of the qasr. A hundred lamps, some hanging from the high ceiling and some on tables or attached to the columns, gleamed with clear light. Geometric designs made of hundreds of pieces of glass, most no bigger than my thumbnail, glittered on the walls. The floor was a white stone, polished so much it shone, and the rugs laid upon it were of the finest silk.

Such a waste, to walk on them.

Lo-Melkhiin took me to a raised dais, where there was a large cushion. He handed me off to the side of it, a girl appearing from nowhere to help me arrange my skirt and ensure my veil was still securely fastened, and then he sat down beside me. When he was settled, he nodded to the man who stood on the floor beside him. The man carried a large wooden staff, bigger than a shepherd would use; at Lo-Melkhiin's signal, he hammered the butt of it on the floor three measured times.

At the far end of the hall, the great doors were pulled open. Six men stood there, and when their way was clear, they walked slowly into the room. It was hard for me to see in great detail through my veil when they were that far away, but I could tell that they were not men of the city. Their capes were the color worn by men who crossed the desert with the caravans.

Those men came into the city often enough. The serving girls talked about markets and bazaars when they did my hair. But they had not said that some traders come to the qasr, and certainly they had made no mention of any traders gaining audience with Lo-Melkhiin.

Thinking of him made me look his way. As the henna mistress said, I did not move from my straight position, but rather I slid my eyes across under my veil. The viper's smile was back upon his mouth, though it was softened by something I did not recognize. Perhaps he could not be fully cruel here, where he spoke with men who brought wealth in trade. Perhaps the dark spot in his mind was stronger here, in the room where Lo-Melkhiin should serve his people.

When I looked back, the caravan men were on their knees, their faces on the floor before us. Their capes caught my eye again. Now that they were close enough for me to

224

see them clearly, I realized the patterns along the borders were ones I recognized, though they were stitched in purple, which was an expensive color to wear into the desert.

"Welcome, master of the caravan," Lo-Melkhiin said. "And welcome to your sons."

They raised their faces from the floor, and I looked into the eyes of my brothers and my father.

vi.

When my people first began to take, when we pulled weavers from their beds, and smiths from their forges, I was young enough to wonder why it was so easy. The older ones told me it was because men were weak, because they could not fight us. They lived only to serve.

But I was not so sure.

My first weaver was old, and he did not scream when I pulled him away from his wife. I set a picture of her before him, younger and with fewer lines around her eyes, and he wove happily for me without stopping to eat or drink. In the end, his fingers bled and stained the cloth, but I liked the pattern, so I cut it from the warp before I set fire to the loom, weaver and all.

My first smith was old, but he could still pull the air and raise the hammer. He worked without crucible or tongs when I showed him his children, still alive. In truth, they had died in a sandstorm and left him alone with his craft and his age. He had no hands at all when he was done, but I had pretty gold.

My first glassmaker blinded himself in the fires he used to glaze his work. My first spinner used his own finger bones for a spindle. And all of them came to me without a struggle, when they thought I had something they wanted.

Lo-Melkhiin was my first challenge: the first time I knew that I was correct, and my elders had it wrong. He did not wish to serve me, and I thought it was not just because he was already a king. Lo-Melkhiin fought until I showed him his mother, wasting away to her death in the hot sand. It was that image, the idea of her death, that weakened him enough for me to grasp him; and then it was only a matter of time until I shut him away inside his own mind.

After that, with Lo-Melkhiin's hands and Lo-Melkhiin's voice, it was easy. Merchants fell over themselves to please me, and I rewarded them. Men did great works, and knew it was because I was their patron. My army was strong and my coffers were full, and if I had cared who was in my bed, I would have wanted for nothing there, either.

But it was not me they served, and I could not forget it. They thought they served Lo-Melkhiin.

It galled me. The man I had taken in the desert was all but gone, a screaming wraith whose voice delighted me alone, and still they told stories of his power and his wisdom in the lands I ruled. I had done my task too well, taken so discreetly that no one even knew what I had done. My own people, content to stay in the desert and pick off artisans one at a time, were ignorant of my accomplishments, and I had nothing but another man's hands and another man's name.

But she knew—the girl I had found in the desert and taken for my wife. The one who did not die. She knew that I was more than what I seemed. That galled me, too, that she could know I was not a man and yet still sit there, weaving, while I stared at her. She could lie beside me in the night and not fear that I would murder her. It almost made me want to do it out of spite, except that then I would have been alone with my secret once more.

I went to the women in the spinning room, but they had made no great things. Their thread snarled and their weavings fouled the looms on which they worked. She had spent too much time with them, and they were part of her world to begin with: the world of women. I had made a mistake, and I would not make it again.

I did as my people had done, taking craftsmen one at a time to steal their work and their hands and their blood. Then, I had taken a king, and his kingdom had laid itself at my feet. That was how I had to go on now. I had to start with her, and when she was mine, she would bring the women with her.

She would fight me; I knew it in Lo-Melkhiin's bones. It gave him hope, which amused me greatly. He knew this girl would defy me, and it brought him joy. He was almost more pleased to see her family than she was. I would crush him again soon enough. First, I

228

had to have her, and I could not fight her from within herself.

I had to do as I had always done, as my people had always done, without realizing we did it. We did not take men because they longed to serve us. We took them because they followed us into the fire for something they thought we offered them. A younger wife. A restored family. Wealth. Honor. Fame. Those had always been what we tempted men with.

And I would tempt her just the same. I would give her a choice that was no choice, so that any way she chose I would get her, and all she brought with her, when she was done. She would not burn as the others had, and neither would she serve. I had called her common, but she was better than her sand-crawling kin. I was done with murdering little girls. This one would be my queen.

twenty-six

I WAS GLAD OF THE HEAVY VEIL, and gladder still that the henna mistress had reminded me that if I was quiet, no one would be able to tell my mood. I bit my tongue, hard, to keep from crying out. I had missed my sister and my mother and my sister's mother, of course, but it was not until I saw my father and my brothers that I knew how much I had missed them too. My father had favored us overmuch after my sister's brother had been lost to the flood, and even my brothers' teasing was something that reminded me of home. To see them, and to see them on their knees before us, gave me both joy and fear. What Lo-Melkhiin might do to my family stilled my blood.

"Great lord, Lo-Melkhiin," my father said. His voice was like a calm wind over sand, and I bit my tongue again to stop the tears that would have clouded my eyes. "This humble trader thanks you for granting an audience to him and to his sons."

"Noble caravan master," Lo-Melkhiin said to him. His voice was loud and cold. "How could I turn you, of all men, from my halls? Come and stand closer to me, father of my heart."

My father hesitated for only a moment—well-traveled feet on a familiar path before they ventured onto an unknown one—and then stood and came closer. Lo-Melkhiin had put his hand upon my arm when he spoke to my father, and I did not flinch from him. I looked at my father and wished he could see my eyes, and find some comfort there.

"It is true, then," he whispered as he drew close. He spoke as one who had been told a thing countless times, and yet who doubted the truth of it until it was before him. Until I was before him. He did not speak to Lo-Melkhiin, though Lo-Melkhiin heard his words. He spoke to his smallgod. "My daughter yet lives."

"It is true, father of my heart," Lo-Melkhiin said. "Your daughter is my queen."

My father knelt again. It was as though his legs had borne him thus far and would bear him no farther. Now he sat upon the dais, right in front of me. Without thinking,

I reached for him. He caught my hand and kissed it. I felt the dust of the road, the whiskers in his beard, and the hot tears that fell from his eyes.

"Come closer, brothers of my heart," Lo-Melkhiin said to my brothers, who still knelt where they had first settled.

They came to sit beside my father and took my hand, each in their turn. They did not weep to see me, but they squeezed my hand tightly, and I knew that I was loved. I hoped desperately that we would be allowed to talk, whatever my father's petition was. Perhaps he merely wished to see with his own eyes that I lived. Perhaps there was something more. If he went with Lo-Melkhiin into conference, maybe they would leave my brothers with me, and I could ask them about my sister and my mother, and the others in my father's tents.

"Tea!" called Lo-Melkhiin, and I saw the serving girl who had fixed my veil hasten to do his bidding. "And bring food also. These men of my heart have crossed the hot sand and braved the hammer of the sun to see us. We must make them welcome."

Pillows were brought, and a low table to put the cups and bread on. My brothers each had their own oil bottle and their own bowl of olives. Always before, they had shared.

"Father of my heart," said Lo-Melkhiin, when the tea was cool enough to drink and my father had eaten four olives, placing the pits carefully back in the bowl as he found them, "it makes my heart glad to see you, and I know my wife's heart is the same, but I must ask: why have you come to us?"

He was the soul of politeness, my husband. The viper's smile was gone. Instead, he was a lion, surveying his pride as if he owned the whole desert and could afford to be generous with it. He spoke to my father like he had come to my father's tents and asked for me, as though they had bargained a dowry and drunk honeyed mead at the wedding feast to celebrate. My father was too good a trader to let his discomfort show on his face, but his eyes moved too quickly and betrayed him.

"I have come to ask a favor of you, Lo-Melkhiin," my father said to him. His voice was still a calm wind, with only the barest hint of the storm underneath.

"Ask it of me, then, father of my heart," Lo-Melkhiin said. "If it is in my power, and much is, it will be granted to you. I would do this for any caravan master in my lands, who works so hard for the people in his tents, but especially for you, because your daughter sits beside me."

My father bowed his head at the compliment, and took a sip of his tea. I had seen him do that when he taught my brothers the way of trading, but I did not like to see it now. I did not like to think what my father had that could interest Lo-Melkhiin in trade.

"As you know, great lord," my father said, "I have two

daughters. One sits at your side; the other is still in her mother's tent, though she will not live there once the moon has passed its fullest."

I caught my breath. My sister had studied the priestly arts with my mother and with her mother. My father could not let her marry and leave to go to her husband's tent. There would be no one to tend our dead.

"My wife, the star of my skies, has told me much about her sister," Lo-Melkhiin said. He put his hand upon my arm and rested it there for a long moment.

My oldest brother wrapped an arm around the youngest, who sat next to him at the table, and held him still, like how he would have caught a goat that sought to stray. I smiled behind my veil, where no one could see me. My brothers did not care for where I sat and how he touched me, but at least some of them were wise enough to try hiding it, and to hold the others back when they might have protested.

"She is very beautiful," my father said to Lo-Melkhiin. "Her mother and her sister's mother have taught her the priestly ways, and thus I did not think she would wed and leave our holy places."

"Yet you say she will go out from her mother's tent," Lo-Melkhiin said.

I might have screamed, except I clung to the quiet that shielded my feelings from the room. Courtly speech drove me mad, and when it was partnered with trading talk, it was even worse. It was my sister they spoke of, not the weather or a camel. I wanted to know, and had little patience for their pretty words. My oldest brother, perhaps guessing that his movement caught my eye, stared like he could see my face. Very slowly, he winked at me. I took a long breath, and forced myself to be still.

"I did, my lord," said my father to Lo-Melkhiin. "My sons and I traveled far on our last caravan. We went to the north, through the sand desert and the scrub desert, because we had heard rumors of a trading post near the mountains there."

"I have heard this also," said Lo-Melkhiin. His hand tightened on my arm. I wondered if he would tell them how he knew.

"We made good trades there," said my father, "and we met a traveler who wished to return with us. He brought his own pack and carried his own water, and so I did not refuse him."

He was lying. I could see it in his eyes, and in the way my brothers shifted. I could not tell if Lo-Melkhiin noticed. The traveler might have had his own gear, but that was not the only reason my father had agreed to bring him back across the desert.

"When we reached my tents, the traveler met my other daughter," my father said. "I am no poet, to speak of love in flower-shaped words, but even I could see the sun rise

235

in his eyes when he saw her, and her step lighten when she walked to him."

"Father of my heart," said Lo-Melkhiin, with the warm voice he used when he spoke to his mother, "love makes poets of us all."

"They will wed," my father said. "And they will pitch their tent beside mine, and raise their children in my wadi. My other daughter will still tend our holy places, but now she will not live alone."

I had tears in my eyes again, and this time I did not try to stop them. I could not be faulted if I cried for my sister's happiness, when I had thought she might have none but the dead when she was old. Now she would have a family.

"Father of my heart, this is wonderful news," Lo-Melkhiin said. "But you have not asked your favor."

"Great lord," my father said. "You know the perils of the desert, and you know how well I must guard against them to have the renown and success that I have. I beg you, let me take your wife to her sister's wedding, and return her to you when it is done."

I couldn't breathe. Lo-Melkhiin would never permit it. He could not be sure I would return. They could say I had died in the sand, was bitten or broken or burned. They could hide me forever.

"Father of my heart, you know the gravity of this request," Lo-Melkhiin said. His fingers bit into my arm.

"I must consider the safety of my wife, the star of my skies. I know how much she loves her sister, but the danger is great."

"We are prepared to make the most careful of arrangements," my father said. "I have brought my best and steadiest camel to bear her. The beast has never failed me. It has never foundered in the sand, never started from its lead. Her brothers will guard her, and I will swear her life to you, again, if you wish it."

I wanted to laugh at them. I had already crossed the desert once, on the back of a horse with only my own will and a pinch of salt to keep me in the saddle, and they spoke of me as though I were as fragile as a sweet-water blossom at the height of the desert wilt. I would walk, I would crawl, if it meant I could see my sister again.

"Father of my heart, you have moved me," Lo-Melkhiin said. "You have taken time from your caravan to come and see me, and you have prepared at great cost should I grant your request. I beg you, give me an hour to speak with my wife, the star of my skies, so that we might make our own plans for her safety."

"It shall be as you say, great lord," my father said. He bowed low over the table.

Lo-Melkhiin clapped his hands. Men appeared, dressed in the same white cloth that the serving girls wore, though theirs was shaped into tunic and breeches.

"These are the father and brothers of my heart," Lo-Melkhiin said, gesturing grandly. "They have journeyed far to see me, and to see my wife, who lights each of my days with her smile the way the sun lights the desert sky. Take them to the guest gardens and see that they have everything they need. I fear their traveling clothes will be too heavy for garden air. Make sure they are shown the baths, and given finer weave, so they might appreciate the qasr to the fullest while they are our guests."

The men bowed low, and waited for my father and brothers to rise. I reached for my father again, and again he kissed my hands. This time there were no tears, just the strength of his hands on mine. And then they left us, and Lo-Melkhiin tore away my veil.

twenty-seven

"WELL, STAR OF MY SKIES," said Lo-Melkhiin to me. "Will you beg?"

I would have thrown myself at his knees and promised him anything he liked, except I did not think he would make me. He wanted me to go, for whatever reason, or he would not have been so polite to my father. Maybe he thought I would not know that. Maybe he forgot that I was the daughter of a master of offer and counter-offer, even though he had just sent my father from the room. I thought it strange that I knew Lo-Melkhiin so well.

"No," I said to him. "If you wanted weeping and wailing, you would find a better way to make me."

He laughed, his teeth bright in his mouth. "Yes, my wife, I would."

He passed my veil back to me, and I went to pin it into place. Cool hands met mine, and took the work. The serving girl had not left us.

"My mother will accompany you, of course," Lo-Melkhiin said to me as if the girl were not there. "She has not been outside of the walls since she was healed of her illness. I think the journey will do her well."

"And she will ensure I return," I said to him.

"No, star of my skies," he said to me. "I have a much better way to ensure your return."

At first I thought he meant to keep one of my brothers in my place, but then I saw the answer. Of course I would come back. If I left him, he would remarry; his bride would die, and he would be that much closer to marking off all the villages on his map, which meant he could start over. My sister, wedded, would be safe, and I would be in hiding, but we could not hide every girl of marriageable age.

"Go and tell your brothers, my love," he said to me. "I will have your things and my mother's things packed."

"Will you come?" I asked him.

If he did, it could be disastrous. I doubted my older brother could control the younger ones that long, and nothing that crawled in the desert sands or flew above them could control my sister, not as I had remade her. If he did not, though, I might lose my power and be ill again, and there would be no one to heal me.

"Alas, my love, I cannot." He smiled wickedly. "Though I would very much enjoy watching your brothers bite their tongues while they try to keep their heads cool. There is too much for me to do here."

He left me, and I stood to go back to my room. I would not meet my father and brothers dressed like this. It was too much for all of us. At the very least, I wanted a lighter veil. They had come this far, and should see my face. I got lost once, in corridors I had never walked through before, but I ended up in the kitchens, so at least I knew how to find my way from there.

"Lady-bless," called the cook as I passed through. "Will you take a cask of honeyed mead to your sister?"

I was forever impressed by the speed at which news traveled in this place. Seemingly, it flew faster than the wind. I told the cook I would be glad to take his mead, one of the prides of his kitchen, and he sent a boy to carry it to the girls who were packing my things.

At last I was back in my rooms. I changed quickly. This dress had no ties, for all its glamor. Its beauty was in its embroidery, and the way the gold thread caught the light. I took it off, and then my leggings, and stood in my shift. I wondered what dishdashah they would send for me to wear at my sister's wedding. It could not be too fine. I should

241

not outshine her on her wedding day. Hopefully whoever packed would keep her head and remember that.

I found a simple gown, blue linen with no embroidery at all, and pulled it on over my shift. This one hung to my feet and needed no leggings. I put on the slippers that were sturdy enough for garden paths, and went out again to find my father.

They had come from the bath by the time I reached them, and were sitting in the shade with a backgammon board, though none of them were playing.

"Sister!" my youngest brother shouted when he saw me.

He ran and caught my elbows, lifting me into the air and spinning me around as he kissed my cheeks and my nose. My left slipper went flying into a bush.

My other brothers pelted me with affection in a similar fashion, though they at least left me on the ground when they did it. My youngest brother fetched me my shoe, and I balanced myself on his shoulder as I stood on one foot to put it on without bending. Then I went to where my father stood, still in the shade, and bowed to him.

"Father," I said to him. "Thank you for coming to ask Lo-Melkhiin if I could attend my sister's wedding. He has a few conditions, but already my things are being readied for the journey."

My father said nothing for a moment, and I looked up at him. Surely he had wanted me to get permission, even if he had not dared to hope for it. He put his hands on my shoulders and held me at arm's length for a moment, and then without warning pulled me into an embrace so tight I thought he would crush my ribs.

"Daughter of mine," he said to me. "I am so sorry."

"Father," I said to him. "There was nothing you could have done. If you had been in the village and fought them, they would have only killed you, and my brothers, and taken me anyway. Who then would keep my mother and my sister and my sister's mother? Who would go out with the caravan?"

"Daughter of mine," he said to me. "You are too wise and too kind."

"I am a queen here, but I am as I have been taught," I said to him. "I am as I learned to be in your tents."

He released me, and my brothers came back to sit in the shade. We sat, and they told me of the man my sister was to marry.

"He is as pale as unbleached wool," my youngest brother said. "You can see how his blood passes through his body."

"My youngest brother is a fool," said the eldest. "I can see my own veins. It is not a miracle."

"His hair is the color of the sun, but his eyes are brown, like normal." This from the tallest of them.

"My sons, you jabber worse than the sand-crows," my father said, but there was laughter in his voice. "Your sister will think her sister weds a ghost. Say instead that his skin is pale and his hair is the color of flatbread when you have mixed in saffron. They are correct about his eyes, though, daughter of mine. They are brown like ours."

"Does he really come from the mountains?" I asked them. "Lo-Melkhiin's mother, who must travel with me, is from the great blue desert. That is also far away."

"He truly does," said my oldest brother. "He brought with him a silver-colored metal that is not like anything I have ever seen."

"Speak no more of that here, I beg you," I said to them. They looked surprised. "I cannot explain why. Only say nothing more of the metal within these walls, or within the hearing of anyone from the city."

"Even you, sister?" asked the oldest.

"I am not from the city," I told them. "Lo-Melkhiin has decided I am his queen, but that does not make me belong here."

"He called you the star of his skies." This brother was the most quiet. He did not often speak, joking that the others spoke enough for him, but when he did, even my father listened to his words. I listened to them now.

"He did that only because you were there to hear it," I said to him.

"He mocks us," said my youngest brother. "And he mocks you."

244

"Hush," said three of my brothers at once, and then they spoke no more for some time.

I had spent most of my time in visions seeking my sister. Perhaps I ought to have looked upon my brothers from time to time. They simmered with anger and inaction, like a pot of lentils left in the embers of the cook fire. I wondered what they had plotted while they were out with the caravan, far from the watching eyes of any who knew even where Lo-Melkhiin's qasr was, let alone any who might speak to him. For a breath, I saw them in the desert, trading spices in purple cloth packets and wrapping unfamiliar ore in broadcloth of the same color.

My brothers doubtless thought to use my sister's wedding as a staging ground for my rescue. I hoped my father would be wiser, and stern enough to hold them back. I must return to Lo-Melkhiin, or I would never grow powerful enough to defeat him. With Lo-Melkhiin's mother along, they would be unable to make much mischief, but I still feared they would do something rash.

I found my father's gaze, and saw he understood my concern, though he did not understand why it was I had to return. He would fear reprisals on the others who lived in his tents, and I hoped that it would be enough to keep the storm in his eyes from brewing full. I hoped also that it would be enough to temper my brothers' fires as well.

A serving girl came into the garden and coughed. She

would come no closer with my brothers there, so I went to her instead. She was pink behind her veil. I suppose my brothers were handsome enough to catch the eye. Three of them were married, after all.

"Lady-bless," she said to me, her voice low, "your things will be ready when the hottest part of the day has passed. You will leave then, if that suits your father."

"Wait a moment," I said to her, and went back to where my father sat. "Will you be rested enough when the sun goes behind the wall to travel?" I asked him. "Will the camels be?"

My father squinted up at the sky. He did not think to check the water clock, if he even knew what it was. It was not my custom to check it either, for all I had lived here so long by now. I still judged the hour by the sun.

"Yes, daughter of mine," he said to me. "We will be ready, and the camels can find their way under the stars."

I went back to the serving girl and told her as much. She bowed to me, cast one quick look at my brothers, and left to see to her tasks. When I looked back at them, my brothers were smirking at one another.

"Shall I tell your wives you found the city so lovely?" I said to the oldest three. They laughed, and kissed me again.

I told them I would see them by the gates when the sun had reached the walls, and went back to my rooms to oversee the last of the packing effort. I wanted to be sure that my clothes were not over-fine. I found the henna mistress had taken charge, though it was not precisely her place. She showed me the dishdashah she had selected for the wedding feast and for the dancing. I nodded my approval.

"Lady-bless, would your sister take one of your gowns to be wed in?" the henna mistress said. It was a heartfelt offer, but I shook my head.

"No, mistress," I said to her. "She will be wed in a dishdashah she has stitched herself, as I was. It is luckier. But I thank you for the generous thought."

She bowed and left me to select shoes for riding. Soon, everything was sent away to be bound to the camels. I walked to the gate with Lo-Melkhiin's mother at my side, and the desert whispering welcome before me.

twenty-eight

THIS TIME WHEN I PASSED through the city, the streets teemed with people who had come to see Lo-Melkhiin's bride. Men stared at my father's camels as they walked slowly past. Little girls waved scraps of purple cloth like flags. Their mothers twined the cloth around their fingers. When I passed, they kissed the cloth and raised their hands. I could not fathom where they had gotten it. Purple dye was the most expensive of all the goods my father traded, and yet I saw so much of it, both in and out of my trance.

My brothers could not stare at me, surprised as they were by the acclaim I was receiving in the streets, because they were too busy with the camels. Lo-Melkhiin had sent my sister and her husband-to-be rich gifts, but also had he given gifts to my father. They were a shadow of what he would have paid, had he bargained a bride price fairly, but they were still worth a small fortune. There were jars of the clear oil that burned in the palace lamps, bales of fine silks and silken threads, wine from grapes that only grew in the lands by the blue desert, and a lion skin. I would not tell them the price of that. They all thought it a marvel, and my youngest brother would not stop petting it. I remembered too well how the lion had looked in my vision, when it yet lived.

Lo-Melkhiin's mother rode beside me, sitting as straight as I did on her own camel. We both had canopies above our heads, and veils to cover our faces. She carried a fan as well, having no need to use her hands; a boy led her camel for her. I had one hand on the camel's mouth rope and one on the saddle horn, but I would need no fan once we were in the desert wind. I had worried that she would be vexed to travel, especially on short notice, but she looked pleased—a true smile was on her face as she swayed back and forth, matching the camel's stride. Lo-Melkhiin had kissed her when we left him, and he had not worn his viper's face to do it. We went out through the gate, the guardsmen drawn up in straight lines, their armor gleaming in the sun as we passed them, and then into the desert.

We could not go across the sand, as Lo-Melkhiin's horses had the day I came to the qasr, because camels are not as fast-moving. Theirs is a plodding, steady pace. A horse can get you somewhere quickly, but you cannot carry very much with you. A camel will take its time, but it will also carry your house if you ask it nicely enough. Instead, we turned into the dry wadi bed and followed its meandering path between the oleander flowers. The scent was overwhelming, but I knew better than to get too close. There was poison in the blossoms, and while they would not kill you if you smelled them, they could make you ill. I turned to say as much to my serving girl, and to the woman who served Lo-Melkhiin's mother, but they sat on the backs of their own camels and did not lean toward the blooms.

The camels plodded forward, and the sun sank. My oldest brother came with water and bread, offering it to Lo-Melkhiin's mother first, as was proper, but we did not halt.

"Sister of mine," he said to me. "We will ride through the dark tonight. There will be stars enough to guide us. Can you keep to your saddle?"

I certainly knew I could, and he knew it too. I knew also that he was uncomfortable speaking to Lo-Melkhiin's mother. My brothers might have liked the lion skin Lo-Melkhiin gave my father, but they felt differently about a woman who wore lion manes upon her head.

"Mother of my heart," I said to her, ignoring my brother's

wince at how I addressed her, "will that suit you? And will it suit the boy who leads you?"

In truth, it was he I was most concerned about. Sitting on a camel is awkward and uncomfortable if you are not used to it, but it is not as tiring as walking.

"He will ride with me if he tires," said Lo-Melkhiin's mother to me. The boy looked up, surprised. "I know better than to play at nobility in the desert. The sun does not care who you are when it bakes you."

"We will go on," I said to my brother. He nodded, and went to offer water to the two who rode behind me.

The sun sank lower, turning the desert a friendly orange, and then a deep red. At length it set, leeching all color from the horizon, until all that remained was white sand beneath us and a dark sky overhead. Behind me, the serving girl shifted uncomfortably. She did not like the empty dark of the desert night. I turned to smile at her. I knew she would not see it, but I hoped she would hear it in my voice when I spoke.

"Do not worry," I said to her. "The desert night takes a moment to wake, but once it does, you will think you have never seen anything so beautiful."

There was no moon yet, but our eyes were still dazzled by the glare of the sun on the sand. I knew that it would take some few moments to fade. When my eyes finally cleared, I looked up and found that I was not disappointed.

Everything was just as beautiful as I had remembered.

The serving girl gasped, and I knew that she had seen it too. There were stars in the city, of course. I had been to a party to watch them specifically, and I had seen how they shone there. Most nights, though, we had not gone outside, and if we had, it was only to the garden, where the view of the sky was blocked by the trees and the walls. The girls went to bed early, to be up before the sun; if they went to visit family in the city, the sky was obscured by torchlight and by the hazy light of the lamps.

There was none of that now. The sky burned above us, full of stars beyond the counting of a hundred Skeptics, even if they were given a hundred years to count them. From horizon to horizon the glory stretched, like a great dark bowl had been overturned above us, sealing the lights in for us alone to see them. This was true beauty, I decided—better than all the fine cloth and finer embroidery, better than all the food and well-made ceramics it was served in. This was something Lo-Melkhiin could not buy, could not copy, and could not steal. It gave me great peace to see it, and it also gave me hope.

It was well the camel I rode was a docile beast, for I confess I did naught to steer him as we went along. I watched the sky, not the path in front of me, but the camel was as steady as my father had promised my husband, and it did not miss a step, even when there were rocks on the bottom of the wadi bed. Beside me, Lo-Melkhiin's mother told the boy to join her after he tripped for a third time, trying to watch both his path and the skies. He climbed up behind her, leaning against the saddle but sitting on the camel's rump, and gawked unfettered while she took the rein.

At last I found myself swaying overmuch in the saddle, and my father called a halt. I slid down, and would have helped to pitch the tents as I used to do, but the serving girl came to me with a lamp and asked a hundred questions about the sky. By the time I had answered half of them, the work was done.

"Daughter of mine," my father said to me, and I went to where he stood in front of the tent that was usually his. It was large, because he had got it when my mothers still traveled with him in the caravan.

"Thank you, father," I said to him, and turned to see that Lo-Melkhiin's mother stood beside me already. The old woman who was her companion, and my own serving girl, stood behind her. The boy had disappeared.

The four of us went into the tent. My father had put down rugs so that we would not sleep on the sand, and had weighted down the side flaps with rocks from the wadi so that no creatures would disturb us in the night. The old woman lit the lamps, and we sat while she and the serving girl laid out our beds.

"Your father is a good man," Lo-Melkhiin's mother said

253

to me. "He keeps his caravan well, and he is kind to old women."

"He is wise," I said to her. "If he is kind to a man's mother, then the man will trade fairly."

"Does he think my son will trade fairly?" she asked.

"No," I said to her, after I had thought about it for a moment. "Perhaps it is only his habit."

"Or perhaps he does not judge the mother the way he judges the son," she said to me.

"That is a wise guess, lady mother," I said to her. "For he has helped teach me how to work in the world, and I do not judge mothers by their sons either."

"Yet I think I will like your mother, and your sister's mother, given what I have seen of your brothers and of you," she said to me.

"It is my hope that you do," I said to her. "My mother is a kind woman, and my sister's mother too, though I did not know how much she loved me until the day I took her daughter's place and came to wed your son."

"You are easy to love, daughter of my heart," she said to me. I looked at her, surprised, but there was no lie in her face. "I think even my son loves you, in his way."

I was silent for a long moment, watching as the bedrolls were unrolled and the pillows brought out and sorted. Lo-Melkhiin's way of loving was to use and to burn. It was not like my mother and my sister's mother and my father. We might work together, he and I, but it was dangerous work, and I did not see how it would come to a good end.

"I am not sure that means I have less cause to fear him," I said to her at last. "If anything, perhaps I should fear him more."

"You are as wise as your father has taught you, then," she said to me.

"The camels will be rested in a few hours," I said to her. "We should not waste our own rest with talk of what we fear."

She nodded, and beckoned to the woman she had brought. The woman came to her side and carefully lifted the lion's-mane wig from her head, placing it reverently in a corner of the tent where we would not kick or step on it if we left in the dark to make water. Lo-Melkhiin's mother shook out her traveling robe and let it fall to the rugs on the floor before the woman could catch it. She did not look back as she went into her bed, but I did, and saw the care with which the woman folded it. Lo-Melkhiin's mother had a loyal household, and that made me glad.

I went to my own bed, letting the serving girl strip my traveling robe from me before I went, so that I would not get too much sand where I was to sleep. She set it down, folded her own beside it, and crawled into the bedroll next to mine. I heard her murmur as she began her prayers, and wondered what smallgods her family had. Before I might have asked her, though, I rolled over, and saw her traveling robe where she had put it next to mine. Tucked inside the cuff, where she might press her lips against it as she rode a-camel back, was a narrow piece of purple cloth.

I went to sleep, and for the first time in weeks I had no fear that I would die.

twenty-nine

I KNEW I DREAMED, because I was with my sister, and we stitched a new wedding dress. This time, the cloth was yellow. It was a common color, neither as expensive as the purple nor as striking as the orange, but one that suited her well. The weave was very fine; I could see where she had put in stitches and then taken them out, displeased with the quality of the work she had done.

"It is not the same when you are gone," she said to me. "My stitches grow sloppy when I do not have you to keep me focused on the task."

"I am sorry, sister of mine," I said to her. "I could think of no other way to save you."

"Do you think I feared him?" she asked. "Do you think Lo-Melkhiin or Lo-Melkhiin's marriage bed frightened me? I know they frightened you, sister. I know they frighten you still."

"You have never feared anything," I said to her, and my words made it true. "Not the lion or the viper or the scorpion. But that would not have saved you, if you had gone with him to be his wife."

"And what saved you, sister?" she asked. "Why have you lived these nights and days, when the ones before you have died?"

"If I live, sister," I said to her, "it is because of the work you have done for me."

Until I spoke those words, it was only the two of us and the dishdashah in my vision. Now I saw the shrine she had made for me in her tent, the rugs we sat upon, and the lamp that gave us light.

"Do not forget that," she said to me.

"I would not," I said to her. That remembrance stood between me and my nightmare. So far, I had taken nothing. It had all been a gift.

We stitched in silence for a time. Under our hands, the hemline was given flowers, and vines twined up the seams. My needle was bronze, a dull glint in the lamplight. My sister's needle shone silver as it pulled the thread in its wake.

"Sister," I said to her. "What did the pale man from the

mountains promise our father if he were allowed to marry you?"

She smiled, a lioness's smile that showed her teeth and tongue.

"It was a higher price than if I left our father's tents," she said to me. "I love him well, but he must learn the desert ways. He cannot herd the cows, or even the sheep, without one of your brothers or one of the children to help him. He does not know which snakes can be eaten and which must be burned. He cannot tell the path that game will take. He must be cared for, and that is why the price was high."

I could not fathom why she would love him. When we had stitched the purple dishdashah and sewn our secrets into it, she had told me that her husband would be a man like our father, who had his own caravan and herds and tents. My father had the social standing to find such a man, and my sister had the beauty to capture his heart. It had been her wish that her husband would have a brother close in age, that I might wed him. That way, we would always have tents close to one another. I had not been gone from her side for so long that I thought her dreams would have changed so much.

My needle stilled as a creeping cold swept over me. I had told Lo-Melkhiin that my sister would wed a merchant my father met when he was out with the caravan. I had said he would be from far away. I had said he would have the bright metal, like the needle with which my sister stitched. I had made a whole man from my words, and then I had brought him to my sister. I had made her love him.

"Sister!"

I jumped, and rammed the needle through my skin. One drop of bright red blood fell upon the dishdashah, and I watched in horror as it stained the fabric and the embroidery both.

"I am sorry," I said to her. "I have ruined it."

"No, sister," she said to me. "No one will see that; it is so small. And it is my fault for startling you, but you did not answer me when I spoke."

"It is the smallgod," I said to her. "Sometimes I lose myself."

"If that is the price to keep you safe from your wretched husband, then so be it," she said to me. "Come: we are almost finished."

We stitched again as silence grew between us. I chewed the inside of my cheek so that I would not drift into the trance again. My sister was wrong about the price of my living. I had not paid it; at least, not in the way she thought. She had paid more than I; her whole life was rerouted, as though a rock in the wadi bed had forced the water to find a new path. If a rock was large enough, it could shift the whole course of the wadi. Any village that relied upon that wadi might dry out for want of water. The wells would run dry, and there would be nothing but scrub for the sheep and goats to eat. The people would move their tents, leaving behind their dead; or they would stay, and die, and join them. She had made me a smallgod, and I had done this to her.

I thought to pray that I had not caused too much ruin with my actions, but I had no one to pray to. Our smallgod was gone, passed over for the new one, his spirit resting at last. I could not pray to myself, and there was no comfort for me.

The lamp burned low as we tied off our threads, and then my sister looked up at me.

"Sister of mine," she said to me. "I will see you in the morning."

"You see me now," I said to her, before I remembered that I was dreaming. I reached for her, and caught nothing. "Sister!" I called, but she was gone, and so were the dishdashah and the tent and the lamp. I woke to darkness, sitting up and grasping at nothing in my father's tent, where he had pitched it.

"Lady-bless," said the woman who traveled with Lo-Melkhiin's mother.

"I am well," I said to her, though my heart raced and my breath heaved in my lungs.

"You are with your family, lady-bless," she reminded me. "You are safer here than you are when you sleep in the stone qasr."

"Yes," I said to her. "I remember. I only dreamed, that is all. Please, sleep again. I am sorry to have disturbed you."

"It is all right, lady-bless," she said to me. "I do not sleep very much anymore."

I lay back down and pulled my hair over my face. I did not know how long I had slept. With the tent flaps shut against the cool night air, it was impossible to tell the hour. I laughed, as quietly as I could. I had become so dependent upon the hour-candles and the water clock, even though I had used the sun as much as possible when I was in the qasr. Without them, and without the sky, I could not guess the time.

I heard the camels shifting their feet in the sand. Most of them would have knelt down to sleep. If they stood now, it meant that they were rested. I breathed deeply and smelled mostly the rug and the burned oil in the lamp and the perfumes that my companions wore, but at the edge of those scents was the fire the watchman would be standing by. It smelled of embers; they had not added new fuel in some time, so that none would be wasted when the fire was no longer needed.

If it was not close to dawn, then it was close to the time my father wished to leave. I would not try to sleep again.

In the dream, my sister had not known that I was the one who had brought her the man she was to marry. Perhaps she

262

thought the smallgod's power was only enough to keep me alive. I had seen no falsehoods when I slept, but I wondered if, by the time I met her in the waking world, she would have realized what I had wrought. I could not bear her anger and her hatred if she did not like the control I had exerted on her life, but I knew I had earned them both. If she spurned me, I would understand it.

It was not just that I had found the pale man in my dreams and brought him to my father's attention, although that was weighty enough. It was that I had made her love him; and he, her. I had told Lo-Melkhiin that the man my sister wed would have a fire only she could reveal. I could not guess how he would burn, then, if it was her choice that was directing him. I could no more guess that than I could have guessed how her determination to make me a smallgod would change me.

Again, I wished that I could pray, but there was no one to hear my words; even if I could have said them to my own shrine, I feared the power they might unleash if I said them. It was as though I were a water jar, nearly full when the bucket had come out of the well. Instead of pouring the water into another vessel, or back into the well, more water kept coming into my jar. I should have overflowed, spilling the precious liquid onto the sand where grasping roots would find it, but instead the jar kept filling. I knew that soon I would swell under the pressure, but surely the water must overflow. It could not be packed more tightly into the jar.

Whichever brother was guarding the fire whistled shrilly three long times and then three short times. Beside me the serving girl woke, forgot where she slept, and then remembered with a sigh. Lo-Melkhiin's mother stirred, and the old woman went to light the lamp.

"That is the signal to wake," I said to them. "We must be ready to go again when the whistle sounds once more."

"Yes, lady-bless," the girl said to me.

She went to the water jar and poured a cup for me, and for Lo-Melkhiin's mother. By the time my father came to strike the tent, the bedrolls were wrapped, the rugs rolled up, and the serving girl had gone in search of the crates where she was to pack the pillows, lamps, and other contents of the tent.

"Daughter of mine," said my father, "we will ride soon, before the sun has finished rising above the horizon."

"We will be ready, father," I said to him.

"I commend you, master of the caravan," said Lo-Melkhiin's mother to my father, when he would have turned back to his work. He looked back at her. The early light made the lion's-mane wig shine pale. "Your tents are as comfortable as any place that I have ever slept," she said. "My son was right to trust you with the keeping of his beloved wife, and with me."

"I thank you, mother-of-the-king," my father said, and bowed. "Your words do me honor and lighten my heart. I had feared you would not be able to rest easy in the desert sand."

"It is no more dangerous than anywhere else," said Lo-Melkhiin's mother.

My father nodded, and went to strike the tent. Before long, we were all on the backs of our camels. My heart was light and heavy with every beat. I did not know what was before me. All I knew was that every step brought me closer to where my sister would be wed.

thirty

WE CAME TO A PART OF the wadi where I recognized every bend and every stone. I knew the slope of the banks, and where the pools would be. Here, we passed sheep and goats brought to drink by the children whose job it was to tend the herds. They looked up at us as we went by, waving to my father and to my brother, but were silent in their awe of me. This made me sad—I had not been gone from them for so long that they should forget who taught them the way of the herds—but then I remembered who rode beside me.

In the qasr, Lo-Melkhiin's mother was imposing, her lion's-mane wig and her straight stance a fixture of the palace. In the desert, she was a startlement to look upon. The hair of the wig was a tawny gold in the sun, reflecting the sand like she was a living lion astride a camel, not a woman. The boy who rode behind her, aware of the looks being sent his way, sat straight too; though I wondered if he might have had fun if he slid down and played with the children who were minding the herds.

Every now and then, one of my married brothers took his camel out of the line and brought it to its knees. Then a child, one of his own get, would climb up, and they would be on their way again. My brothers' wives were all from different villages that my father traded with when he was out with the caravan, and they did not share a tent the way my mother shared with my sister's mother, but their children ran wild in the desert together, and sometimes it was hard to remember which of them belonged to which of my brothers.

There were plenty of children left on the ground to tend the sheep and goats. I could tell that these were not just our herds that grazed. My father's mark was on many flanks, but there were at least eight other herds besides. My sister's wedding, it seemed, was to be a grand affair, with guests from up and down the wadi, and across the sand besides.

We passed by the rocky hill with the caves where we buried our dead. I looked, half-afraid that I would see a jealous smallgod glaring down at me—the lowly girl who had stolen his power—and what I saw nearly made me jerk the rein and halt my camel. It was tradition, when villages gathered, that at least the priestly members of each clan would bring a stone from their wadi bed to leave on the path that led up to the caves. I had expected, given the marks on the sheep I had counted, perhaps eight or ten, certainly no more than a dozen. Instead, I could not count them, there were so many. Hundreds of stones, pebbles that a child might carry and rocks the size of my father's fist, lined the path. Only if every man, woman, and child my father had ever met when he was out with the caravan had come—only then could they have brought this many stones. I could not fathom why they had been invited.

My father was a proud man, but he was not foolish. He would not seek to impress me, whatever my new status, and he had not known Lo-Melkhiin's mother would come, so he could not have sought to impress her, either. He would not care if I told Lo-Melkhiin about the wedding he had given my sister, knowing that he could never match the splendor of the qasr. The pale man from the mountains that my sister was to marry had no family close by, and no ties to the caravan that were not also shared by my father and brothers, so the numbers could not have been swelled by him.

We saw the tents before I had finished reasoning my puzzle through. They stretched away from the wadi in both directions, spaced carefully around the wells and around the privies, so that the two would never meet to the befoulment of the former. I saw cook fires beyond counting, the smoke from a hundred roasting goats and more besides filling the air. Everywhere I looked, women kneaded bread or milled grain for more flour. Younger children than those out with the herds carried baskets of dates and figs and pomegranates between the fires at the direction of their mothers. Men butchered cattle, while others built pens to house the animals that had come with the guests.

Each tent was marked with a strip of fabric. I thought, like as with sheep, that this was so a person might tell to whom the tent belonged; but then a breeze came through, and I saw that all the flags were the same. Purple fabric— not too much, because of the expense—marked every tent in the encampment. Beside me, Lo-Melkhiin's mother looked around her, a worried expression on her face. I turned to ask her, but then my camel knelt and I heard a cry I knew as well as my own heart.

"Sister!"

And there she was, flying across the sand with her hair streaming behind her as no bride's should. I did not care what Lo-Melkhiin's mother thought of us, or if our mothers would scold us for our scandalous behavior later. I was off my camel almost before its belly hit the ground. The sand was a burning fire on my thinly shod slippers, but I did not care. My sister's arms were around me, and mine were around her again.

"I have missed you, sister of mine," I whispered for her ears alone. "And I am glad to come to see you."

"Sister," she said to me. "I am glad that you are here to see at all."

The sheep and goats surrounded us then, as the children went to touch her. It was good luck to touch a bride, but it should have been more difficult for them; as brides we were meant to remain in our mothers' tents until the wedding. I did not know if it was good luck to touch a smallgod, but I hoped it was. The children brushed against me as they went to her. There was no longer any taking us for one another, though. Her laughing eyes had not stilled, as mine had. Her hair hung freely beneath her veil, where mine was braided and pinned against my skull. And my dishdashah was much finer than was hers, though the quality of the embroidery was more or less the same.

"Come," she said to me, pulling free of the small hands that reached for her. "I will take you to your mother."

I followed her, my feet finding their old skill of walking on the shifting, burning sand as though I had never left it. She led me past tent after tent, each with the purple flag, and each with men and women I did not recognize standing near them. The scent of cooking food was strong, still, as we walked, but another scent began to take its place. Fire, not for cooking, burned close to our destination. When we were close enough to see it, I saw a small stove built above the fire, and a bowl on the stove. A man stood there with pale skin and hair the color of saffron stirred in water, and I knew that he was the man my sister was to wed. He looked into the bowl, waiting for something, and though I could not see over the rim, I knew the bowl was full of the bright metal from the mountains, and that he would shape it when it could be shaped.

My sister did not look at him overlong for a girl who was meant to be in love. Part of me was glad at that, if it meant she loved me still, but part of me worried. If I had made her love him, perhaps she only felt it when I wished her to.

I pushed such thoughts aside when she pulled me past him and into a tent that was so familiar I would have known it with my eyes shut. My mother waited there, and my sister's mother, and they both wept when they saw me, drawing the veil from my face so that they could kiss me and pull me into their arms as though they would never again let me go.

"Mother," I said to them. "Mothers of my heart, I have missed you both so much."

They did not speak, only tightened their arms while my sister waited beside me. When they had secured me in their memories enough to let me go, they relinquished me back to her, and we sat on the rug as we once had, when we stitched secrets into cloth.

My sister had smiled then, as she smiled now, and I knew she meant to tell me a secret as we sat. Before she spoke, though, she traced my braids, feeling each pin that anchored the style.

"I can show you how it works, if you like," I said to her. "I have learned how to do it, and the girl who has come with me will help. You can borrow my pins."

"I want nothing of Lo-Melkhiin's when I wed," she said to me. Her voice was bitter, like the hard yellow fruit my father bought when he traded near the blue desert.

"You will have me," I said to her. "And I am his."

"You are mine," she said to me. "As I am yours. We have done too much for even a demon to separate us."

I knew then that she had seen, at least in part, the visions I had; and that when I saw the dress she would marry in, there would be my stitches in the thread, and my blood staining the hem.

"Sister," I said to her. "I must return to him."

"Do you like the qasr so much?" she asked me.

"I do not," I said to her. "But if I do not return to him, he will wed another girl, and she will die."

"I care not," my sister said to me. "Lo-Melkhiin will not live to wed another after that."

I saw it then, clearly in the light of the desert sun. I knew why Lo-Melkhiin's mother had been worried before she even got off her camel. I knew why the herds had come, and why the men, women, and children had left so many stones on the path to the cave where we buried our dead. I knew why there were so many roasting goats and so many baskets of dates, which would not go bad even if they were left out in the sun.

My father had come to the qasr and begged my husband to release me for a wedding, but he had lied. The peace I had struggled to hold myself to in the qasr was at risk from the desert, and I could not stop it. My husband had let me come—unwittingly or not, it did not matter. What mattered was that I stood with my family, with my sister and my mother, my sister's mother and my father, my brothers and their children, and every man, woman, and child my father had ever met while he was out in the desert with the caravan. They might dance and feast. They might play backgammon and talk of the fires of summers past, but this was no wedding.

This was war.

vii.

The human sand-crawlers thought they were so clever. They thought if they buried their business in sand, and conducted it far away from the walls of my city, that I would not learn what they were doing.

They were wrong.

I did not need the eyes and ears of men to spy for me, though I had plenty of both at my disposal. My people were haunting the desert still, preying upon men as they were moved to, though none of them had risen as high as I had done. I had shut myself off from them so they would not follow my example and supplant me, but now I opened myself to them again. It was they who brought me word, whispered in my mind where only Lo-Melkhiin could overhear us;

and he could not stop us, so I did not care.

The desert rats were gathering for a wedding that was not a wedding.

When my bride's father had come to me, and brought his sons to ask my favor, I had had a choice. I craved their blood to be spilled at her feet, more than I craved sunlight and pretty things. But if I had washed her with their blood, she would never have turned to me; their rebellion might have faltered without them, but it would not have died.

I had to let them go, to let them all go. I had not even kept a hostage to toy with and mutilate, or perhaps to turn over to another of my kin, while they were gone. I sent Lo-Melkhiin's mother, as would be expected of a human king who sent his wife into the desert. When they were gone, I found the qasr empty without them. Without her.

I did not muster my army. I refused to use a force of men to quell this desert uprising. Men might have seen me for what I was at last. I could have laid waste to their desert on my own, but that would have taken time I did not care to spend, and much of my power. Instead I called my people to me, meeting with them in the night, where once I had listened to my Skeptics talk about the stars. They saw how powerful I had become, and listened to my words with hungry ears.

It did not take me very long to convince my people to join me. They craved blood as I did, and did not much care that this time, they might have to kill quickly rather than linger over every wound.

There would be blood enough in every form to sate them, and power beyond what they had known after.

"But my queen is not to be touched," I said to them. "I will have her whole in mind and body when this is done, and the desert is red with the blood of her family."

There were some quiet complaints at that—that I might choose a pet to lavish suffering upon while my kin were forced to deal the mercy of a fast death to those they caught. I let them whisper. They must not guess the truth of why I wanted her. They must not take her, as I had taken Lo-Melkhiin. She was mine for that, if any were to get it, but I hoped instead to control her through other means.

I nearly swooned to think of what we might do together. I could force people to do what I wanted, but I had to be close enough to touch them. She could reach across the desert and do her work as easily as I might reach for more bread at the dinner table. I had not bothered to learn of smallgods when I had taken Lo-Melkhiin, but perhaps it was time to make Sokath, His Eyes Uncovered have great thoughts about them. His heart might burst when he was done, which was why I had avoided him in favor of the younger Skeptics—he was nearly clever enough without me. For this, though, I would risk his death. I had many others at my beck and call.

But first: the desert. I would take my kin onto the sand, and we would turn it red with blood. Men would not sing of the battle we fought there. They would whisper it around their campfires. They would be afraid to speak of it any louder than that, lest the wrath of the victors be called down upon them. Women would wail in the desert, grieving their dead husbands and sons. They would cling to those children who had been too young to fight and had not died—if we did not kill them anyway, of course. My kin were sometimes difficult to control.

Lo-Melkhiin worried about his mother, overhearing our plans as he did. He knew that I would save the girl at any cost, but he did not think I would expend the same effort to bring his mother back to the safety of the qasr. It struck me how deeply he seemed to care for them both. A man might love his mother and not be judged weak by other men for it. Most men did not have the luxury of loving their wives—at least, not so soon after marrying them.

And he did not love her, not quite. But he thought very highly of her. He was impressed with her bravery, and with her unwillingness to change her desert-spirit within city walls. He thought her power was mysterious, but not terrifying as mine was. He wished he were able to know her better, as himself, without the specter that was me hanging between them. He thought she was born to be a queen.

It was so different from how I coveted her. I looked forward to rubbing it in his face later—that he would only ever have her through me. I would touch her with his hands, and use his mouth when I kissed her, and she would fight his body with all the strength in hers when I did it.

Now, though, I had my work before me. My army was not great in number, but we were great in power. We would drive the rebels

back with the strength we gained from devouring their own ancestors. We would rid the desert of their treachery.

And when we were done, I would return to the qasr with my bride,
whether she willed it or not.

thirty-one

WHILE I HAD BEEN DREAMING OF my sister's past, and watching the stars fall from the sky, and spinning useless thread in Lo-Melkhiin's qasr, my father and my brothers had been busy. They had returned with the caravan to find me gone, but my mother and my sister and my sister's mother had not let them mourn, as would have been traditional and proper. I lived—my sister was sure of it—and if I was to keep living, they must take their camels back into the desert and trade once more. This time, with every bolt of cloth, crock of honey, and packet of myrrh that changed hands, they must tell what had happened, and what my sister was trying to do.

I know now that my father did not grieve. My brothers had been chafing under the rule of a king who lived so far away and was so cruel. Two of them had daughters. When they went back into the desert they bartered no less shrewdly than usual, but with every bargain they told of my marriage: how I had made Lo-Melkhiin's eye turn from my sister to me. My father told the men he traded with that I was brave. My brothers said that I was clever—that I had made Lo-Melkhiin love me, and that was why I did not die.

And everywhere they went, they built a shrine, and they left purple cloth, and they prayed.

Soon, they found that women came to trade with them instead of men. The women listened to the story of my wedding with an attentiveness the men had not shared. Rarely now were my father and my brothers tasked with building the shrines to me. Often they were already built, nestled in the sand or in the corner of a tent, or even in the caves where the dead were buried, though I had not died. They left the purple cloth—as a gift, they said, for the living smallgod I had become.

Just when they were about to turn back, when they had reached the edge of the sand desert, could see the scrub desert and, at the full length of their sight, the low blue lines that were the mountains to the north, they met a pale man who carried bright metal, the like of which they had not seen. They wondered if he was ill, his skin was so pale. He wore his kafiyyah like a woman would, veiling his face to them. Men only covered their faces if there was too much sand in the air, or if there was a sickness about.

"If he stays too long in the sun, he burns red like a coal in the fire," my sister said to me as she told me what had gone on after I had been taken away. "His skin peels away, and he says he is very sick when it happens. Your brothers laughed at first, because it was something only a woman would do, to be concerned about her skin—but he showed them his hands, and how they burned, and they held their tongues after that."

My father traded for the bright metal, as much as he could carry. The pale man took honey and spices and dyes, light things that would not burden his camel, and said that if my father wished for more metal, he had only to return in one month. My father could not say how he knew the metal would be needed, only that the smallgod had told him. In any case, my father returned to our wadi with strange tales to tell my mothers and my sister, and with baskets of bright metal shaped as knives, arrowheads, and pins.

My sister told me that she was captivated by my father's words about the pale man, and by the bright metal he had brought. She begged my father to go back, to trade for more, and to bring the pale man with him if he would come. He listened to her, and went out into the desert with the caravan long before there was a need for new trade.

Everywhere he stopped to let his camels rest, my father saw new shrines built to me. There were offerings of pickled gage-root and sweet-water flowers, though the desert burned around them. Girls sang new hymns at the shrines, their light voices carrying on the wind. In the evenings, when they sat around the fires and wove, they chanted prayers instead of working-songs; though my father could not hear them, he knew what they said.

At last, my father came again to the edge of the scrub desert, and met the pale man there. This time, the pale man had two camels laden with metal and with ore, which he said he could shape however my father liked.

"Come with me to my tents," my father said to him. "It is a long journey, but your camels look strong, and we will do what we can to protect you from our sun. I promise you, you will trade well while you are there."

"Revered caravan master," the pale man had said to my father, "I had hoped you would invite me. There is much of your desert that I wish to see."

And so they went, my father retracing his steps back to his tents. He showed the metal to all the men he met, but the pale man would not trade.

"Come with us," he had said to them instead. "Come and we will see what we might make."

Around this time, word spread of the bird that had attacked Lo-Melkhiin and brought him low. My sister said she had prayed to me, unceasingly, that I would help him die. I could not tell her that I had done the opposite of that, but now I knew where the swell of power had come from. It heartened me to learn I was not bound to grant the prayers that brought me power. I was bound enough as Lo-Melkhiin's wife. I did not wish to be bound any farther, even to my sister.

"Others have been attacked by the birds," my father had said to the men he traded with, and to the women who listened to his words. "Why is Lo-Melkhiin so ill when no one else has ever been?"

"The birds are from the mountains, as am I," the pale man had told them. "I have seen them drink the water that comes from the caves where I get my ore. I have seen them sharpen their great claws on the mountainside, and the claws gleam brighter than the daggers that I make."

"Could it be that the metal makes Lo-Melkhiin ill?" my quietest brother had asked.

My father said nothing for a very long time.

"If it is so . . ." the youngest said then. He was less wise, but kinder. "Then we might save our sister from him."

The words had not been true when I thought of them, but in the silence between what I thought and what I said, I had made them real.

"If it is so," said my father at last, "then we might save everyone."

They could not test the metal against the king, of course, but they could test it against other metals. It was much harder than silver. It was far stronger than copper, though it could not be made to shine as bright. It bent bronze, which is what most people were using for weapons. The arrows that Lo-Melkhiin's archers carried, and the daggers and swords at their waists, were bronze. If my father could get enough metal, and the pale man thought that he carried enough with him, then he could make weapons that Lo-Melkhiin's army would not be able to withstand.

Now, instead of trading, my father was recruiting.

"Come with us," he said to the men they met. "Come and bring your women and your children and your herds. Bring them to my wadi, where they will be safe, and we will go to meet Lo-Melkhiin and stop him from stealing our daughters to die as his wives."

Many of the men we met were from villages that had given a daughter already. Those who had not yet, knew that they would have to soon, if I died. They came to my father's cause slowly at first, but my sister said that it was their women who begged them to join. I did not doubt that. Men prospered under Lo-Melkhiin's rule, and if it cost them a daughter, it was no more than a hard winter might demand as payment for survival. The wives and mothers, though, grieved each loss and prayed at my shrines to avoid further losses. They told the men to go, and, after a time, the men went.

When my father returned to his tents along the wadi, his caravan stretched so far behind him that my sister said she could stand on the sand and look, without seeing its end. Then she smiled, and said she had not looked too long, because when she saw the pale man who rode with my brothers, she forgot that the caravan was there at all.

"I knew it must be the man with bright metal," she said to me. Her eyes gleamed with love for him, and I recoiled like she had struck me. I had made this in her, and I feared she would hate me if she knew it. "No one else could look like that," she said. "He was so pale, I saw why your brothers thought he must be ill. He had taken off his kafiyyah so that it did not cover his eyes. He told me later that he wanted to see my father's tents, but that he forgot to look at them, because instead he saw me where I stood waiting."

"Sister," I said to her. "Why do you love him?"

She looked down at her hands, which were lined with henna for the wedding. She did not hear my desperation.

"I did not know at first," she said to me. "I saw him and I wondered if I loved him only because he was so different from any man I had ever seen."

That, at least, sounded like my sister. She had always been more adventurous than I. It seemed fitting that she would see a man so strange and love him for it.

"He spoke of his mountains and of his time in the desert," she said to me, "and my heart was heavy. I thought he meant to return to his home in the north. But he told me that he wished to stay in the desert. He could go and get more ore to make the bright metal, but he wanted the desert to be his home.

"Then I was truly glad, sister of mine," she said to me. "Because if I married him, I could stay here with my mother and with your mother, with your shrines and with our dead. I would not leave my father's tents, and my husband would not ask me to."

She had not answered my question. She had not told me that she loved his eyes or the sound of his voice. She had not said that his touch lit a fire on her skin. Then it came to me: she loved him because he did not seek to change her. If I had made him, or if my father had found him, it did not matter. My sister would have a husband who would not make her sit, veiled and weaving, in his tent. He would not take another wife, as my father had done. She would be his, and he would be hers, alone. This was why she loved him, and it made my heart glad to hear it.

"Come," my sister said to me. "Let me show you how we will end your husband's rule."

My gladness turned hard in my chest; and around it, the copper fire of a hundred prayers burned.

thirty-two

MY BROTHERS HAD TAKEN Lo-Melkhiin's mother to a tent and left her there, with the boy and the old woman and three guards to stand outside. The tent flaps were closed, and it must have been stifling, but I knew that no one would go in to see her unless my father ordered it. When my sister would have taken me around the camp and shown me off like a prize cow, I begged her to let me go to Lo-Melkhiin's mother instead.

"Do you think she has not counted the men, as I did?" I asked her. "Do you think she has not guessed what this wedding of yours will entail? Do you think she has not suffered too?"

My sister relented, and took me to the tent. The eyes of men followed us as we went, my sister in her priestly-whites and me in my fine city dress. How different we had become in so short a time.

"Here is Lo-Melkhiin's mother," she said to me when we reached the tent. "I will stay out here and wait for you, sister. Come to me when you have said your words."

I nodded, and held the flap open to go in. The tent was well-appointed; and less hot than I had feared. Lo-Melkhiin's mother would not wilt in the stuffy desert heat. There were rugs on the floor, and a faint incense burned, as though someone had thought she would be offended by the smell of so many sheep and goats and men. Someone had brought tea and dates, like all visitors were given when they came to my father's tents, though I did not know if anyone had stayed to drink the formal welcome with her. Though I no longer dwelt amongst my family, I was still bound by their duties to their guests.

"Welcome, lady," I said to her, bowing, and then sat down across from her. "Welcome to my father's tents."

The tea was gone, but I held the bowl of dates out to her and she took one. I took one as well and then gestured to the boy, who fell on the bowl like he had not eaten in days. Lo-Melkhiin's mother coughed quietly, and the boy remembered to take at least one of his prizes to the old woman, who smiled as she ate.

"Shall we discuss the desert storms, then?" asked Lo-Melkhiin's mother. "Or perhaps the state of the herds? There seem to be a great many of them here."

"Mother of my heart, there is no reason to hide my family's purpose from you," I said to her, "for you have seen it with your own eyes. They do marry off my sister, as my father said, but they also plot against your son."

"They are not the first," she said to me. "The first died so quickly their blood did not even stain the marble floor inside the qasr. Why does your father think he will fare better?"

"He has many friends who will help him," I said to her. "And they have a new metal from the mountains to the north, brought by the pale man who will be my sister's husband."

"Ah," she said to me. "The same metal that the Skeptics say was on the talons of the great bird that attacked Lo-Melkhiin?"

"The very same," I said to her. "There are daggers made from it, and fletched arrows that will fly true."

"True enough to hit Lo-Melkhiin?" she asked. "True enough to slay all his men?"

"Lady mother," I said to her. "I do not think he will fight with men."

The old woman stood quickly, grabbing the boy and pulling him into her lap. He struggled, probably having decided that he was too old for such treatment, but she was much stronger than he was. She put both of her hands over his ears so he would not hear us. He fought her for a few moments more, and then gave up, the way the goats did when they realized that they could not escape us, and that we held them for their own good. He settled, waiting, and she did not relax.

"You think there are other demons that will come with my son?" Lo-Melkhiin's mother said to me.

"I know it," I said, though until I said the words, I could not have said how I knew.

Lo-Melkhiin had never said that there were more of his kind directly, but he had hinted at it. He had said that he would find a way to take my sister, and I knew he could not do it himself, bound as he was by the laws of men. Yet he was so sure he could, if he wished me to suffer, that I knew he must have other demons at his call to do it. They might not be as strong as he was, perhaps because they were living in the desert, but I knew in my bones that they would be stronger than my father and my brothers, and all the men who would fight beside them.

"I do not want my son to die," Lo-Melkhiin's mother said to me. "He is a good man."

"He might have been, my lady mother," I said to her.

"But the demon has used his skin for so long, used his hands for such awful things. Do you think he is a good man still? Do you think when he is free of the demon, his heart will be whole?"

Sometimes men go mad in the heat of the sun, and beat their children as they would their goats and sheep. My father never tolerated such behavior in his tents, because those children sometimes grew up to be cruel too. I feared that Lo-Melkhiin, the true one, had been locked so long inside a monster that he would be a monster himself, even if the demon were driven away. We had a demon for a king already; I did not wish to replace him with another. Yet I had seen the dark spot within his mind, and I knew not to fear it. Perhaps Lo-Melkhiin's mother's wish was not so desperate, but I wanted to be very, very sure.

Lo-Melkhiin's mother had a strip of purple cloth around her wrist. I saw it now, when she raised her hands to me. Her face was lit by the lamps that burned inside the tent, and the lion's-mane wig cast a tawny aura around her.

"I will pray," she said to me. "Not to the smallgods of my own family, as I have done before. They are far from here, near the blue desert, and maybe they are too busy with the blue desert's troubles to hear me. I will pray to the smallgod who sits in my tent, and who is married to my son."

I was not surprised that she knew. It seemed that

my sister had done her job well and spread the story of my smallgod to everyone who might listen, just as she had promised on the day Lo-Melkhiin took me to be his wife.

"Lady mother," I said to her. "I cannot fight a war."

"Daughter of my heart," she said to me. "You have been fighting a war since you decided to take your sister's place. Only keep fighting it now, and we shall see who stands at the end—demons or smallgods."

I went out from the tent, where my sister was waiting for me. I did not ask if she had heard. I did not care if she had. I looked into her face and saw a light of hope, one that sang for blood and fighting to get the end she desired. I was less willing to face deaths other than my own. I did not know how we had changed so much since I had left her, and yet I knew that I had caused her to change.

We went back to the tent that our mothers shared, and there was a basin of clear water there. I halted, confused by it, and my sister laughed at me. Her laugh was still the same.

"Sister of mine," she said to me, "I will still wed tonight."

Our mothers came, and we washed together. It was not as easy as the baths in the qasr, but it was familiar. We shared the water bowl and the soft soap made from ashes and sheep fat. We rinsed the lather from our bodies. My mother sang to us—the old songs, not any of the new ones they were singing for me—and when the desert air had dried us, we began to dress.

As she had said, my sister would take no pins from me to do her hair. It hung to her waist, straight and black and uncoiled. We put her veil over the top, securing it with the bone pins that she had worn the day before. Her dishdashah was yellow, as I had seen in the dream; there, if I looked to see it, would be the spot of blood. I did not look. She wore no shoes, and so I left mine off too. They could not have borne dancing in the desert sand, in any case.

My dress was blue, and as plain as I could manage. The serving girl had brought it, but I sent her back to wait with Lo-Melkhiin's mother, and told her that my sister and mothers were help enough for me. I did not braid my hair either, but let it fall as my sister had done. It was unseemly that a married woman should wear her hair loose under her veil, but I thought that if any man tried to criticize me, I would only remind him whom it was he sought to wage war against.

As we dressed and my mother sang, the words of Lo-Melkhiin's mother weighed heavy on my spirit. She was so sure he was a good man. I had seen flashes of that, or else I thought I had, but I was not certain that there would be enough to resurrect him. If my father and his men were successful, there would be a dead king and no one to take his place. It would be as Sokath, His Eyes Uncovered had feared—a dead king and no one but the grasping merchants and petty lords to take his place. We would fight until the children who tended the sheep were old, if they did not die fighting themselves.

My dress was such a simple thing, for all it had come from the qasr, because I did not wish to outshine my sister on the day she wed. If I could think of a solution as simple as the dress, it would be better for everyone, but my mind was too full of worry to think. When I closed my eyes to focus, I saw my father's blood on Lo-Melkhiin's hands, and my brother's children with no fathers left to care for them. There were too many people here, and too much noise. I could feel the copper fire burning inside of me, but I could not direct it. When I tried to spin it, it unwound. When I tried to weave it, it tangled.

My mother painted my face with kohl, and my sister's, too. I had to be patient. I had to get through the wedding feast and the dancing, and then, when the night was quiet, I would try to find a good path for my copper fire to take. If it made me ill, Lo-Melkhiin would not be here to heal me, but there was nothing I could do about that. I had to make hard choices at every turn, it seemed, but I needed make none of them yet.

My mother pulled me to my feet, and turned me slowly around before her. "My daughters are here together again," she said to us. "And I am glad."

My sister smiled, her heart showing in her eyes. I tried to do the same, but all I could manage was the smile itself. Quickly I pinned up my veil, hiding from all of them at once.

thirty-three

I DO NOT REMEMBER THE WORDS the priest spoke at my sister's wedding. He did not speak for very long, I am sure, because it was already nearing sunset when my sister went to stand before him, and he could not marry anyone in the dark. Such rituals must be completed while the sun is in the sky.

The pale man wore a tunic and breeches in the desert style, but with a wide belt from his homeland that was nothing like any we might make. I thought it suited him. He had broader shoulders than my father or my brothers, and the belt showed them off. He still looked pale, but as he stood beside my sister, he did not look like something the desert would eat or dry out to dust.

When the words were said, and the first mead was poured, my sister brought the cup to my father and to her mother, and then to my mother. They drank, and she took the cup to me and to each of my brothers. She poured a little into the sand, for her brother taken by the flood when we were small, and then again for the smallgods, though the wink she directed at me when she did it belied her sacred motions. The cup should next have gone to the pale man's family, but he had none here, so she gave it to the priest instead, and the priest drank until the cup was empty.

Then my father clapped his hands, and the women brought out the roasted goat and the baskets of sweet figs and dates. There were baskets of breads and pots of honey. Everyone pretended not to notice when the children ate only sweets, but when my youngest brother would have done the same thing, they laughed at him. It was a merry party, but I could not forget the army in whose midst I sat.

"Sister, put your thoughts away," my sister said to me. Her eyes were dancing, and her face was lit with joy. "There are sentries and guards aplenty. We would know if Lo-Melkhiin marched against us tonight."

I did not tell her that I was less certain. She might not have believed me, and even if she did, she could not have helped. I remembered that I wore a veil, and that if I pretended, none would know the expression on my face. I had only to make sure my body sat the way a happy girl at her sister's wedding would sit. I looked across the fire at where Lo-Melkhiin's mother sat. If she could do this, knowing what she did, then so could I.

A drum was brought, and pipes, and my father stood to begin the dancing. My brothers joined him, and they paced up and down the lines where people sat eating. Their steps were measured and familiar to me, the dances that my family did to welcome a new person to it. I had seen my father dance at all of my brothers' weddings, and at the birth of each child. After they had gone up and down one full circuit, my oldest brother pulled the pale man up to join them. His steps were not perfect, but he did an admirable job of trying, and we clapped and cheered from where we sat.

When they were done, the drums beat faster. This time all the men, from the oldest greybeard to the youngest walking boy, took to their feet and danced. These steps were simpler, not special to any one family, but rather shared amongst all who called a wadi home. This was the dance of men in the desert, those who were strong enough to live here, those who did not fear the hammer of the sun. I felt cold as I watched them, though I never stopped clapping and cheering. I knew that if they fought Lo-Melkhiin, many of them would die.

The men danced until all the stars were out, and the moon had more than cleared the horizon. Then they took their seats again, and fell upon the feast as though they hadn't been eating their fill less than half an hour before. Mead was brought, and cool water from the well, and they laughed as they drank.

My mother and my sister's mother brought out tambourines made from tortoise shells and copper beads, and shook them as they sat. The men laughed as my sister took one of them and threw me the other. She ought to have given it to one of my brothers' wives, but I supposed that no one here considered me to be married for long. Lo-Melkhiin's mother did not protest. She only looked a little bit sad as I rose to stand beside my sister.

We had done this dance only once before, when my third brother was married. It was the first time we had been old enough to do it, but we had seen it many times before, and my mother and my sister's mother made sure we knew the steps. I knew my sister was praying to my smallgod out of habit, asking for her pins to stay steady and the ties of her dishdashah to hold. Again, my prayers stuck in my throat, so I settled for calling up the copper fire and using it to fix the pins and ties for both of us. In Lo-Melkhiin's qasr, I had thought of those things as armor, the only way a woman might be shielded. Now, I knew it to be true.

My sister beat her tambourine four times upon the palm of her hand, and I beat four times in answer. This put the rhythm in our bones, and the feeling of the dance in our blood. We beat four times together, and then we began to spin.

We walked in a broad circle, feet light on the sand and hair flying behind us under our veils. We dragged our toes in the right places, outlining the shape of a tent as we moved, and then stepped inside the marks to continue dancing. Now the women who sat and watched us had the rhythm, and began to clap.

They had set torches burning, because lamps would not be bright enough, and I saw the light gleam off the copper beads as my sister shook her tambourine. I matched each of her movements, spinning in the sand, as we mapped out the tent and the things that would be inside it. Here was where my sister's cook fire would be, and here she would put her loom. When children came, they would sleep in the corner, while my sister and her husband would sleep closer to the door. We laid down rugs to keep the sand from getting into everything, and lined the sides with heavy pillows to keep out creatures that might harm those who slept within.

I was careful as we danced—not to keep track of the steps, but to control my copper fire. I did not wish to call any of the things we danced for into being. My sister's wedding was grand enough without adding anything uncanny, and I feared that if I did, I would be too sick afterward to reason with anyone about their planned attack. Instead, I kept the copper fire spooled inside of me, apart from the dance, and separate in my thoughts. I found that I could do the steps without thinking about them, and I put all of my concentration into keeping the fire where it was. The men began to clap too, and with the added rhythm I sank into the fire entirely, my feet never missing their mark.

I no longer danced upon the sand; or rather, I did, but I was above it as well. Like a sand-crow, I circled the tents in the dark, seeing where the torches burned and how the men standing guard were given roast goat and water, but only enough mead for luck. I saw the new tent that had been set up for my sister and her husband. It was not the tent they would live in, but it was enough for them until they could pick a place to set their stakes. I looked down at myself, dancing steadily beside my sister, and then cast my gaze out into the desert to see what was coming toward us in the night.

The guards would not have seen them. I knew that, the way I knew that they could not stop them, either. There was only one man in their number, who rode on a horse and set their pace. That was Lo-Melkhiin. Those who came with him were not men. For whatever reason, the demons he brought did not walk in men's bodies. I guessed it was because they were stronger that way. Or because they wanted to take the bodies of those they found here, offered up like the feast my father served for my sister's wedding.

I felt the tambourine shake and was back in my body, the dance complete. My sister stood beside me, unbent, though

I knew she was as winded as I was, and she smiled under her veil.

"You see, sister," she said to me. "Tonight we have all the luck we need."

Again, I held my tongue. I could have said to her that demons were coming, but when she looked into the desert, she would see only Lo-Melkhiin on a horse, and she might try to kill him herself. She had never lacked for spirit, and the idea of that scared me to my bones.

"Yes, sister," I said to her, calling on the copper fire again, willing it to be so. "Tonight we have good luck."

My mother took the tambourines, and the other women stood to do their own dance where we had trod. I took no outstretched hand, ducking away from all of them when they might have pulled me back into the dance. Instead, I went away from the fires, away from the sights and sounds and smells of the wedding, and into the dark, where I might have a clear head to think.

Perhaps if I went to Lo-Melkhiin, he would take me and turn back, content to hold me hostage in his qasr. If I took his mother with me, we would have an even greater chance. When I looked for her, though, I saw that she sat with four of my mother's brothers and their wives. They would not let her out of their sight, even if she went with me. If I went into the desert, I would go alone.

I returned to my mother's tent and took off my fine dishdashah and veil. My sister's priestly-whites were there, and I put them on. I feared no blasphemy. She had worn them when she prayed to my smallgod. I was allowed to wear them now. I pinned on the white veil, and put on the slippers that completed the regalia. I would take no piece of the shrine with me, as my sister would have done. I did not need a scrap of the purple cloth, or the eggshell lamp, or any of the flowers that had been left as offerings. I was enough on my own.

I left the sound of dancing and celebration behind me. I did not pray or sing as I walked. I only called on the copper fire in my chest, and felt the spool unwind. Threads of fire went to each of my fingers and toes. My eyes bloomed with it, and they sharpened the hearing in my ears. This was all the armor I needed now, or so I hoped.

And I walked into the desert alone to meet my husband, where he rode with my doom behind him at last.

thirty-four

I HEARD LO-MELKHIIN LAUGHING, and knew he saw me where I walked. My sister's priestly-whites were newly washed, and gleamed in the moonlight. I was not hard to see. When I heard my husband laugh, I stopped and waited. I had come this far. My doom could come to me.

"Star of my skies, you did not need to come out to greet us," said Lo-Melkhiin when he was close enough that he did not need to shout. There was no hint of a good man about him. If I wanted one, I would have to make one, as I had made the pale man for my sister. "We are quite happy to go among the tents your father has pitched on the wadi. We wish to see them."

"Please," I said to him. "Take me back to the qasr and use me as your hostage there. Make them send you your mother. Tell them that they must never rebel, or you will kill me."

"Human lives are nothing to us," said one of Lo-Melkhiin's kin. "Our brother does not care about your life, even if he wears a human body and has married you in a human rite."

"My kin speak true," Lo-Melkhiin said to me. "Except I do find some value in your life. I will take you, and I will still burn your father and your brothers and all who stand with them until they are ashes to be mixed with the desert sand."

"Please," I said again to him. "Spare them, and I will give you the power that I have."

"Humans have no power," said another of Lo-Melkhiin's kin. "Or at least they have no power in comparison to ours. How else would we take them and spend their lives so easily?"

I could see them more clearly now. At first, it had looked like Lo-Melkhiin sat on a horse and was surrounded by a white mist, like the steam that rose from the coals in the qasr bathhouse when you poured water on them directly. Now I could see figures in the mist. They were tall, arms and legs too long, and though I could not see their faces clearly, I did not like what little I saw.

"This one has power," said Lo-Melkhiin to his kin. "But she cannot give it to me. She is not to be worried over, though. If she uses too much, she becomes ill, and only I can save her from it."

"Please," I said to him, a third time. "Leave us; leave, Lo-Melkhiin, and return with your kin to wherever you came from."

At this they all laughed, the sound screeching along my nerves.

"We will never leave," Lo-Melkhiin said to me. "Why would we, when we have everything we want here? Your people may struggle and rise up against us from time to time, but we do not die. We will crush them. We can crush them right now, if we choose."

Lo-Melkhiin got off his horse and came over to where I stood. None of his kin followed me. He came right up to me, grasping my shoulders. His fingers bit into my skin, but I would not flinch.

"Wife," he said to me, and to me alone. "Here is the only bargain you will get from me tonight. Fight with me, overthrow my kin here in the desert where we stand right now, and I will leave your people. You will tell them their rebellion is over, that you are my hostage and they must not rise up again. Only help me defeat my kin first, and I will save yours."

I did not doubt that we could do it. Even the slight touch of his fingers on my arms surged with power, and neither of us was really trying. The beings in the mist were only half formed. I knew my fire and the cold light Lo-Melkhiin had at his command would be enough to send them into the sand for an age, if we put forth the effort. My family would be safe. I would be safe. But Lo-Melkhiin would have a demon in him still, and with my power beside him, I shuddered to think what the demon could do.

"How can I trust you if you betray your own kind?" I said to him. I would compromise with him no longer. He had given me what I needed, and my sister's wedding had provided me with the rest. I was stronger here than I had ever been in the qasr, powered by the dancers that circled the fires between my father's tents. "How can I give the safety of my family to someone who has no regard for his own? You have not even asked about your mother. I will never join you."

"Very well," he said to me, and went back to his horse. He climbed astride it, and turned to the mist. "My wife has forsaken her own kind, spurning my offer as she has. Go to the tents of her father. Take whatever you want from them."

I screamed then, but I could not stall the mist. It streaked away from us through the night, toward the place where my family danced at my sister's wedding. I put some of the copper fire into my scream, so that they would have some warning, but it did them no good. They could not stop the mist as it pulled children into cook fires and buried men alive in sand.

"Lo-Melkhiin!" I screamed at him. "I beg you, husband, make them stop!"

"I cannot," he said to me, the viper in his eyes. His mother was wrong. There was no part of the boy she had loved still inside him. "They are mad with it, can't you see? Nothing can make them stop now. Watch your world burn, light of my heart. Tomorrow we will find another one and burn that too."

I turned from him, and stretched out everywhere with the copper fire. He did not stop me, or he could not, and I went amidst my father's tents to the ruin and terror I saw there. I pulled my oldest brother from the sand. He coughed, spewing grains of it in all directions, and then lay still. I quelled every fire I could find, lamps and candles, cook fires and hearths, but so many of the children were already burned. My sister stood with one arm around both my mother and her mother, and the mist parted around them. I could not imagine that they would be spared, but then I looked closely and saw that each of them wore a necklace made of that bright metal.

"Sister," I cried to her, hoping that she would hear. "The metal will protect you. Get it to as many as you can!"

She did hear, for she began to run. I could not stay with her. There were too many others that had been burned or buried. I could not save them all.

"Not so human after all," the mist said to me, with voices

beyond counting and no faces at all. "And yet, not powerful enough to fight us. Only good enough to clean up the mess."

I needed more hands, but even with the copper fire, I had only two. It was not fair. There were so many of them, and I stood alone in the desert, having nothing to fight them with. A wooden ball rolled to a stop at my feet. A lamp sat beside it. And a bolt of orange cloth with gold thread. Above, I heard a great bird scream. I knew that I had made them, not called them or found them. They had not been, and then I wished for them, and they were. If I wanted help, I would have to make it.

I brought forth all the copper fire I could muster, and threw it out into the desert. The demons did not know the desert well, for all that they lived here. They did not use it as my people did. They did not know its moods and its temper: which animals were common, what secrets those creatures carried. I would fight them with the very things they scorned, and the desert itself would be my hands.

I found the lizards that baked in the sun and crawled into the oleander at night. They were large ones, the size of a sheep at full growth. I set a fire in their bellies, and turned them out to do battle for me. They burned so hot, they streaked through the mist and seared it. I could hear Lo-Melkhiin's kin scream, and the sound was like my sister's laughter to my ears.

I took the horses that the southernmost traders had

brought with them. They were fleet-footed and could run in the sand even during the hottest part of the day. I gave them horns made from the pale man's metal to strike at the half-formed bodies of Lo-Melkhiin's kin, and where they pierced the mist, dark ichor fell into the sand.

Sand-crows I woke and brought forth from their nests. When Lo-Melkhiin's kin struck them down, they caught fire and flew again, their talons shod in the same bright metal that their northern cousins wore. They sliced at the mist, herding it away from my people.

The goats came to me, curious and eager, and they took cleverness from my copper fire like it was a salt-lick I held for them. They made traps to catch the mist in baskets, and shut it up in tents. The mist howled in fury, but my spritely goats only laughed at them and took to new mischief.

There were fires again, burning out of control in the hearthstones and fire pits. I called on the wadi toads, who always knew when the floods were coming, and made them hands to carry water with. They extinguished the flames, and when they poured water on burned skin, the skin was healed.

Last, I waked the hives, and brought out the bees. They could not see in the dark, so I used my copper fire to light their way. They went to every person they could find, carrying small scraps of the pale man's bright metal, and made sure that everyone was warded against the mist.

My head was pounding, and my throat was dry. The creatures I had made battled for me, and I stood in the sand and wept from pain and exhaustion. My people wailed and screamed their losses, mourning for those I had been too slow to save from living burial or the fire's fury. I wanted to kill Lo-Melkhiin for what he had brought down upon my family. Finally, I shared my sister's anger.

Lo-Melkhiin was close to me, and somehow a war raged across his face. His body was unmoving as his mind fought against itself. His horse was dead; pure terror had burst the poor beast's heart. Around us, the fighting was starting to diminish. If we were to have peace, it would be soon. There was a bright dagger, not a copper one, in my hand.

"Lady-bless," said my bees. "The mist is caught. Where shall we put it?"

I could think of only one place where Lo-Melkhiin's kin might be safely taken. It was so far that I did not know if my power was sufficient to the journey, but I knew I must try, even if it was too much for me. The knife vanished. I had chosen my end.

"North," I said to them. "Take them to the mountains where the bright metal sits in the ground. May it bind them there for all the ages of men."

"We go, we go!" said the bees and the fiery crows and the lizards, which had grown wings from their burning bellies.

They went up into the sky, and Lo-Melkhiin screamed

to see them go, but he could not reach them. I watched them disappear from my eyes, but I could feel when they landed in the mountains. Lo-Melkhiin's kin writhed there, weakening, and could not escape.

"Star of my heart," Lo-Melkhiin said. His rage was spent, but he was a viper still. "Now we have only one another."

I would not go back to him. I would die first. My death was no longer his; I would have it here, in my desert, on the sand beneath the starry sky. It would never belong to him.

My copper fire was at its end. There was enough left for only five more words, the shortest story ever told, made with threads that frayed almost before they could be spoken. I could save myself with them, I knew. Or I could save Lo-Melkhiin.

I thought of a qasr without a king. I thought of merchants who did not care what the desert did. I thought of my father, who deserved better, and of my sister, who deserved the best. I thought of a ball and a lamp and a bolt of cloth, all made because I wanted them to be. It did not matter if Lo-Melkhiin's mother was wrong. I could make it so that she was right.

Five more words, and then I could sleep. My head would no longer pound. My throat would no longer burn. It would be quiet and still. Perhaps I would dream of the creatures I had made. I would like to see what they became in the morning when the sun came up. Lo-Melkhiin's artisans had made such new wonders, yet I did not think there had been new animals since the world was born; now I had made six of them. I hoped they would do good when I was gone.

Five more words. I could feel them on my tongue. There would be peace in the whole desert, not just in parts of it. Not just for the nobles of Lo-Melkhiin's court, but for the common folk of the qasr as well. For everyone. My father's caravan. My mother's tent. All through the sand desert. In every village and in every district inside the city walls. I would speak for them. Five more words, and it would be done.

Lo-Melkhiin is a good man.

thirty-five

THERE WAS A LION ABOVE ME when I woke, a lion with the face of a woman, and so I thought I dreamed.

"Daughter of my heart," said Lo-Melkhiin's mother to me. "You have my thanks."

I sat up. I thought my head would split, but after a moment, the ground stopped heaving and the pain left me. I reached for the copper fire inside me, but it was gone. Nothing remained that could be burned.

"Sister?" The lamp that lit my sister's face burned with a clear light. "Sister, you live!"

I was as surprised as she was to learn it. Yet I could feel my heart and hear my own breath. I had faced Lo-Melkhiin and lived, again. I wanted to run and dance on the shifting sand, but I was not sure my legs would hold me up to do it.

"Daughter of mine," my father said. "Let us bear you back to your tent."

He stooped to carry me, as he had not done since I was brought out of my mother's tent for the first time, but I held up a hand.

"Where is Lo-Melkhiin?" I said to them. "Where is my husband?"

"He is dead," my sister said to me. "Sister, you have killed him."

"No," I said to her. "He lives, I am sure of it. Where is his body?"

Lo-Melkhiin's mother pointed to where he lay, and I crawled toward it. My father was surprised, and did not think to help. Lo-Melkhiin's face was the color of ashes. There was blood on his lips, and his breath was so shallow that I listened for nearly a minute before I heard it.

"He lives!" I said to them. "Help him, please!"

They stared at me as though I had stood in the sun too long and baked out my thoughts, all except for Lo-Melkhiin's mother, who looked at the ground.

"Sister," my sister said to me. "Why?"

"I have saved him," I said to them. I made my voice as loud as I could, so that any who were close by would hear me. "You saw the battle that was fought. You did not fight men. You battled demons, and so did I. You saw the power and the new creatures that were made. I tell you, he is saved. When he wakes, he will be the good king again. The demon is gone and will worry us no longer."

"Daughter of mine," said my father. "Are you sure?"

"Father," I said to him. "I know it as I know my sister's face. I know it as I know my mother's voice. I know it as I know myself. Lo-Melkhiin is a good man."

My father carried him, leaving me to my oldest brother, whose lungs had been cleared of sand. Many of the tents were down, struck in the fighting, but enough stood to house the wounded and the dead; there was one for me and Lo-Melkhiin.

We were set there, and then left, except for my sister and for Lo-Melkhiin's mother. The boy came in, his arms burned, and behind him the old woman and serving girl. They wept to see me, and I kissed them. Then I turned to where my husband lay, and waited for him to wake.

Outside my tent, my mother and my sister's mother began their rites for the dead. Everyone who had died here would be buried with my family's bones, including my youngest brother and my oldest brother's sons. It would take them more than one night to do it, even with help from the other visitors who wore the priestly-whites, but it would be done.

"I am sorry, sister of mine," I said to her. "I did not mean to turn your wedding into a funeral."

"Do not be foolish, sister," she said to me. "If not for you, we would all lie dead, and no one would be left to perform the rites."

Then she went out to find her husband. She could not help her mother and mine, because I wore her priestly clothes.

The boy brought me a slice of melon. It soothed my throat, and I thanked him. He ran away from me, hiding behind the old woman. She took him in her lap again—this time he did not fight her—and began to sing. It was a song about the morning, and even though the sun was still hours from the sky, I was glad of it. I did not want to be thinking dark thoughts.

A buzzing sound came close to my ear. I looked, and there was one of my bees, a bee no longer. It was still golden, but it was person-shaped. It held a tiny staff in place of a stinger, like a shepherd for tiny sheep, and it trailed fine golden dust behind it. A wadi toad crouched by my feet. Its hands were webbed, but not quite toad-like, and its knees bent, like an old man's. It held a water jar, but before I could take it, one of my goats did instead. It walked on two legs now, fine limbs white and gleaming in the lamplight, and poured the water on Lo-Melkhiin's face. The other creatures could not fit inside the tent, but I heard the scream of a fiery sand-crow, and smelled the brimstone it left in the air as it flew. I heard the stomp of my new-horned horse, and felt the heat that came from the belly of my lizard. My creatures were still with us, and they would do good.

Lo-Melkhiin coughed, and his eyes opened. I looked into them, afraid that I might see a hollow thing there. If there was madness or cruelty, I would have to kill him, and I did not know if I could. The eyes that looked at me were kind. I could see his mother in them, the way she hoped and wished. I could see what must be his father, the foolish king that everyone had loved anyway. And I could see the wisdom and peacefulness that were his alone. Though we had been married for nearly three moons and I had seen him almost every day, I felt that I looked upon my husband for the first time.

"*Al-ammiyyah*," he said to me. *Common*. The old insult had no edge, and I judged it a good beginning.

"Lie still," I said to him. "You must rest, and drink more water."

The wadi toad waddled more than it hopped now, but it went to fill its jar and returned without spilling any, like my sister and I had done when we carried one jar between us.

"Go," said Lo-Melkhiin's mother. "Tell your people what you have seen."

I went out from the tent and saw them. I told them that Lo-Melkhiin would live, that his heart was restored, and that he would be the good king they remembered. I told them that when the dead were buried, they could go home, and tell everyone they met that peace had come. I told my sister that her wedding would be a sacred day now, the day that men remembered how peace had been won. My new bees flew around me as I spoke, trailing their golden dust through the air, and no one doubted my words.

I went to my father and to my living brothers, embracing them. My mother and my sister's mother labored still, so I would have to wait to speak to them, and my sister had gone with her husband into their tent, so we could not put our heads together and talk as we once had. Those days, I knew, were past. We would have other secrets now, and other tasks to tend as we whispered them.

For three nights, my mother and my sister's mother buried the dead, and for three nights, Lo-Melkhiin recovered. At last, their work was done, and he was well. I went to them and thanked them, and they put their arms around me and wept. They knew then that they would lose me again; but this time, I would go because I wished it.

I traded three pots of the golden dust for five horses. The boy had collected it for me, chasing the bees like it was the greatest game he had ever played. Lo-Melkhiin took the gelded male, putting the boy in front of him as he rode. I had a black mount, and Lo-Melkhiin's mother and the two other women rode mares that were brown. We set out across the desert as we had before, except this time my sister did not pray as we went. This time, I looked back at my father's tents until they were gone from my view, and when Lo-Melkhiin promised me that I could visit, I knew he meant to keep his word.

We came into the city as the sun was setting. The guards at the gate were surprised to see us. They said they had seen strange lights over the desert on the night when we had battled, and that they did not think Lo-Melkhiin would ever return. A few of the city lords had clearly thought so too, but once it became clear that the king had come back, they behaved themselves.

Lo-Melkhiin called Firh Stonetouched to him, and said that he no longer had to carve stone if he did not wish it. He also gave the carver all of his statues back, and said that Firh could do as he wished with them. I did not ask what became of them, but the statues disappeared from the gardens overnight, and I hoped he had turned them into dust. A statue appeared in my water garden at the same time. It was another great cat, but this time it was a lioness, not a lion, and her eyes were not haunted as the other statues' had been.

"This one is yours, lady-bless," Firh Stonetouched said to me. "I carved it with your blessing, and I will do no others."

"It is beautiful," I said to him, because it was. "And I am grateful."

He bowed, and left me. I sat staring at the statue until another shadow came into the garden, and Lo-Melkhiin was there.

"Will you stay with me, Al-ammiyyah?" he asked me. "I will not make you. The Skeptics say the wedding does not have to stand, and that you can return to your father's tents, and to a match of his making—or none at all—if you choose."

"I will stay, husband," I said to him. "I have become accustomed to the qasr, and to the people here. I thought the desert was my home, but it is no longer. Your home is mine now, and I will live in it."

"Let me make you the queen in truth, then," he said to me. "Marry me again, if you will. I will give you a crown and a place on my council."

"The petty lords will never allow that," I said to him.

"They are afraid of you," he said to me. "They are afraid of what the palace women say you have done. If we tell them now, they will do it."

I considered his words. When I had lived here before, I had had little to occupy my time. I did not wish for the same thing again, but I had thought I would take part in running the household, only. A seat on the council—to hear petitioners and advise judgment—was much more to my liking, though I had not thought it was within my grasp. A golden bee flew amongst the flowers of my water garden. My creatures had followed me to the city, and lived even inside the qasr walls. They would remind everyone what I had done.

"Then, yes," I said to him. "I will marry you again, and take the seat you offer at your side."

Lo-Melkhiin smiled and took my hand. I had tasted power and I had used it up, but now I would get more of another kind. We would share it, and keep each other from the dark. The sun gleamed in the desert sky, and the stones of the walls reflected the golden light all around the garden, but there was no fire where our fingers met.

1.

Already, the story is changing.

When men tell it in the souks and in the desert, they shape it to fit their understanding. It passes from caravan to caravan, to places where they have never heard of the one called Lo-Melkhiin. The words change language, and meaning is lost and gained in every vowel's shift. They change the monster into a man, and they change her into something that can be used to teach a lesson: if you are clever and if you are good, the monster will not have you.

You should not believe everything you hear.

Good men fall to monsters every day. Clever men are tricked by their own pride or by pretty words. That is what happened to the king in the tale she tells. He was clever and good, and the monster plucked him from the desert like he was little more than sand. She was clever and good as well, so good she wished to take her sister's place, and so clever she made it so. That is not what saved her from the monster.

The story will mean different things to every person who hears it. That is how she meant for it to be. I can tell you of the meaning I found, the new purpose and direction for my life, but it will be nothing to you if you do not understand why she told it in the first place.

There is life, and there is living—and that is what she learned.

She told the story in small pieces; that much is true. It came to her in undyed wool, which she could spin, or in threads that she could stitch or weave. She did not tell it every night, and she did not tell it always to the same person. Sometimes she told it only to herself, using the tools and the strength given to her by others. That did not make its power any less, and that power gave her life.

Living came later, when she learned to tell the story on purpose.

The monster tested her, pulling at her soul and rending her spirit. She clung to life, and in the clinging she might have become a monster too, except she chose the path her story would take. She chose white stone walls and a golden crown. She chose to debate words of law, and to never grind her own grain. She chose to fight men every day, and then fight their sons, who thought they knew better than their fathers.

Her own legend was swallowed up by the creatures she made. All six of them went out into the world and were given new names by the people who saw them. Each had special powers that she did not intend, which waited to be unlocked as people learned to communicate with them. They spread out across the earth, to places where men did not live at all; each prospered in its own way, but they never forgot the girl who made them.

If you listen long enough to the whispers, you will hear the truth. Until then, I will tell you this: the world is made safe by a woman. She bound the monster up and cast him out, and the man who was left was saved. For one thousand nights, I lived a nightmare in the dark, but when the nights numbered a thousand and one, the nightmare was ended.

Al-ammiyyah, the common tongue, had saved the king.

Finis

acknowledgments

MASSIVE THANKS TO:

Josh Adams, who championed this book before it was even a book, and called me while I was napping at least four times a week during March of 2014 to talk about it.

Emily Meehan, who took me very seriously when I told her that no, no one was ever going to get a name. Also, Marci Senders: I remain stunned by the book design.

My family, especially EJ and Jen, who loaned me their cottage; Sarah and Dan, who loaned me rent money; and Ian and Emily, who checked in to make sure I was okay. And to my London aunt, uncle, and cousins (plus Team Bentley!), who took care of me before and after my surgery.

Emma and Colleen, who read each chapter as I wrote it, and Faith, Laura, RJ, and Tessa, who read it when I was done and told me how to make it better. Also Carrie Ryan, who gave excellent career advice to a rookie author, even though she does not remember the conversation, and who answered a super-cryptic email in a very helpful manner.

The writers of the Fourteenery and the Hanging Garden are all ludicrously fabulous, and I am better off for knowing them.

Finally, I could not have written this book without the time I spent in Jordan, working with Dr. Michèle Daviau and Dr. Michael Weigl on the Wadi ath-Thamad project. Four years of school and six summers in the desert, and more learned than I really understood at the time. Thank you.

E.K. JOHNSTON

Kingdom of Sleep

It has been generations since the Storyteller Queen saved her country from fire and blood – but now the kingdom of Kharuf is threatened by a demon gathering power. When a princess is born, the demon is ready with her final blow: a curse that will cost that princess her very soul, or force her to destroy her own people to save her life.

The threads of magic are tightly spun, binding princess and exiled spinners into a desperate plot to break the curse. But the web of power is dangerously tangled – and they may not see the true pattern until it is unspooled.

Coming soon

Read an exclusive extract of E. K. Johnston's spellbinding new novel on MyKindaBook:
www.mykindabook.com/kingdomofsleep